PRAISE

SLOWER

TED SHEPHERD

Ted-Shepherd.com

ISBN: 978-0-578-42481-1

Published by Ted Shepherd

Interior formatting
Mark Thomas / Coverness.com.

For my family, who make me want to live life slower.

CHAPTER 1

The second hand of the classroom clock seems to be moving slower than a lethargic snail. My science teacher, Ms. Beans, is not helping move things along. She sits on her beat-up wooden chair, which her rear end has squashed for decades as she inflicts science on pathetic victims like me. She looks down her pointy nose through her purple glasses at her copy of our textbook. At random times while she's reading aloud, Ms. Beans pauses on a word and spends at least thirty seconds pronouncing each syllable.

"Sa-lin-i-ty."

This is unbearable. I'm going to explode. Or go to sleep. Or maybe I'll explode while I'm sleeping. That would be a mess.

So far, I have not exploded. Fallen asleep? Definitely. Why does she do this? The words are right in front of our faces in the book, so why does Ms. Beans insist on reading them to us? Is she actually getting paid for this? I'm fourteen and a mature ninth grader. Others in the class are tenth graders, who are even more mature. She doesn't need to read to us like toddlers.

She's so perky about science. She seems to love it, and she's trying her best to be so enthusiastic that we'll be infected by her weird science-liking disease too. It does nothing for me. This is the most boring that the world can possibly be. I will really explode.

I notice that I'm subconsciously jiggling my leg, and I have probably been doing that for half an hour already. I hope that my leg-jiggling hasn't annoyed anyone, especially the girls. I don't want to get a reputation as Emit the dorky leg-jiggler. Again I think I'm going to explode. No, don't do that. That would be a mess. An embarrassing mess.

I glance over at my cousin Ellen. She is diligently examining a one-inch flap of peeling paint on the wall behind Ms. Beans's head. I have spent hours examining this same flap myself. The flap is much more interesting than Ms. Beans and science. It's a great flap.

What is wrong with everybody else in the class? Other than Ellen and me, everyone else seems interested in what Ms. Beans is saying. Or maybe they're just better than me at faking that they're interested. I wish I could text Ellen, but the rule is that you can't have your phone out in class.

I close my eyes and imagine walking to the front of the class, grabbing Ms. Beans's textbook, and hiding it. Oh, the freedom from her deadly droning! I could hide the book in a backpack, in a locker, or even in Ms. Beans's car, a twelve-year-old green Subaru with a green miniature Rubik's cube hanging from the rearview mirror, and a bumper sticker that says "I *Heart*

Science." She would never think to look for it there. I could put it in her glove compartment, or even better, under a seat. I could rip down the stupid Rubik's cube. She would never think—

"Emit!" roars Ms. Beans, "WAKE UP!"

My head shoots up from the desk like a gopher at the sound of danger, sticking his head out of his hole. "Sorry," I mumble.

"You're in high school now, Emit. Naps are for pre-K, not ninth grade. This is the third day in a row this has happened." She stands up. "You know what, I'm done with you for today. Go to the principal's office."

I'm not worried. Our principal, Mr. Zachs, is a family friend; he has known our family, starting with my grandfather, forever. He's been the principal at Briar Grove High School since the building was built forty-seven years ago—the longest-serving principal in the state. Briar Grove is an old suburb of Princeton, New Jersey. Mr. Zachs must be over eighty, but nobody really notices. He doesn't want to retire, and he's still vigorous and does a good job. He's always been here, and it seems he always will be.

He understands that I, like half of my friends, have ADHD, or attention deficit hyperactivity disorder. I also have a sleeping disorder. And I've had these troubles since I was a kid, along with bad headaches several times a week. My illnesses make it hard for me to concentrate for more than a few minutes. I'm drowsy all day, but I can't sleep at night. My mind wanders a lot, and after I have daydreams, I tend to get the headaches. I've had all sorts of tests done for hormone imbalances and brain tumors, but the doctors didn't find anything. My mom, who's a doctor, has decided that I shouldn't be medicated for my ADHD. She thinks ADHD meds are bad. About half of my friends get to take lots of Ritalin and Adderall. But not me. Sometimes I'm jealous of my friends, because they say that the stuff works.

Teachers like Ms. Beans make my symptoms worse. Because of my ADHD, I get extra time on tests as an accommodation. But it doesn't help, because the tests are just as tedious as everything else. Mr. Zachs knows about my medical challenges, and so he will give me only a gentle scolding.

"Emit, get out of here," continues Ms. Beans. "You've completely interrupted the class and made me lose my train of thought. And where's my textbook?"

"Serves you right," I whisper to myself as I stumble out of the classroom.

As I leave, I hear a kid whisper, "There goes Herky-Jerky."

"Shut up. You're the jerk," I mumble under my breath. Since I can remember, the stupid people have teased me about making a jerking movement when I stop daydreaming. I know I don't do anything like that. They're just being bullies, because they know they can make up anything to make me feel bad. As my mom would say, what they're doing is illegal and wrong because they're creating a hostile environment for an ADHD disabled person.

As I do the walk of shame out of the classroom, I think again about Ms. Beans. I've never understood teachers. Sometimes they act so nice. Other times they get angry for no reason. Why does she get angry just because I rest my eyelids a bit? I'm not hurting anybody. For other teachers, I can often predict their mood and how they'll react. But not Ms. Beans. With her sincere smile and calm personality, you would assume that she's a gentle, caring teacher. Sometimes she is. But other times, she's just the opposite, snapping at students for the smallest offense and holding a grudge for months.

I stroll as slowly as I can down the empty hallway, past the closed classroom doors, behind which are seated rows of fidgeting students. All of us are used to the school's 1950s design. A big three-story rectangle with red brick on the outside, and cinderblock hallways and classrooms on the inside. It's all dingy and worn out. But we don't usually notice that, because it's all we know.

The walls and lockers are painted a cream color. There is virtually no other color anywhere. A few months ago, I asked Mr. Zachs why everything was cream; in the high school TV shows, the lockers are usually some bright color. He said that cream is the most soothing color, and a soothing environment discourages rowdiness. I don't know about that; the "soothing" color makes me so bored that I want to rip my hair out in chunks. It also makes me very tired.

But I guess everything makes me tired. For as long as I can remember, I have only slept for two or three hours at night. I then get exhausted during the day and always fall asleep in class. Somehow I still get pretty good grades, but they could be better. My classroom performance is made worse by the ADHD. My doctor said that my sleep problems and the ADHD are all linked; he says my sleep problems are caused by my ADHD, that I fall asleep because I'm so bored. I'm not so sure. When I wake up in the middle of the night, I feel completely rested and like I've slept plenty. But then by 1 p.m. or so, I'm completely exhausted and I feel like it's after midnight.

My constant sleeping in school makes my classmates think I'm a bit odd. They also think it's weird that I look a year or two or three older than everyone else in the ninth grade. I was the first boy to start shaving two years ago, and my face gets stubble by 3 p.m. each day. I already look like a grownup, while other kids my age are just going through puberty. Unfortunately for me, fully grown doesn't mean especially tall. I get that from my parents.

I get to the front office and tell Ms. Burner, the receptionist, that I'm here to see the principal. She nods, and I knock on the door of Mr. Zachs's office. After a few seconds without an answer, I peer through the door's small rectangular window. I scan the room quickly. Mr. Zachs isn't in there.

"Hey, Emit!" I jump and almost hit my head on the door as I turn around.

"Sorry. I didn't mean to scare you," says Mr. Zachs from behind me in his slight Russian accent. "Please come in." He moves in front of me and uses his key to open the door.

"How are you doing, Uncle Dimitri?" I ask once we're inside behind the closed door.

Dimitri Zachs has been a friend of my family for as long as I can remember. I think I heard once that he was a college friend of my grandfather in California, after my grandfather moved to the US from Germany. Through a coincidence, Mr. Zachs ended up being my principal fifty years later even though we're across the country from where they met. Although most students are probably intimidated by his faint Russian accent and piercing eyes, I know he's warm and friendly. I feel completely comfortable around him, and I often think he understands me better than my own family. I sometimes call him Uncle Dimitri, although he's not really my uncle. He's asked me not to call him that at school, so that the other students or teachers don't think I get special treatment. Well, actually, I do get special treatment from him. I'm grateful for it. But he's careful not to let his kindness to me be too obvious to others.

"Do you want to come in and take a nap?" he asks. "I heard about your little sleeping incident."

I look down at my toes. "Sorry, I couldn't help it."

Mr. Zachs grins. "Don't worry about it, Emit. I often got into trouble too when I was your age." He pats me on the back.

"Want anything to drink?" he asks. "I have lemonade, apple juice, and water."

"Lemonade, please," I say.

"Sure." He walks over to the little minifridge in the corner of his office.

"Uncle Dimitri, oh, I mean, Mr. Zachs?"

"Yes, Emit?"

"Actually, do you have any Diet Coke?" I ask.

"Sure," he responds with a smile, understanding my request for what it was: a desperate cry for caffeine.

Mr. Zachs's office, a rectangle, contains little furniture: a large wooden desk, a chair in the corner, and two metal chairs facing the desk. On the desk, there is one small picture frame.

Years ago, I asked him about the faded picture of a woman in the frame. He responded that it was his wife, who died when he was forty. I saw great sadness in his eyes. I didn't like to imagine Mr. Zachs suffering when his wife died.

"So …" I utter, searching for something to talk about.

"Tell me more about why you got into trouble today," he says.

"Well … you heard what happened. I couldn't help going to sleep. Same as always. Nothing different."

"Yes, but we discussed you trying to limit your sleeping by keeping your mind engaged. Now, I know that Ms. Beans is not the most interesting person in the world." He slips into a whisper. "To be honest, I would probably fall asleep in her class too. The point is, you have to find a way to keep yourself focused so you don't fall asleep in class. Maybe you should think of games to play in your mind to keep yourself alert. Maybe imagination games?"

I don't want to tell him that I had been imagining stealing Ms. Beans's textbook when I fell asleep.

Suddenly Mr. Zachs's old-fashioned office phone rings. He answers and immediately puts his finger to his lips. "Shhhh."

Oh great, it's probably Ms. Beans continuing to complain about me. I don't understand why she dislikes me so much. Accidentally sleeping in her class is not a good reason for her to hate me so much. It's like I personally offended her somehow. I can't help falling asleep. I'm not trying to offend her. Sleeping is just a natural, uncontrollable bodily function. She wouldn't be offended if I had to cough in her class. Neither should she be offended if I have to rest my eyes a little. Doesn't the law entitle people with handicaps to a reasonable accommodation?

"Yes, Ms. Beans," Mr. Zachs responds on the phone. "I assume you are talking about Emit Friend. Hmmmm … OK. You can come down anytime; Emit is here in my office right now. All right, see you then." Mr. Zachs hangs up the phone.

"Well, she's coming down to the office," Mr. Zachs says. "She claims she's had enough of your stunts. Emit, what is she talking about?"

"I don't know," I reply, and bite my lip nervously. I just wish I could go home. I don't want to be in this situation. Why can't I be a normal kid who sleeps at night and is awake during the day?

I hear a knock at the office door. Mr. Zachs nods in the direction of the door. Slowly, I get out of my seat, take a deep breath, and open the door.

"Hello, Emit." Ms. Beans smiles coldly. "Have you told Mr. Zachs what you did today?"

"Yes." I stare down at my feet.

"Good." Ms. Beans strides through the open door and sits

down on one of the metal chairs. "We need to have a chat." Ms. Beans points to the chair next to her, so I sit down.

"What do you want to talk about?" I ask, probably a little too loudly.

"Do not be sarcastic with me, young man!" she answers.

I roll my eyes.

"Emit, out!" she says coldly.

I stomp out and close the door a little loudly, not a slam, but almost. "Are you kidding me?" I mumble to myself. That woman might be the most annoying person I've ever met. I bet she's telling Mr. Zachs that I'm a terrible student and that there's no hope for me. Why can't she just understand that I fall asleep because I have a sleeping disorder? I'm not trying to be disrespectful.

Suddenly Ms. Beans bursts out of the door. She glares at me for a moment, then strides down the hall, shaking with anger, but also looking confused. I walk back into Mr. Zachs's office.

"What was that all about?" I question as I take a seat.

"Emit," he asks, "did you steal her textbook?"

"Uh, no," I reply, confused.

"Emit, be serious," he says. "She says that you took her science textbook sometime today."

"What! I didn't do that!"

"That's what I told her. But she insisted that you did." Mr. Zachs raises his hands in surrender. "Seriously, Emit." Mr. Zachs becomes very serious and looks at me strangely. "Please tell me if you took it. I won't be angry."

"I didn't do it. I promise. Serves, her right, though, losing that old, dusty, boring book. I certainly dreamed about stealing it," I confess. "But how could I? She had it in her hands the whole class. And I was in her class the whole time. Everyone saw me there. All the people in the class are witnesses that I didn't steal her book. I came directly from her class to your office when she booted me out of class."

"Emit, listen to me now." Why is Mr. Zachs so serious? "If you had taken it, where would you have hidden it?"

"I didn't take it!"

"I believe you, Emit," says Mr. Zachs softly. "But where did you imagine putting it?"

"I don't know. I think I dreamed about putting it in her car, under the seat, to trick her."

Mr. Zachs stares at me. It is as if he is looking into my soul. "That's what I thought," he says slowly. "Ms. Beans found her textbook under the seat in her Subaru."

CHAPTER 2

I sit in silence, stunned. Is it possible? Could I have stolen the textbook? Wouldn't I know if I had? Ms. Beans had the book in her hands the entire time. My daydream had been only about how I wanted to take it. But there's no way I could have taken it, is there?

Mr. Zachs looks at me intently and steeples his hands together on his desk. "The reality of the situation seems a lot like your daydream, Emit." Mr. Zachs makes quotation marks in the air with his fingers when he says "daydream." Mr. Zachs is keeping up with popular culture; he must have seen some teenager on TV use air quotes.

"How could I have stolen it?" I say, agitated. "She had it in her hands the entire time."

"Emit, please calm down."

I try to control myself. Being rude to Mr. Zachs isn't going to help.

"Emit, when you get home, try to think about how this happened," Mr. Zachs urges.

"I will. I promise." I rise from my chair. But how could Mr. Zachs be taking seriously the possibility that I had taken the book? That was nuts. I had been in Ms. Beans's room the whole time. And everybody in the class saw me there.

"Oh, and Emit," Mr. Zachs adds. "Try to get some sleep tonight."

I nod, then stroll out of the office. I look down at my watch. 3:50 p.m. The school day at Briar Grove ends at four. I decide to wait in the bathroom for ten minutes until my bus comes.

Ten minutes later, as I stroll out of the restroom, I see Ellen walking down the hall, her brown curls swaying back and forth. Ellen is my cousin—the daughter of my dad's brother, Uncle Ethan. She is one year older than me, but we have been very close for as long as I remember. Many boys call her weird because she does a lot of typical boy things. Like me, she plays a lot of video games; we sometimes play *Warriors' Bloody Struggle 3* online together, and her online name is DeathDude13. Her latest sport is rugby; she is one of the founding members of Briar Grove's new rugby club. She also plays tennis. We're both on the high school team.

Recently, though, I have been worrying about Ellen. The reason is that she doesn't seem to want to hang out with me as much anymore. I have two theories about the cause of this, both of which are bad for her. Theory number one about why she's not hanging out with me is that Ellen wants to seem cool, and she feels that hanging out with her cousin will look weird to the Popular People. I hope this isn't true, but I'm fearing that she might be beginning to care about what the Popular People think—those catty, shallow people who care about appearances above all else.

Theory number two is that she has a boyfriend. She matured before most other girls. So the guys have been paying a lot of attention. Of course, it's totally fine with me if she gets a boyfriend. That's good and natural, as long as he's a good person who treats her well. I know that at some time this will happen, and she won't want to hang out with me as much. But I'm worried that she's started to hang out with a bad person who might hurt her. I thought that she would tell me if she had a boyfriend, yet I haven't heard a peep. I do have some guesses for possible contenders though. Well, actually, one possible contender: Jake Judson.

I've known Jake since the day we both started kindergarten. On that day, he peed on me in the bathroom, making it look like I'd done it, so that I had to go home. Our relationship has gone downhill since then. We fought a lot when we were kids, either verbally or physically—although now we just usually stay away from each other. He's really not a nice guy. But he tricks people into liking him, because he's really smart and a good athlete. I had always been smarter than him until this year, but I guess he really stepped up his game. Before, when he punched me or made fun of me, I always knew that I was smarter than him. Now I don't even have that anymore.

It also doesn't help that he's good looking, with carefully combed blond hair. And he's really good at sports, way better than me. Although he's not that tall, he'll probably be the captain of the tennis team next year, and he's on the swimming team, and he also runs cross-country.

He fakes people into thinking that he's a nice guy by always acting fake polite and fake thoughtful. He's especially nice to parents. He says stuff like "Hello, Mr. Smith. I'm so glad to see you, sir." But I know it's all phony, because he doesn't act like that to me in private at all. He acts all nice to people at school too, especially to the girls. Many people are tricked into thinking he's this great guy.

That's why I don't like Jake, and why I hope that he's not the reason that Ellen doesn't want to hang out with me anymore. And if he is, well, I guess there's nothing I can do about it. But that would be really bad for her.

On the bus ride home, I think about Ms. Beans and the textbook. The only way I could have stolen it is if taking it from her in my daydream spilled over into reality. But weird stuff like that happens only in science fiction novels, not real life. My daydream is a little blurry, but I vaguely remember in my dream everyone sitting completely still as I crept to Ms. Beans's desk and took the book. It didn't seem strange at the time, but now that I think about it, no one sits completely still for more than a few seconds.

I stick my hand in my pocket, looking for my keys, and feel something like a cube. That's weird. I pull out a green Rubik's cube attached to a string. My eyes widen as I recognize it. It's the Rubik's cube from Ms. Beans's car.

As the bus rolls along, I sit stunned. I haven't been to her car. Again, I only daydreamed it. Rubik's cubes from dreams don't end up in your pocket. Could I have somehow used my mind to take the book and her Rubik's cube?

When I get home, I immediately go upstairs to my bedroom. I try to remember exactly what I did in my daydream before I stole the textbook. How could I possibly have taken it with no one noticing? I guess I must have gone to her car. The Rubik's cube is evidence of that. But how did that happen with nobody in my class seeing me? Did something that was going on in Ms. Beans's class cause this to happen? I was just listening to Ms. Beans give a long, boring talk. Maybe I have some unique ability that only kicks in when Ms. Beans is droning on. I smile. Hey, that would be cool to have a superpower. Maybe I'm like Spider-Man, except my power doesn't come from a radioactive spider but from a monotonous teacher.

"Emit!" screams my mom from downstairs.

"Yes, Diana!" My mom hates it when I call her by her real name.

"C'mon downstairs!" she yells back. "And don't call me Diana."

As I walk into the kitchen, Mom says, "I was just at the church. They told me that you weren't at choir practice on Sunday night. I thought you said that you would go."

"I decided not to," I say. "Too busy with homework. I went to Starbucks instead."

"Emit, I thought that we had an understanding that you

would go to church choir and youth group," she says. "You know how important it is to be part of a church community."

"Mom, I'm not into church as much as you." This really isn't quite accurate. I actually really like our church. The youth group and choir are fun, and I get to see a lot of my friends there. But I have fun irritating my parents, who are both religious.

"Mom, why are you and Dad so religious?"

"It's just the way your dad and I are. It's the way I was raised by my parents. It's my faith."

"But Dad's dad isn't religious," I say. "Opa doesn't go to church at all."

Mom crosses her arms. "I don't want you to end up like your grandfather."

"I hope I do …" I mutter under my breath.

My dad's father, who lives about fifteen minutes' drive away from us, is quite the opposite of my parents. His name is Henry Friend. But I call him Opa, which is a German nickname for "grandfather." Not religious at all, he's a little funny looking, until you get used to him. He is eighty-something years old, but he's wrinkly like he's a hundred and acts like a twenty-year-old. He's one of these people with a huge metabolism and naturally huge muscles. He uses a wheelchair and never does any exercise, but he always looks super fit and muscly. The first time I saw him take off his shirt at the pool, I was shocked. I expected an old guy to be flabby and out of shape, especially a guy in a wheelchair. But he has big biceps and a six-pack. Way stronger looking than me, or anyone else in my family. And he's over eighty. He eats huge amounts but never gets fat. At the dinner table, he eats anything that's left over. We call him "the vacuum cleaner."

I don't know very much about my grandfather except that he's from Germany. Otherwise, he is very private and barely talks about himself. He never will talk about his early life. My parents say that this is because some traumatic things must have happened to him when he was growing up in Germany in the 1930s.

My grandmother, my father's mother, is more like my parents. She's relaxed and kind. I call her Oma, which is the German nickname for "grandmother." They say opposites attract. My German grandparents definitely fit into that rule. They had my dad when Opa was forty-one, long after they left Germany; my dad is in his midforties now. If you look carefully at Opa and my dad, you can see a faint family resemblance. But the resemblance is masked by how wrinkly Opa has become and also by how Opa is really lean and my dad is chubby. But if you look at pictures from when Opa was in his early thirties, he looks a lot like my dad does now.

Opa and Oma are completely devoted to us. For example, when my parents got their first jobs here after they finished graduate school, Opa immediately retired and moved to about fifteen minutes from us. He retired very young, and nobody understands how he had the money to retire so early. He bought a lot where a house had burned down in an old neighborhood. He built a beautiful new house there, which he helped to design. It's new, but he designed it to look old so it fits into the neighborhood. He enjoyed the construction process so much that he even helped the contractor out a lot, cutting wood and pounding nails—at least, as best he could from his wheelchair.

"Emit," my mom says, bringing me back from my thoughts. "Do you know anything about carpenter bees?"

"No, Mom. Not much, Mom. How come?" Maybe a long, boring speech from my mother will activate whatever crazy thing happened to me in school today.

"I think that's the explanation for that hole in the kitchen wall," she says. I look at her blankly. "You know, the one right there," she continues as she points at the wall behind me. "Remember, we noticed the hole last month when Opa and Oma and Ellen were over here for a few minutes. When I was outside today, I saw a big bee climb into the hole on the outside of the wall. I think the bee must have made the hole there and then dug through and made the hole on the inside. What do you think?"

"I don't know, Mom," I say. "I just think we need to get it fixed. Let me look into it."

Bugs are too interesting. I need to get my mom to talk about something boring. I know just what to do.

"Mom, I heard a little about President Brown's new policy proposal at school today. Can you tell me a little more about it?"

My mom smiles. "I knew you would be interested in that," she says enthusiastically. "What exactly are you wondering about?"

"You know, the usual," I say. "What's up with all of the new efforts to combat white supremacy? Isn't Brown proposing to change the constitution so people could be put in jail for racist hate speech?" I sit down on the kitchen chair, force my face into the most earnest, interested expression that I can, and try to get comfortable for the long speech that I know will flow forth from my mom's mouth.

"Ah." My mom smiles. "Well, you know that President Brown has been cracking down on one of the neo-Nazi groups. In fact, he just signed an executive order that allows police to arrest people if they show any Nazi-like behavior or display any Nazi symbols. It's all very controversial, because Brown's opponents say that the executive order violates the constitution and free speech. President Brown says it doesn't violate free-speech rights, because it's an issue of national security; he says that it's just like the rules that they now have in Germany. But to be doubly sure that stopping hate groups is legal, that's why he now wants a constitutional amendment. He thinks that Congress might act now because of the Trenton school shooting—you know, the one where the teenager killed nine people at the Jewish school? The shooter said that he'd been inspired by reading a lot of anti-Semitic neo-Nazi websites."

As a Brown supporter, my mom jumps at every opportunity to preach to me about his genius. She is so obsessed with Jacob Brown that I often call her a "Brownie." I don't think she especially likes that. She claims that she admires him because of his brilliance and because he has broken through barriers as the country's first Jewish president, and he's a liberal Democrat like her. But I don't think that's the whole story. I think she mainly likes him because he looks like Brad Pitt.

Usually, when she gives her typical lecture about how terrific Brown is, I try to listen to at least learn a few things. This time, I have something more to do. As she talks, I try to clear my mind of any distractions except my mom's droning voice. I wait to see if something strange happens—for all the drinking glasses in the kitchen to shatter or for something to explode. I tense my body and focus intently on activating my superpowers, or whatever it is that went on at school. Nothing happens.

A thought pops into my head. When I stole the book at school, I wasn't paying attention; I was completely zoned out. My "power" activated when I completely relaxed and cleared my mind. Maybe it's relaxing and emptying my mind that's the trigger.

I let my body go loose like a rag doll. I lean back on my chair and close my eyes. I try to completely stop thinking.

Never mind; that's impossible. By trying not to think, I'm just thinking about whether I'm thinking. Instead, I try to slow my thoughts, and rather than actively thinking, I just passively observe what's going on in the room. I listen to my mom's droning voice; I feel the breeze from the open window on my face; I analyze the texture of my jeans on my legs; I feel my breath enter and leave my lungs. Suddenly a feeling of peace comes over me.

When I open my eyes, everything in the room is as still as a statue. My mom's voice is paused on the letter *R*.

"… rrrrrrrrr …" My mother's voice does not waiver, not even for a breath. I slowly stand up. I can move normally but she is paused in one moment.

After thirty seconds or so, her voice slowly changes to a different sound. "… owwwwwwwwww …" This doesn't make sense. Why is everything frozen except her voice?

I suddenly realize what is happening. I must have slowed time. Time hasn't stopped. Instead, it's just slowed way down. While everything else is slowed down, I'm still doing things at normal speed. My mom is in the middle of saying "Brown," except slowed down. She's slowed down a lot: her lips are barely moving.

Wow! Stunned, I sit for a couple minutes in the sloweddown world, gathering my thoughts. I suddenly feel warmly happy. I could have a lot of fun with this! I sit back down on the kitchen chair so my mom won't be suspicious about a sudden change in my position, if time speeds up again. If relaxing and calming my mind causes time to slow, then maybe tensing and actively thinking will make time return to normal. I flex my muscles and start thinking about my day, about school, and about the bus ride home.

"… n is doing his best to fight white supremacists. He has started receiving death threats from an underground group of neo-Nazis. This is the kind of thing you might expect from these bad people. I don't think anything will happen; I can't imagine they would actually go after the president."

She's now back to normal speed.

It worked! I have a … superpower? Well, it's not a power like a superhero might have, but it's certainly some sort of power. I pinch my arm to make sure I'm not dreaming. A million questions are running through my mind. How did I get this power? Have I had it forever? What can I do with it? Can I really slow anything and anyone? Like, could I slow Niagara Falls or a tornado?

I decide to go investigate. "Thanks, Mom. That's very interesting."

"No problem, baby. I love talking to you about absolutely anything. I can tell you a lot more about this issue, if you're interested," she says, sounding like a cooing pigeon.

"All right." I sprint upstairs, run into my room, and slam my door. I relax my body, calm my mind, and slow time again, and again, and again. I'm getting better at this. After four time-slows, a crushing headache grabs my head. It feels like someone is smashing my head with a hammer. There must be a restriction on how much slowing I can do. I massage my temples and stumble downstairs into the living room.

"Are you all right, Emit?" my mom asks.

"Yes, I'm fine," I reply. "Just a headache."

"Do you need some Advil?" she asks. I shake my head and collapse onto the couch. I click the power button on the TV's remote control.

"… Gutenberg Bible was stolen from the Russian State Library in Moscow. Russian police released this footage from a security camera in the gallery." A blurry black-and-white video pops up on the screen. An old bible sits in a glass case in the center of a large room. I wait for something dramatic to happen—for criminals in ski masks to burst through the auditorium doors, or a Russian spy to be lowered slowly from the ceiling on a thin cable. But nothing happens. Instead, the Gutenberg Bible simply disappears. The bible is there in the video, and then suddenly it's not. The camera switches back to the CNN reporter. "Police suspect a hacker altered the video footage so the criminal cannot be identified." Then the show goes into a commercial break.

What a cool crime. It's like a heist movie, except it's real. I know a little bit about how hackers work, because I had tried to learn coding for the web for a few months. But I do not understand how a hacker can break into a government camera and change a video feed. The most I could ever do was create a website.

My headache is just about gone. I tell my mom that I'm going upstairs to lie down. Once I close my bedroom door, I continue practicing my skill. I repeatedly slow time. I can tell I'm slowing time by looking at the second hand of the old electric alarm clock that's sitting on the table next to my bed. When time slows, the hand starts to move so slowly that it's hard to tell that it's moving at all. Otherwise, the world seems normal. I can move at normal speed through the slowed world.

I start to understand some of my skill's details. I can slow time about five times in quick succession before I get a headache. Then I have to take a break for half an hour or so. I practice for a couple more hours, interspersed with the half-hour breaks. Occasionally my mom knocks on the door and asks about my headache, and I tell her it still hurts and it feels good to lie down.

I'm getting good at quickly slowing time. I can now slow time almost instantly by concentrating on a certain feeling of emptiness in the part of my brain that's right behind my eyes. I focus on the emptiness; then time slows immediately. I also figure out how to reliably release the world back up to normal speed. I let my brain flip out of the empty feeling, and the world speeds back up. With a little practice, this has become easy.

I'm amazed that I didn't notice this skill before. Had I been slowing time before without knowing it?

I decide to conduct some more experiments with the new gift. I want to understand exactly what slows down when I slow time. I grab my baseball, bound down the stairs, and head toward the backyard. As I pass the kitchen, my mom asks, "Is your headache feeling better now?"

"Yeah," I say. "Miracle recovery."

I go to my favorite part of the backyard, which is concealed from the house by mom's azalea bushes, with a wooden fence blocking the view from our rear neighbors. I put the baseball on the ground, relax my body, calm my mind, and flip to the empty feeling. I open my eyes. I can tell by the stillness of the trees, birds, and even the wind that I have slowed time. I pick up my baseball and toss it underhand a few feet, and watch it roll to a stop on the ground. As I expected, in slowed time, the baseball moves at a normal speed, at least from my perspective. I adjust my body and thoughts to allow time to speed up again. I pick up the baseball. Then, I throw it overhand hard, and while it is in midair, I flip to the empty feeling to slow down time. The ball is still in the air, but it is inching forward ever so slowly. It seems to be moving about an inch per second. I walk over to the barely moving baseball and put my hand in front of it. The baseball pushes my hand firmly. It must keep its momentum even when time is slowed.

My final experiment may be a bit dangerous. I bring three cardboard cereal boxes from the recycling bin and place them one in front of the other in front of the wood fence. I relax, calm my mind, and flip my brain to the empty feeling. Time slows. Then I throw the baseball at the cereal boxes and immediately return time to normal. The ball disappears from the air, but a jagged hole—the size of a baseball—has been bored through each of the boxes. There's a dent with some splintering in the wooden fence behind. Wow! If I throw something in slow time, it will have a much higher velocity in normal time than something actually thrown in normal time. The baseball I threw was undoubtedly faster than a ball thrown by the fastest professional pitcher. I guess this also means that if I punch someone in slow time, that punch will be much, much stronger than a punch thrown in normal time. That could definitely be useful in the future! Dave Slye, a thuggy guy at school, won't bully me for long if I can punch a hundred times harder than him.

"Dinner time in fifteen minutes!" my mom yells from the kitchen. I return inside.

"What's for dinner?" I ask.

"Beef tacos. Will you put the water glasses on the table?"

I grab two glasses and start to take them to the table. "Uuumph!" I trip over a chair. The water glasses fly into the air. They are about to hit the floor when I remember my slowing power. I flip to the empty feeling, and just like that, the glasses are suspended in midair. Wow, I'm getting good at this. I can really slow things quickly now. I walk over to the two glasses and grab them before they hit the ground. A few water droplets are also sailing through the air. I grab a paper towel and pick the water droplets out of the air. Then I move back to where I was when I tripped. I tense my body, busy my mind, and return to normal time.

"Are you all right, Emit?" stammers my mom. "How did you catch those glasses?"

"I slowed down time and grabbed them out of the air," I casually reply.

"Say again?" My mom has a worried look on her face. I suddenly realize she thinks I'm crazy.

"I'm kidding; I just have quick reflexes."

"Ahh." My mom smiles. "Well, I'm glad you're OK." She goes back to preparing dinner.

Whew, that was close. I could tell she was about to suggest I visit Mrs. Cardigan again. Mrs. Cardigan is a local children's therapist whom I had to visit for a while when I was seven. I made the mistake of messing with my mom by telling her that I had an imaginary friend named Lupert. She took me to see Mrs. Cardigan, where I endured several weeks of miserable therapy visits. We started off innocently coloring pictures of our feelings, but after a few sessions, it escalated into a debate about whether having an imaginary friend was abnormal. I haven't spoken to Mrs. Cardigan since then. I'm sure she would have a great time with my new ability.

After dinner, I help with the dishes. Then I notice that it's still light out. I ask, "Mom, can I go over to Peyton's house and get my football? I left it there yesterday."

"Sure," my mom replies. "Just don't stay too long. I know it's the weekend tomorrow. But you still need your sleep."

"All right." I sprint out the door, run down the walk, and dash across the street toward Peyton's house. Peyton Durst is one of my closest friends. I've known him since his family moved in across the street, when we were both five.

I'm so focused on my thoughts that I don't notice the car until I hear the roar of the car engine and the screeching of tires. I look up, and the car is just a few feet away, coming right at me.

CHAPTER 3

Think slow. I flip my brain to the empty feeling. Time comes to a halt. I take a moment to catch my breath, then stroll up to the formerly speeding car. I peer through the driver's window. My grandfather, Opa, sits frozen in the driver's seat of his big black Mercedes. I suspect that he'd just seen me, because there is a look of horror on his face. I realize that when I return to normal time, I have to make it look like I had just dived out of the way. But I also have to be far enough away that he can't swerve and hit me. I can't make Opa suspicious.

I decide to lie facedown on the grass between the sidewalk and the street. I focus on flipping my brain back to normal time and tense my muscles.

"Emit! Emit, are you all right?" My grandfather rolls down his window and looks over at me anxiously. I maintain a scared expression on my face.

"Yes, I'm fine," I whimper. "Just a little shaken up." I stand up and dust myself off.

"Thank God you're all right. You almost gave me a heart

attack," he admits. "Would you mind helping me into my wheelchair?"

"Sure, Opa." He hates having to use a wheelchair, despite having painful arthritis in both knees. My parents told me that the arthritis started after he fell down the stairs and injured his knees. He had to have surgery for the injuries from the fall, and the arthritis started about ten years later. He hates being old; he's over eighty. About ten years ago, the arthritis caused him to fall while crossing a busy street. He agreed then to use the wheelchair most of the time, but he's still grumpy about it. At least he can still drive; his legs provide enough power for pushing the brake and accelerator, just not enough for walking. And he's really good at moving around in his wheelchair.

"C'mon, Emit. You can ponder life later," states Opa matter-of-factly.

"Yes, Opa." I dash over to the Mercedes and open the back door. I pull out the folded green wheelchair and carry it over to the driver's door. Opa pushes open the door and starts to use his strong arms and hands to maneuver his body into the wheelchair.

I see his missing left little finger. Opa has told me with twinkling eyes that during college, it was severed in a sword duel involving the affections of a Spanish dancer. However, my parents tell me that when Opa was five years old, a bee bit his left pinky, the bite got infected, and the rotting finger eventually had to be removed. Opa seems very accustomed to having only four digits on his left hand. He can drive, grip objects, and even hit a baseball. He can still do that from his wheelchair. He looks really old. But other than his bad knees, he's in remarkably good shape for an old guy.

Opa grabs my shoulders and lifts himself up as he positions himself directly over the wheelchair. He releases me and grunts as he drops into the chair. I follow him as he rolls up the driveway, pushing himself firmly with his hands on the wheels up the incline. At the front porch, Opa gets out of his chair, and I help him climb the four steps onto the porch. I am about to open the door when he grabs my shoulder.

"Could we, um … not mention to your parents what happened with the car back there? Your mother has been getting on me lately about my, uh … reckless driving," he says, looking down at his toes. "I'm afraid she would try to make me stop driving. I've had my driver's license since I was seventeen, and I don't plan to give it up now," he proclaims.

"Sure," I reply. I open the front door and kick my shoes off into the pit. The pit is an area to the right of the front door where we all leave our shoes when we enter.

"Diana," Opa bellows. "Diana Friend!"

"Opa!" My mom runs in from the other room. She kisses him on the cheek, then looks over at me. "Thank you for helping Opa out of the car."

"No problem," I mumble.

"Rob! Your father is here," yells my mom over her shoulder.

"Dad!" my father says, and clomps down the stairs. "Why

are you here?" My dad puts his hand on his forehead. "Sorry, that sounded rude."

Opa rolls over in his chair and hugs my dad around his waist. "It's really good to see you, son."

"You too, Dad," says my dad. "So, what's up?"

"Well, I was wondering if Emit wanted to go to the Giants game tomorrow? I already bought the tickets." Opa grins. "It would be nice to spend a little time with my grandson."

"Can I go, Mom?" I look up at my mom expectantly.

"Yes, that's fine," she says.

"Yesss!" I yell. "Awesome. Thanks, Opa. I can't wait!" Opa nods and grins. "Well, I'm going to get my football at Peyton's," I say, and jog outside.

*

When I get to Peyton's house, I knock on the door. The door opens before my second knock. I'm surprised he's right there at the door. He's quite a computer guy, and usually when I go over, I have to go up to his room to get him from in front of his computer. Peyton is pretty good at sports too, but he doesn't play on any teams, because his computer stuff takes so much time. So most of the physical activity he does is just playing around with me. When we compete with each other, I usually win. But he's good enough that it's fun for me. He sometimes gets frustrated that he doesn't win more. It's tempting for me to let him win more. But I always try my hardest; it would be disrespectful to him for me not to. He's better than me at computers. I'm better at sports.

"Hey, Emit," says Peyton. "Do you want to throw the football for a few minutes?"

"Ummm … yeah, sure. I think I can," I reply.

"Awesome," he says. "I've been cooped up too long upstairs, working on my computer. I need to get off my rear end, and you came over exactly at the right time. Let's use your football. It's here already." He picks it up, and we walk through his driveway and to the backyard. He throws the football to me hard, which catches me off guard.

"Oof!" I let out.

"Come on, Emit. Slow reflexes, huh?" Peyton teases.

"Faster reflexes than you," I shoot back.

"It's so obvious I have faster reflexes, Emit. We can do any contest you choose. I'll win easily," he says.

"Fine. Get ready!" I put the football down. I nod at his soccer goal and the soccer ball on the ground in front of it. Peyton stands in front of the goal and takes a wide stance.

"Bring it on," he challenges. I take a step back, then sprint toward the soccer ball. My foot smacks the ball cleanly and it soars into the air. Peyton dives at the last minute and barely gets his hand on it. The ball is deflected away from the goal to the left. Peyton smiles as he gets up.

"That was crap," I mumble.

"Let's see you do better," Peyton says. I switch places with him, guarding the goal. He retrieves the ball, places it, and prepares to try to kick it past me into the goal. I look at his waist. I remember my soccer coach from fourth grade kid soccer repeatedly said that all movement originates in the waist.

"Ready?" Peyton asks. I nod my head. "One to zero, I'm ahead," he adds. Peyton darts toward the ball and kicks it solidly. I dive the correct direction, but the ball flies right past my outstretched hands into the net.

"Yesss!" Peyton drops into the classic celebration kneel with his arms stretched out to the sides.

"Don't celebrate yet," I warn him. "I can still come back."

"We'll see about that," he boasts. Peyton stands up and strolls over to the goal. I get ready to kick again. "I'm behind two–zero," I say. "First to three."

I sprint forward and kick the ball cleanly. Peyton dives one way and the ball flies the other into the net.

"Yesss!" I pump my arm. "Two–one." Peyton gets up, pulls the ball out of the net, and places it and himself in position to kick again.

"You're going down this time," Peyton warns. Before kicking, he picks up the ball, kisses it, and points to the right corner of the goal. When he then kicks it, the ball, of course, starts to the left. Instead of diving, I immediately slow down time. I calmly walk over and nudge the ball off its trajectory. I return to my original position in front of the goal and resume normal time.

The ball sails just outside the left corner of the goal. "Dang, I could swear that kick was right on target," Peyton grumbles.

"Two–two," I laugh. "Looks like it's comeback time."

"You're cheating somehow," he gripes.

"How could I possibly cheat?" I retort. "Am I Luke Skywalker, and did I use the Force to push the ball?"

"Yeah," he laughs. "Well, let's finish this."

I nod. I inhale deeply, then dash toward the ball. My foot makes solid contact. I slow time, and the ball stops in midair. I need to find a way to get it past Peyton without raising his suspicions. First I wait about forty-five seconds until I see him gradually lean right. This means he is beginning a dive to the right. Now, if I can force the ball to the left, I win. An idea pops into my brain. I get on my knees next to the nearly frozen ball. I begin to blow on the right side of the ball. After several seconds, I can see it slowly changing direction. I continue to blow until it is pointed exactly at the left corner of the goal. Next, I blow on the back of the ball to speed it up so there is no way Peyton will have a chance to change course and block the ball. I could have tried to use my fingers to push the ball, but little puffs of air are more precise. I take a moment to make sure the trajectory of the ball is perfect. Satisfied, I return to my original position before resuming normal time.

The ball shoots into the goal.

"Noooo!" Peyton lies on the ground in defeat.

"Ha! Who has the best reflexes now?" I tease.

"You," he admits with a scowl. "At least for today."

"That's right." I flail my arms out in my classic victory dance. Peyton stands up and saunters slowly to the back door. He looks so defeated I almost feel bad for cheating.

"I was sure I would win that," says Peyton sadly.

"Yeah, bad luck," I agree.

"I hate to admit, but that was a great shot that you just did," says Peyton. "I could swear that you made the ball curve, just like a pro. I thought the ball was heading to the right, so I dove there. But then it curved to the left."

"Thanks," I say. "I've been working on shooting."

Peyton suddenly turns and chucks the ball right at me. I immediately slow down time by instinct. I'm getting good at this! After pondering what to do next, I decide to just return to normal time and catch the ball. If I were to do anything else, Peyton would probably be suspicious. I speed time back up.

The ball hits me in the stomach, knocking the air out of me. I barely make the catch.

Peyton looks at me glumly. "I guess you did win fair and square."

I stare at Peyton. "Don't be a sore loser." He turns around and walks inside his house. He slams the door. He must have woken up on the wrong side of bed, I think to myself.

I chuckle and stroll across the street to my house. I have one more experiment to try.

"Maddy Friend!" I yell as I enter the front door of our house.

"What do you want, Emit?" my sister yells back.

"Can you come downstairs?"

Lately my sister is always upstairs in her room, watching YouTube. She's obsessed with some stupid YouTuber named Meggie. All of her friends also love the Meggie videos. She must be an amazing singer or comedian, or whatever, for so many eleven-year-old girls to love her.

"What, Emit?" Maddy asks sarcastically as she plops down in the comfy green leather chair in the living room.

"Watch your tone, young lady," I command. She hates when I impersonate Dad's signature phrase.

"Shut up, Emit," Maddy shoots back. "What do you want?" I slow down time. I stroll over to my sister and poke her lightly on the left arm. I then return to where I was standing and return to normal time.

"Ow!" Maddy grabs her left arm. "What was that?"

"What was what?" I ask innocently.

"I just got a pain in my arm." She sits down on our couch. "It feels like I got stung by a bee."

"That sucks," I say.

I do it again. I slow time, poke her in the arm, return to where I was, and resume normal time.

"Ouch!" she says. "There it is again." She looks at me with a flare of anger. "Emit, are you messing with me?"

"What, me? I would never do such a thing. How could I?"

"I think you did," she says. "At the exact same time that my arm hurt, you did a jerk." She demonstrates a sudden, jerky movement. "You did that both times my arm hurt." Did you put a whoopy cushion under my seat and you pushed a button so that I got zapped or something? I remember you did that with that stupid fart app on your phone before." She starts to rummage behind the chair cushions, but she comes up empty.

"I would never do anything to hurt my sister," I respond.

"Family first. Family ties are sacred ties."

"Yeah. Blah, blah, blah. What do you want, anyway?" Maddy asks.

"Oh, I forgot," I answer quickly.

"Well, that was a waste. You're stupid, Emit," she gripes, executing an excellent annoyed-younger-sister combined eye-roll and head-roll as she trudges back upstairs.

I try to figure out what she was talking about when she said that I jerked sometimes. That's what they harped on me at school about too. They would call me Herky-Jerky, and say that I jerked. Then I understand. The jerking movement that she mentioned must have been how she interpreted my being in a slightly different position when I speeded time back up compared to when I earlier slowed time down. Even if part of me was just three inches different, she would see that as a quick three-inch movement.

So I've learned a couple lessons. The first one is that I should not slow time when people are looking right at me. If they are not looking at me, they won't notice what looks like a quick jerk movement when I stop slowing time. The second lesson is when I speed time back up, I need to be careful to be in the same position as when I slowed time down. The greater the change in my position, the greater the jerk that people see.

I begin to understand the great strength of my slowing power. Now it hits me. Yesss! I can beat my friends at any game. I can spring pranks on my sister whenever I want. My thoughts race ahead. Maybe tomorrow, when I go to the Giants game with Opa, I can experiment some more. I could tackle some football players in slow time. I smile.

CHAPTER 4

"Time to wake up, Emit!" yells my mom from downstairs. I groan and put my pillow over my head.

"No …" I moan in the depths of teenager agony.

"It's nine o'clock, and the Giants game starts at eleven!" she shouts. "It's early because the TV network demanded it. Come downstairs and eat breakfast."

"Yes, Diana." I get out of bed and stumble over to my closet.

"Don't call me that," my mom adds after a minute.

I smile, throw on a green T-shirt and some khaki shorts, then stroll downstairs. I smell fresh bacon.

Mom smiles at me and says, "Good morning." She makes herself a smoothie with her new Ninja blender. My dad sits at the table, reading something on his phone. "Opa is going to pick you up in about an hour. The game should be fun," adds my mom.

"Mm-hmm," I mumble.

"I remember when your grandfather used to take me to football games when I was your age," says my dad. "We had so much fun yelling at players. One time I showed up on the big screen at one of the games. I was so surprised I peed in my pants on live TV."

"How old were you?" I ask, horrified.

"Ten." My dad sees the disgusted expression on my face. "Nine." He looks over again. "Actually, eight."

*

An hour or so later, Opa and I are inhaling hot dogs at the Giants game. They're playing the Cardinals. We always get good seats, because they save good spots for people in wheelchairs. I stare up at the time on the big screen.

"Ten minutes left until the game." I don't exactly know why, but this is kind of boring. Opa grunts.

Suddenly the Giants theme song booms out over the speakers, and the players rush onto the field.

"Look," I call out to Opa. "Eli Benny!" I point at the famous quarterback.

"I don't pay attention to the players anymore," Opa replies. "I've seen so many Giants quarterbacks through the years I can't even count them." I chuckle.

"Kickoff in ten, nine, eight ..." yells the announcer.

"All of this energy exhausts me," complains my grandfather.

"... three, two, one," screams the announcer.

A Cardinals player kicks the football, which soars down the field. The Giants kickoff returner, Van Clyborn, catches the ball and weaves down the field.

"Get him! Get him!" scream the few Cardinals fans. Clyborn

runs right through the first defender, knocking him to the ground.

"Go!" Opa yells down to the field. Clyborn runs past the fifty-yard line. He dashes straight toward a hole in the Cardinals' defense. Suddenly a huge, 250-pound Cardinals player, Mean Jim Keen, blocks the hole, opening his arms to prepare to engulf Clyborn and crush him.

"No!" Without thinking, I slow time. The stadium freezes and becomes silent. Stunned at what I've done through instinct, I freeze, mimicking the appearance of everyone else in the stadium. Have I really done this? This is crazy. It's one thing to slow time to trick Peyton. It's a whole other situation to do it at a pro football game. What should I do? After a few more seconds of stillness, I decide.

I dash down the aisle toward the fence separating the fans from the field. I hoist myself over and drop down to the turf below. Sprinting over to the frozen Van Clyborn, the kick returner with the ball, I consider my choices. I need to find a way to stop the tackle without being too suspicious. Moving any of the frozen players would draw too much attention and look unnatural to the fans when time returns to normal. I have to do something major though, or I might not succeed in stopping the tackle. Blowing on the ball won't help.

An idea pops into my head. I walk carefully over to Mean Jim Keen, the would-be tackler. I kneel down and untie his left shoe and loosen it. I then move to his left side, and I grab his left foot, bracing my feet against the ground. Using all my strength, I pull his foot as far as I can to his left, about nine inches. I also point his foot out to the side. I have to be careful not to topple him over. But I find that this isn't so difficult, because his momentum tends to keep him upright; it's the same persistence of momentum in slowed time that I learned about with the baseball. With all my tugging, his left foot has now come almost completely out of his loosened shoe. I hope that when I speed up time, he'll lose his balance and trip on his shoe.

Now I jog back to the fence, jump over, and hop back into my seat. Opa is still there, frozen just like everyone else. I return time to normal. Just as I hoped, Mean Jim Keen trips, landing on his face. I grin as Van Clyborn jumps over Keen's prone body, and sprints to the end zone. Touchdown Giants!

Wow! This is totally cool. Van Clyborn carried the ball into the end zone, but I was responsible for the score because I tripped Jim Keen. Without me, it wouldn't have happened. I may not be much of an athlete, but I have scored a touchdown in a pro football game. Cool!

My attention is drawn up the field to a clump of people. I feel a cold sweat as I see the Cardinals trainers and the team doctor tending to the prone form of Mean Jim Keen. Several of his Cardinals teammates are standing nearby, looking deeply concerned. Keen is writhing on the ground, clutching his left knee. This is the same knee that I had pulled to the side when time was slowed. The doctor and trainer try to straighten Keen's leg but can't. I see them signal for the meat wagon. This is the little electric golf cart that teams use to drive injured players off the field. I join with the crowd as we cheer in respect as Keen is placed on a stretcher and put on the cart.

"That's tough," Opa says. "It looks like a torn ACL." I hear the people near me talk about the end of Keen's season, maybe his career. Mean Jim Keen doesn't look so mean as he is driven off. He looks sad and in pain, with his world turned upside down. My stomach sinks as I start wondering whether my movement of Keen's leg snapped his ACL. I moved his leg only nine inches. But when I speeded time back up, did Keen experience the sudden change in the position of his leg as a violent snapping? It dawns on me that having your leg moved nine inches in an instant would have the same force as your leg being hit by a sledgehammer.

The next two hours of the game go by without me really noticing much of what's happening on the field. I can't stop thinking of the sadness and pain on Jim Keen's face. I was just trying to have fun. But I really hurt him badly.

At the start of the fourth quarter, I snap out of my daze, and I start paying close attention again. The score is close: 35–34 Cardinals. One-point difference! Five minutes into the fourth quarter, we kick a field goal. We're ahead by two!

I am finally able to stop obsessing about Jim Keen. There's nothing that I can do now. I just need to be more careful in the future.

"Our kicker is on fire!" I yell over to Opa.

"Yep! This is exciting!" Even Opa is on the edge of his seat. The fans are going bananas.

"Go, Giants! Let's go!" scream the fans.

The sound is overpowering. I don't hear a single cheer from a Cardinals fan; the Giants fans drown them out. The energy in the air is overwhelming. We're all so nervous. All that the Cardinals need is a field goal to beat us.

We kick off. The ball flies all the way to the center of the end zone. Instead of kneeling, the Cardinals kick returner decides to run. He's tackled at the twenty-five-yard line. First down, Cardinals.

"Defense! Defense!" yells the crowd. First down: incomplete pass. Second down: the Giants stop a run up the middle after only two yards. The Giants fans scream as they smell victory.

On third down, the Cardinals QB receives the snap, fakes right, and hands the ball to the fullback. The fake pulls the Giants linemen to the side, leaving a hole wide open for the Cardinals fullback. He runs straight through, and there's nothing but air between him and a touchdown. There is not a single Giants player within twenty yards. We're going to lose after all. Dang it. Ahead with three minutes to go, but we can't hang on to the lead.

Eyes fixed like lasers on the runner, Opa screams, "Get him, Giants! Knock him dow …"

I feel a tingle in my upper back. Opa freezes midword, as does the rest of the stadium.

Suddenly time has slowed. I didn't realize that I had done it. Usually time slows only when I concentrate hard on doing it. But this time my brain must have done it automatically, subconsciously. Now that time is slowed, I might as well go with it. I walk down to the field. I pause to think carefully. I need to take down the Cardinals fullback. But I also realize now that it is easy to injure him. Even a modest change in position when time is slowed is experienced as a sudden forceful movement when time speeds up again. There are no Giants players anywhere nearby, so I can't make it look like they tackled him. If I don't get this right, we lose the game.

The Cardinals runner is frozen in midair in midstride, with his front and back feet both suspended above the ground. If I move his front foot a few inches to the left, he should lose his footing and fall as soon as I speed up time. On the other hand, there is a chance he would get hurt—break his leg or something as it is jerked to the side. I don't want to feel responsible for two injuries today. No, I need a better option.

Light bulb! I have an idea. I walk over to the runner, carefully grasp his helmet, and twist it a bit on his head so that it partially blocks his view from one eye. I then grab him around the waist and rotate him about two inches to the left. He is still in midair, but he is now pointing more toward our approaching linemen. To move him even this small amount, I have to use a large amount of force, because of the runner's momentum. I don't think I have moved him so much that he will be injured when time returns to normal.

I hope that my adjustments will make the runner run straight into the linemen. I figure that it will take at least a moment or two before he can get his helmet straight, and during that time, he'll be sprinting in the wrong direction.

I admire my handiwork for a few moments and then run back up to my seat. Unfortunately, in my excitement, I forget and sit on the opposite side of Opa from where I had started. Opa is frozen yelling in the direction of my original seat.

Wait a second. I'm confused. Wasn't Opa frozen looking toward the field when I left? But now he's looking to the side. I must have remembered wrong. I speed up time.

"… n, Giants!" Opa suddenly continues. Opa stops, looks around, and sees me on his other side. In his excitement at the game, he doesn't notice that I have magically switched sides.

My strategy works perfectly! The Cardinals runner stumbles, shakes his head to reorient his helmet, regains his balance, but then runs straight into the group of three Giants linemen. They submerge him in half a ton of Giants beef.

When the pile disperses, the Cardinals player gets up and walks off the field, still fiddling with his helmet, and limping slightly. Two minutes left and we are up by two. Fourth down. Instead of punting, the Cardinals fake the punt and run. We stop them just short of the first down. All of the Cardinals fans groan.

Two minutes later, our quarterback, Eli Benny, takes the last of four snaps, kneels for the final time, and runs out the clock. We win! Opa and I look at each other, smile mischievously, and sprint for the exits, with me on foot and Opa racing me in his wheelchair. In his chair, he's faster than I am. Very fast for a guy who's a million years old. I'm glad I have his genes.

We exit the stadium before the rest of the crowd and avoid most of the traffic. I feel great! *We* really did win. It wasn't just the players, it was me too. I did it as much as Eli Benny. I'm Eli Benny's secret teammate. I'm the Giants' phantom weapon. I'm their secret savior. Without me, the Giants would certainly have lost.

Slowing time is awesome! I'm thrilled I have this ability. I'm also glad a Cardinals fan doesn't have it. Or what if a criminal or bad person did …?

"Can I turn on the radio, Emit?" Opa startles me.

"Uh, ya, sure," I reply. Opa flips to a local news channel.

"… new evidence uncovered in the Gutenberg Bible heist. Russian police officials have disclosed that they have apprehended a suspect." Boy, this story has really captured people's curiosity.

I suddenly make a connection. An expensive bible there one minute and gone the next in the surveillance video. Maybe it wasn't computer hacking of the video feed. Maybe I'm not the only person who can slow.

CHAPTER 5

"Put everything away. You're about to get your final," proclaims Ms. Beans. Together the class lets out a loud groan. "Yeah, yeah, yeah," she says.

"We just had a quiz on Friday," I blurt, sinking down in my chair.

"So," retorts Ms. Beans, "this is your final exam."

"This isn't fair."

"Well, you're not the teacher, Emit," she responds. "So do what I say."

I glare at her but zip my lips. She glares back at me, but with a little twinkle in her eyes, as she passes out the test papers.

"Hold on to your test when you're done, and I better not hear any talking," she warns. "And remember, try your hardest on this test. It counts for thirty percent of your grade. All right, you all can start."

Ten minutes later, I start to get really bored of testing. I decide to take a break and stretch my legs. And Ms. Beans can't stop me, because I also see an opportunity to practice my new abilities. I slow. Now that Ms. Beans can't yell at me, I stand up and make my way to the back of the class. I really like slowing. It's like taking a picture of the world, but being able to see it from every direction, and being able to interact with the things in it. Being god, if there is one, must feel something like this. I can make changes and do things to people without them being able to respond, or even see me.

I smile when I think about how a major great thing about this power is observing the people and things around me at a single instant. It's like I can take a 3-D picture of the world, and then walk around in it.

I turn my attention to the slowed classroom. The first thing I notice is that Ellen's seat is empty. She must be sick.

I see one boy in the middle of a yawn. A girl has spittle flying out of her nose after a sneeze. Ms. Beans, in the front, is picking her nose. Ms. Beans, that's gross. And Jake Judson is cheating!

How have I not noticed this before? I walk up right next to him and it's obvious. Jake has taped a little slip of paper discreetly to the side of his shoe. Upon closer inspection, I see letters, which I assume are the answers to the multiple-choice final, written on the paper. Apparently, whenever he is unsure of an answer, he just peers down at this sheet that has answers on it, probably given to him by a student in another class. I'm guessing that he has cheated on many tests in exactly the same way.

I know that I should be mad about Jake cheating, but I instead feel relieved. I've been worried because my grades are worse than his. Jake is a jerk, and I was proud that I was always better in school. I began to doubt myself when Jake started getting better grades. Now I know it's cheating making his grades better and not intelligence or hard work. The question is, what do I do about it? A smile spreads across my face as the idea comes.

Slowly, so there is no way Jake can feel it, I remove the paper with the answers from his shoe and toss it in the trash. Next, I get a different sheet of paper, the same size as the original one, and write random answers on it, trying to write in the same handwriting as whoever wrote the answers on the original sheet. Finally, I tape the paper back onto the side of his shoe, in the same position as before. I return to my seat and speed time back up.

After the final, Ms. Beans makes us sit quietly while she runs our tests through an app on her phone that immediately grades them for her. When she's finished doing this, we get to see our grades. I am pretty happy with my grade, a ninety-two. However, I am even happier when I hear Jake yell "What the heck!" Biting his lip, he walks up to Ms. Beans and whispers in a voice that I can just barely hear, "I think you might have made a mistake with grading my test. I'm pretty confident that these answers are all right."

"I'm happy to look at it again, Jake. Please give that here," demands Ms. Beans in an unusually harsh voice that everyone can hear. As she reads through his test, a sinister smile appears on her face. "No, no, no. I'm sorry, but all of these are wrong,

Jake," she says. "For example, the twentieth question asks, 'What do the *M* and *C* stand for in Albert Einstein's theory E=MC2?' You chose the answer that says that the *M* stands for 'math' and *C* stands for 'cockroach.'" The rest of the class laughs. "Do you really think that's the right answer?" she asks.

"Ummm … yes," he answers after thinking about it for a few seconds. The class laughs again.

"Go back to your desk, Jake," Ms. Beans commands.

"I know my answers are right," mumbles Jake as he walks past me. I smile at him as he passes.

After class, as I walk down the hall, I spot Ms. Beans talking to Jake. She seems to be quite angry. Very innocently I position myself ten feet behind Jake, facing away. I strain to hear what they're saying.

"… failed this test," I hear Ms. Beans scold. "How could you do that when you've been getting high A's on all the other ones?" Jake mumbles something incoherent. "Be honest, Jake," warns Ms. Beans without an ounce of humor. "Have you been cheating on the other tests?" I experience a feeling of warm happiness. Finally Jake Judson is getting what he deserves.

"Emit!" yells Ellen, jolting me out of my reverie. I smile as she approaches. "Are you about ready to go to tennis practice?" she says. "We should probably go now."

"Yes, I'm ready."

"Great, but first I need to stop at my locker," she says. "Just come with me so we can go to the courts together."

"All right," I say.

We make our way through the clumps of teenagers and to Ellen's locker, which is at the opposite end of the school from Ms. Beans's classroom.

"I forgot how far it is to your locker. I should've brought my hiking boots," I say.

"I'm sorry that you had to walk such a long, long way, you baby," says Ellen with a smile as she enters in her combination. Accidentally I look up and see that her combination is 31-22-8. I file the numbers in my brain, in case I need the combination later. I don't know why I do this. Just instinct, I suppose. "I'm running out of tennis balls," she says as she pulls out her tennis bag. "Do you have any?"

"No. I'm just glad I remembered my racket."

"So irresponsible," she teases. "What would you do without me?"

"It would be kinda nice to not have an annoying sophomore nagging me all the time," I say with a grin.

Ellen closes her locker and looks at me. "Put a lid on it, freshman."

"You know I hate it when you call me a freshman," I say.

"Yeah, so what?" she says. "What are you going to do about it?"

"I'm gonna do something," I promise.

"I bet you won't."

"Just wait. You'll see."

*

I spend all of the next day thinking about how best to prank Ellen. I hesitate to prank her, but she did dare me to do something. The prank shouldn't be too harmful, just fun. I have fun thinking a lot about it, and I come up with a plan that will let me practice my new skills.

On the following day, she catches up with me as usual outside Ms. Beans's class so we can walk to tennis together. I run my plan through my head as we casually stroll toward her locker.

"Emit, you know that guy, Jake, in Ms. Beans's class?" asks Ellen.

"Yes … Why do you ask?"

"Oh, I was just wondering whether you think he's"—she makes air quotes—"cool or not. He's pretty cute for a freshman. And he's nice. I've been getting to know him a bit. Just hanging out a few times."

"Ewww …" I pretend to gag. "Ellen is trying to date a freshman."

She punches me in the arm, hard. "Shut. Up," she warns. "I never said I was trying to date him. We're just hanging out a lot."

"That's why you called him cute," I say with not a little sarcasm. "And that's why you're spending time with him. If you ask me, spending a lot of time with someone who you think is cute equals dating."

Suddenly we turn a corner, and I see Ellen's locker. Oops, I almost forgot. I slow. I sprint back down the long hall to the tennis room, sliding between groups of frozen students and skidding around corners. I have to move fast because I have a lot to do. The world is slowed, but not stopped. Once inside the tennis room, I grab an entire cart of tennis balls and pull it behind me as I run back to Ellen's locker. I begin to fumble with her lock. Oh, what was the code? I remember there was 22, an 8, and a 31. I try 22-8-31. Nope, doesn't work. 22-31-8? No, wrong again. I glance back at her and see her face very slowly turning toward where she thinks I am. Ugh, come on, what was the code? I need to get this locker door open right now, or she is going to see that I disappeared, which would lead to a bunch of questions I really don't want to have to answer. 8-31-22. No. 31-22-8.

Yes! It opens. I wipe a trickle of sweat off my face, glance back at Ellen, and then get to work. Two at a time, I put the entire cart of tennis balls into her locker, using my stomach as a barrier to make sure none roll out. When I have unloaded them all, almost filling up the entire locker, I quickly shut the door before any can escape. With sweat pouring down my face from the exertion, I sprint back to the tennis room, pulling the empty cart behind me. I put it back where I found it, then race back to Ellen, positioning myself where I estimate I was standing when I started slowing. I notice that I'm really huffing and puffing, compared to Ellen's normal breathing, so I try to regain my calm. Then I stop slowing.

"Emit?" inquires Ellen, looking over her right shoulder.

"Yes," I answer.

Ellen turns back around. "Where did you go? You just disappeared for a second."

Oops. I now remember that I was on her other side when I slowed time.

"Oh … I …" A trickle of sweat runs down my cheek. "I … um … I just, uh, needed to adjust my socks," I explain.

"And why are you so sweaty?" she continues. "We've only been walking for a few minutes."

I freeze, not quick enough to think of what to say.

"Emit, why are you so sweaty?"

"I don't know, it's just hot in here."

"Hmmm. It's not that hot," she responds skeptically, looking at my sweat-soaked shirt. "Are you OK? Are you getting a fever?"

"Can we get to tennis practice, or are you just going to interrogate me all day?" I ask.

"Sorry, we can go." She turns toward her locker. I'm grinning from ear to ear at the thought of what's about to happen. "Why are you smiling?" Ellen asks, starting to spin the dial of her lock.

"No reason."

"Then why—" Suddenly, with a roar, hundreds of tennis balls pour out of the locker and all over the floor. The other students in the hall jump with surprise. Not able to contain myself, I burst out laughing, nearly collapsing onto the floor. The other students then join me, laughing and pointing at Ellen. Ellen, however, suppresses her surprise. She looks calmly at the mess. Then she glares at me. Gosh, she's strong, able to control her emotions even when she's stunned by the perfect prank. She then turns and punches me in the chest, hard.

"What was that for?" I complain.

"I know you did that," she says.

"How could I have possibly done that? I've been in class the entire day." Ellen glares at me one more time, then bends down and begins to pick up the balls. "And if I did have something to do with it," I add, "you did kinda ask for it."

CHAPTER 6

"They won't even let me go to Florida with them this summer! I-I'm being mistreated. I should talk to somebody about their … their … abuse of me!" Standing ten feet away at my locker, talking to Peyton, I grin from ear to ear as I overhear Jake finish this last stuttering sentence to Ellen.

"Well, come on, Jake," whispers Ellen, standing next to Jake's locker. "Don't you think you're being a little dramatic?"

"No! We go to Florida every year, and now they won't take me, because I failed one class. I can't stand them! They're such bad parents."

"You know that's not true, Jake," says Ellen. "They give you everything you want."

"WELL, I WANT TO GO TO FLORIDA!" yells Jake. Suddenly the hallway goes quiet, every eye on Jake. Then, out of the silence comes a chuckle, then a few more; then everybody starts to laugh. Jake's face turns crimson red.

"What a brat," I say to Peyton, beside me.

"What did you say about me?" Jake turns to me, his face still bright red from embarrassment.

"I said that you're a spoiled brat," I repeat firmly.

With a sound not unlike a bear would make, he lunges toward me, grabs my neck, and pulls me to the ground. On the ground, I roll quickly to my left with my feet straight out and collide with the back of his knees, sending him to the floor. Forgetting to use my power, I wrestle around with Jake on the floor, bumping into the legs of other students, who retreat a few paces to watch.

Eventually, our struggle on the floor slams into one of the lockers. Extracting myself and finally able to get my footing, I begin to stand up, as he stands too. Jake delivers a quick jab to my solar plexus, knocking the air out of me.

"Oof." Sensing a moment of weakness, Jake shoots off a massive punch straight at my face. I am able to sidestep it, only to trip and end up on the ground again beside his feet, on my stomach. Not finished with me, Jake stomps me in the lower back. I grab his foot, and he falls to the ground beside me. Ellen and several other students grab us and hold us down, preventing further fighting.

"What is going on here!" shouts Ms. Jointer, a twelfth-grade math teacher. Jake and I both look up at her. "Why are you both bleeding and on the floor?" I reach for my face, and I feel blood running from my nose. Jake has a cut lip.

"Well," starts Jake, "I was just getting some water, and then he attacked me!"

"Liar!" I yell. "You knocked me down because I called you

what you are, a brat! I was just defending myself."

"No! That's not what happened. You were the first …"

"Stop!" bellows Ms. Jointer. "Come with me; we're going to the principal's office."

"You started it," I mutter under my breath as we walk behind her.

Jake intentionally steps on my foot, trying to make it look like an accident. "Oh, I'm so sorry," he says with contempt, his blond hair sticking out at all angles, instead of his normal careful combing.

"C'mon guys," calls Ms. Jointer. She points to the door of Mr. Zachs's office. "Go in and tell the principal what you did."

"This isn't over," I whisper in Jake's ear as we enter together.

"Well, well, well," says Mr. Zachs. "What do we have here?"

"Emit. He just attacked me," starts Jake. "I was just standing at my locker, and suddenly he was on top of me. I think he went crazy. He was just punching and kicking. I just curled up into a ball on the floor."

"Then why does Emit look so much more beat up than you?" asks Mr. Zachs skeptically. "Did he accidentally hit himself?"

"He … ummm … I guess I might have swung once or twice out of self-defense. But he started it!"

I look over at Jake, his pretty-boy features, and his golden hair. "That's not what happened," I say.

"Well, what happened, then, Emit?" asks Mr. Zachs, trying to be impartial. "Please elaborate."

"OK," I say calmly. "So Jake was saying some really snobby

things in the hallway. He was, like, complaining about his parents and complaining about how he can't go on vacation this year, because he failed a test. It was just really bratty. I just pointed that out. Then Jake attacked me, and I had to defend myself. Jake, just 'cause I say something you don't like doesn't mean you can attack me."

Jake erupts. "Emit, you're a lying, stinking piece of—"

"Jake, you know as well as I do that I didn't attack you," I say quietly. "You hit me first." I look seriously over at Mr. Zachs. "I promise, I didn't start it."

Jake suddenly attempts to gather himself, trying to resume his normal fake-earnest personality that adults love so much. "I'm afraid that Emit must be misremembering what happened." But the damage has been done. With his earlier unharnessed fury, Jake revealed to Mr. Zachs his true character.

"No, Jake," I respond. "It was—"

"All right, enough," proclaims Mr. Zachs.

"He knows you started it," says Jake. "I'm the victim here. I was just—" He stops suddenly as Mr. Zachs shoots him an icy glare. If looks could kill, Jake's family would need to start planning a funeral.

"I don't know who started this. I don't care. If I hear of another altercation between you two," says Mr. Zachs slowly and coldly, "I will suspend you both. Am I clear?"

"Yes, sir," we confirm.

"Jake, you can go." Jake gets up, glares at me, and leaves the room.

Mr. Zachs walks to me and looks straight at me. "Don't think I let you off the hook because I know your family. I am the principal, and my job is to enforce the school's rules, regardless of my relationship with a student. I meant what I said about the consequences if this happens again. You may go." Mr. Zachs turns his attention to some papers on his desk as I walk out.

Well, that didn't go very well. I've known Mr. Zachs for a long time, and we've spent a lot of time together. We've become friends. In his office though, it seemed as if that was not the case. He treated me just like he treated Jake, as an untrustworthy teenage boy. He didn't believe my story about what happened, and instead decided to not believe either of us. Well, I suppose it could have been worse. At least he didn't suspend us or—

"Emit!" yells Ellen. She runs up to me. "I can't believe you had a fight with Jake."

"Yeah," I respond. "Did you see how much of a brat he was being? I mean, he really showed what a jerk he is. And all the other kids know it too. Did you see them all—?"

"Emit, please stop insulting him," says Ellen. "I came over here to tell you that what you did, insulting him and hitting, it's not acceptable. If you value our friendship, please respect that I like Jake. Please don't start another fight with him."

Stunned that she's taking his side, I respond, "He started the fight. He's the one who threw the first punch."

"But you were the one who provoked him and made him punch you. It's your fault that the fight happened." She takes a deep breath. "I'll see you tomorrow. Bye."

What the heck? Did she actually just criticize me for the fight even though Jake started it? And she was standing right there, she saw what happened. Apparently, the person that speaks the truth is worse than the person who tries to punish the truth. She is willing to overlook the truth and instead side with a guy who she knows did wrong. Their relationship must be much further along than I thought. I can't let this go any further. It's too dangerous to her. I need to do something about this. I need to protect her.

But what to do? Whatever I decide to do needs to drive a wedge between Ellen and Jake. I need to trick one of them into breaking up with the other. I still really like my cousin, though, and don't want to do anything to hurt her, or her reputation.

Immediately a bunch of options pop up in my mind. I could trick Ellen into thinking that Jake is unfaithful. I've already heard Ellen rant before about all the things she would do if she found out that her boyfriend was cheating on her. But what would be the best way to frame Jake as a cheater? I immediately remember back to a movie I saw four or five years ago, where a boy found a love note from another guy in his girlfriend's purse. I decide to go with a variation of this.

*

At the end of the day, I meet Ellen like usual so we can go to tennis together. Immediately I notice the raised upper lip and her avoidance of eye contact. She must still be annoyed with me.

"What is it?" I ask, breaking the silence. "Are you still mad at me for criticizing your boyfriend this morning?"

"What are you talking about?" she responds, feigning ignorance.

"Nothing. If you forgot about it, I'll forget about it." We continue down the hall in silence for another minute.

"About this morning," Ellen starts, "I just think it's funny how you think that …"

I immediately start slowing time. I don't want to listen to another passive-aggressive insult. I know that when a girl starts with the 'I just think it's funny' line, it is best to get out of there. With the world slowed, now it is time to frame Jake and—

Out of the corner of my eye, I see Ellen blink. What the …? How did she …? Why wasn't that blink slow? Puzzled, I get up close to Ellen and stare at her face, trying to find any normal movement. Nothing. The blink must have been just a little glitch in my powers. I bet I just lost my concentration for a second. I return to my task of framing Jake.

I begin the first step of my plan, which is figuring out how to write out a love note on a sheet of paper in a different handwriting than my own. This step proves to be more difficult than I anticipated, as I cannot find a sheet of paper in my backpack or Ellen's bag. I finally find a notecard in the purse of Coco Avery, who is frozen in place next to the water fountain. Standing next to her is her boyfriend, Dick Braun, a very large senior.

Coco is the classic high school cheerleader. She is pretty, always wears a lot of makeup, and has lots of friends. Even though she's just a sophomore, she has dated several older guys on the football team. It's Dick Braun now. I've seen Jake talking to her on numerous occasions, as Ellen most likely has too. In addition to finding a sheet of paper, I think I've found the person I'll frame as Jake's cheating partner.

Pulling out a blank notecard from Coco's backpack, I do my best to recreate her handwriting on the notecard. I write:

Dear Jake,
I had a lot of fun last night. You are a great guy, and I am
really into you. I hope we can do it again soon.
Love,
Coco

That'll do. There is no way that Jake can refute this evidence, and even if he could pull some explanation out of his sphincter, Ellen would never trust him again. Now I just have to make sure that Ellen finds the note in a natural, but foolproof, way. The note must be placed where she can't miss it, but where it seems logical and realistic. I decide to put it on the floor next to Coco, directly in Ellen's path. I decide to add a bit more drama. Very gently, so as not to create too much force while time is slowed, I press the bottom of the notecard to Coco's lips, creating a kiss lipstick mark. I then set the card on the ground, return to my place beside Ellen, and resume normal time.

"… it's OK to insult my boyfriend. I understand why you think that he's a brat, but he's actually a really good guy. He's gentle, kind, and sweet. He's not like those self-obsessed guys who think it's OK to cheat on their girlfriends. He would never do …" She pauses as she bends down to pick up the note with "Dear Jake" written in big letters on the top. "What's this?" She begins to read. I await her furious reaction. I can't wait for her face to turn red and her eyes to widen.

But instead she says, "There must be a mistake. Or someone's pulling a prank." She looks back up at me. "Emit, as I was telling you, Jake is really gentle and kind. I don't know anything about this junk." She tosses the note back on the ground. "See you, Emit. I've got to run." She walks away from me, down the hall.

That was weird. That didn't go at all as I expected. It seems that she wasn't mad at Jake at all. It seems that, despite the note, she really trusted that he wouldn't cheat on her. Or maybe she was inwardly furious at Jake, and she just didn't show it, and she was going to express her fury at him later when she saw him.

Still trying to understand Ellen's reaction, I turn around and walk off toward the school exit. After I've gone about thirty feet, I hear a commotion behind me. I turn to see Coco Avery and Dick Braun standing together near the place I just left. Dick is holding my fake note, which he picked up. Dick is angry. Coco is crying. I better get out of here. I speed up and leave the building.

Maybe, instead of going to tennis today, I'll walk down to the Gamestop next to my church. *Warriors' Bloody Struggle 3* just came out on Xbox, and I've been meaning to get it, and I bet Gamestop is selling it. Last night, I double-checked the price online, and I packed the necessary sixty dollars in my bag this morning.

Outside it is starting to sprinkle. Instead of walking, I jog down to Gamestop, staying relatively dry and cutting my trip time by almost ten minutes. Opening the door, I see the enticing interior of the video game store. On the far wall is row after row of the newest games. Ten guys are standing there, captivated by them. Usually I would join them, staring at the beautiful games, even though I know I would have to wait until Christmas to get one. But today, things are different. I've been saving up my money for close to four months for this one game. Now I get to splurge.

I strut up to the front counter and to the teenage employee, who is wearing a red Gamestop shirt. "One *Warriors' Bloody Struggle 3*, please, Xbox version," I say.

"Good choice," says the employee. "I've been meaning to get that myself. I hear it has a great multiplayer storyline."

"It does," I confirm. "I've played it at my friend's house. It was totally fun. How much is it?"

"Let's see." The employee pulls down one of the games and turns it over. "It's, uh, fifty-nine dollars and ninety-nine cents." Yes! I can afford it. I'll even have one cent to spare. With a smile on my face, I unzip my backpack's front pocket and dig through it. I can't find the money! I put the backpack down, fully unzip the pocket, and check it thoroughly. The money isn't there. I remember now. I left it on my bedroom table. I had put it there carefully, intending to put it my backpack. But

I must have forgotten to do that.

"Did you hear me?" he asks. "That's sixty dollars."

"I, uh, don't have the money right now. Can I come back tomorrow and get it?"

"Sorry." He replaces the game on the shelf. "This is the last copy."

"Can you hold it for me?" I ask.

"Sorry," he says. "Can't do that. Against store policy. I'd get fired. You're gonna have to find the game somewhere else. Sorry."

"It's OK," I say. Darn. I really wanted that game. I was really looking forward to playing the multiplayer mode, but I guess not. There isn't another Gamestop near my house. I guess I could wait until Christmas or my birthday. But both of those holidays are far away.

Well, there is another option. I could just steal it. I do really want the game, and with my powers they would never suspect a thing. I could just walk up there and take it off the shelf. Eventually, they will notice it's missing, when they do inventory. But they won't know to blame me. Anybody could have shoplifted it. And it's really their fault that I have to steal it. I would have been happy to pay for it. It's totally unreasonable that they wouldn't hold it for me until I came back with my money later.

I slow and hop over the counter. I stroll past the cashier and pull the game off the shelf. This is so easy. My powers allow me to steal anything without getting caught. And even if somebody did somehow catch me, I could probably slow time and escape the jail. I could probably take the guard's key. My abilities let me have anything in the world that I want. I have such power that I can do anything that I—

Suddenly a hero from my childhood pops into my mind. Spider-Man's Uncle Ben once told him, "With great power comes great responsibility." Spider-Man wouldn't want my power to be used for this thievery. It needs to be used for something better than this. And if I did steal the game, somebody else would be accused of taking it. Maybe the teenage cashier. I put the game back on the shelf.

But the cashier probably won't get blamed. It'll just be blamed on shoplifting. So only the company would be harmed. And Gamestop deserves it because they have such a bad policy of not holding games for customers to buy later.

Spider-Man was just a comic book character. It's silly to feel guilty because of something said to a made-up dude in a stretchy suit. And, anyway, the guy who wrote Spider-Man just stole the line from the bible and Winston Churchill.

I grab the game back off the shelf. I leave the store with it.

CHAPTER 7

I jump out of bed Sunday morning and immediately get to work on a task that I've been planning ever since I started thinking about how stealing the Gutenberg Bible might be the perfect crime for a slower. I bring up the video of the Gutenberg Bible heist on YouTube. When I run it, I don't see anything unusual. But that's to be expected if the thief slowed time. I use the YouTube feature to watch the video at a quarter speed. Still nothing. I find a slow-motion software download on the internet and run the video through that. I still can't see anything different. Argh. Even the slow-motion software must not reduce the speed enough to see the slower. Maybe if I can find the original video, I can slow it more; maybe the original has more frames per second. But getting access to the tape will be tough. I'm sure the Russian police won't give it to me. Maybe the Russian museum where it was stolen will. I go to the museum's website.

The website doesn't say anything about the tape or the robbery, but it does give a history of the book. There are only forty-eight known copies of the Gutenberg Bible in the world. It was the first substantial book printed in the West with moveable metal type and was printed by some guy named Johannes Gutenberg, hence the name. This particular bible was stolen from the Nazis in 1945—the Russians use the term *liberated*. It has been held in the Moscow Museum of Religion for seventy years. Russia only has one other Gutenberg Bible. It was also obtained from the Nazis, but this second bible isn't complete. So the first bible—the stolen one—is more valuable. In fact, it's supposedly the most valuable book in Russia.

I call the number at the bottom of the site. "Hello, this is the Moscow Museum of Religion. How can I help you?" asks the museum employee in a thick Russian accent.

"Hello," I try to lower my voice to sound like an adult. "I'm a reporter in the United States. I was wondering if you could provide me the video of the recent robbery? I can give you my email address to send it."

"We've had a lot of requests for the video. You are aware that we posted the video on YouTube a few days ago, no?" inquires the museum employee.

"Yes," I reply. "I am just doing a little research on the robbery. I need the original video file to make sure I didn't miss anything."

"Sorry, I have to talk to my manager. One minute please." Some foreign music plays over the phone. After a few minutes, the operator comes back on the line. "I'm very sorry, sir. My manager tells me that he cannot release the video file without authorization from the Moscow police."

I groan.

"What? Excuse me?" the operator asks.

"Never mind," I reply. "Thank you for your time."

"Sure." The employee hangs up. Now there's no way I will get the video. I will never find out if there's another slower out there. It must be a horrible person if they would use their ability to commit a major crime. But on the other hand, the slower would be the only one that I could talk to about my ability. Maybe he could teach me something or help me understand it. Argh. If only I had taken a few more coding classes. Couldn't I then hack into the museum's website and access the video?

Wait a minute—my friend Peyton is an expert computer coder. Maybe he could hack the website for me. I text Peyton and ask him to give me a call.

Peyton spends most of his days working on his computer. Talent plus time equals genius. By the time he was eight, he was starting to win coding competitions. I expect Peyton will be more than happy to help, because he loves hacking. He does not always use his skills strictly for the forces of good. Just last year, in eighth grade, I was in awe when he hacked into the online gradebook and changed his Spanish grade from a ninety to a ninety-five. He said he used a random password generator. The teachers never suspected a thing. That hack seemed to me to be relatively complicated, and Peyton did it with ease. I have a feeling Peyton could hack into much more sophisticated systems.

While I wait for him to call, I decide to try another approach. I pull up the YouTube version of the bible robbery. I watch the video normally first and note that the bible disappears at exactly twenty-nine seconds into the video. I play the video again. At twenty-seven seconds, I slow time. At first the video seems frozen, but then the frames start shifting. Every three seconds on my slow time, the picture changes slightly; it must be that in slow time, a new video frame appears every three seconds. After about a minute, I move my mouse to the screen to make sure the video is still playing. Yep, still running. I look back at the screen and—

The bible is gone! I quickly rewind back to twenty-eight seconds and wait for the bible to disappear again. There's a brief flash of white in the left corner of the screen, and the bible vanishes. I'm closer. Either there is another slower out there, or some guy with the fastest hands ever is stealing bibles. Unfortunately, I won't be able to see any more on my own. I need the original tape.

I suddenly realize that all the slowing I have done in the last twenty-four hours has taken a toll on me. Now I'm paying the price with a bad headache and nausea. I can barely think straight. I have to be careful not to kill myself with a stroke. I decide that after today I won't slow for forty-eight hours. I went fourteen years without slowing; surely I can go forty-eight hours without it. It will do miracles for my head.

My phone vibrates in my pocket. I grab it and see Peyton's name listed as the caller. "Hey, Peyton. What's up, bro?"

"Nothing much. You know, the usual," replies Peyton. "Did you need me for something?"

"Yes, uh … I was wondering if you could possibly come over and … um … help me on some computer stuff," I say awkwardly. I can't think of the right way to phrase the question.

Peyton pauses for a minute, and then I can hear him yell down to his mom. "Mom! Emit needs some help on some school stuff. Could I go over there and help him for a few minutes?"

"Are you sure you want to go, PP?" says Peyton's mom. Her voice is loud, so she must have joined him in his room. Peyton's mom babies him. His family also uses a most unfortunate nickname for him that stuck when he was a toddler. I honor his request that I not use it.

"Yes, Mom. It's perfectly normal for teenagers to help their friends with homework on weekends," replies Peyton.

"Going out by yourself is how children get kidnapped, PP," responds his mom.

"Mom, I'm just going across the street. I promise I won't get in a white van with someone who offers candy," Peyton replies with a smile in his voice. "And I know there's never any puppies inside."

"Fine, go. But don't do anything dangerous." I can hear Peyton's mom clomp downstairs.

"Emit, are you still there?"

"Yep."

"Sorry about my mom."

"At least you get to come over. Come now before your

mom changes her mind. And you might want to bring your computer."

"All right. I'll be over soon." Peyton ends the phone call.

"Mom!" I yell downstairs. "Peyton is coming over in a few minutes."

"Fine," she yells back. "But come downstairs for a minute. Your grandfather is leaving."

"OK." I had been working so hard up in my room that I didn't even know that Opa had dropped by for breakfast. He calls it "Frühschoppen" when he visits on Sunday for breakfast and drinks a beer. It's a German custom. I amble downstairs and give my grandpa a hug. "Bye, Opa."

"Bye, Emit." Opa gives me a kiss on the forehead. "Your grandmother and I are taking a vacation to France soon. Do you want a little present, or are you too old for that?" Opa winks.

"I'd love a little present," I answer with a smile. "I don't think I'll ever be too old for gifts." I smile.

As Opa drives off, I see Peyton walk across the street and up our driveway. We immediately go upstairs to my room, and I explain my predicament.

"So, I am ... extremely interested in obtaining a certain video from a certain website. The video is the original tape of the break-in at the Russian museum, and I think we can get it from the museum's website."

"Oh, I saw that on the news," Peyton says. "I'm pretty sure they released the tape on YouTube." Peyton pulls his laptop out of his bag. "Why are you so interested?"

"I just …"

"It *is* interesting," Peyton interrupts. "Looks like some clever thief hired a hacker to cover his tracks."

"That's what I was thinking," I lie. "I just wanted to see if there is anything different on the original tape that's not in the YouTube version."

Peyton pulls up the museum website. His fingers fly over the keys; clearly, he has a lot more practice typing than I do. He thinks for a moment. "To get my hands on the video, I'll have to find the museum's employee-facing remote version of the site. Unless they are totally stupid, they are always inside a firewall, with a bunch of security features. This can make it a bit of a challenge. But I have a lot of experience with this, if you know what I mean. I even developed some nifty code to help with this."

"That's cool," I say, wondering who this person is. I've never seen this side of Peyton before. He seems so intense, so happy. Even when we're playing sports, it's always like he couldn't care less. I like this giddy enthusiasm; it's contagious. "Think of all the things we could do together …" I say, melding our powers in my mind.

"We?" He smirks. "I like accessing other people's computers. It's a fun game to try to outwit the organization's IT people. I'm even getting a little bit of a reputation among computer security people. They all think that I'm fifty-seven years old from Uzbekistan, not little Peyton sitting in my bedroom."

I laugh and pat little Peyton on the shoulder.

"Thanks for asking me to do this. It gives me a reason to use my skills." He fishes in his pocket until he pulls out an unassuming flash drive. "This will make it a little easier," he says, inserting it into his computer's USB port. A themed page from the museum pops up on the screen, and Peyton starts typing.

"Hopefully, this will work," he whispers. He presses enter, and a new page opens. There are links to different calendars and staff events. Peyton scrolls down the page.

"There!" I point to a video link titled "Robbery." Peyton clicks it as we hold our breath.

Argh, another firewall block.

"Do you happen to know the administrative code?" Peyton jokes. I glance over at him.

"I don't even know what that is."

"Let me try my software for random code sequencing," he says. "It can try a million possible passwords per second."

After fifteen or so seconds, a new video page pops up and the tape begins to play. "Yes!" Peyton says.

"That was way easier than I expected," Peyton adds. "The museum site has security from twenty years ago."

"All right, Peyton! Thanks so much for helping me out on this."

"Sure," Peyton replies, puffing out his chest slightly. "Do you need me to enhance it or slow it down or anything?"

"Oh! Sure. That would be a big help," I respond. He

downloads the video to the computer and opens it in a video-enhancing program that he has on his flash drive. The video gains a lot of color and clarity as Peyton plays it in the program.

"Let's slow it down," I say, trying to hide my excitement.

"Sure," Peyton says. "It should slow down well because it's really high-quality video, 4K at sixty frames per second." Peyton starts the video over. At thirty seconds a white flash shoots across the screen. The bible disappears. "What was that?" Peyton shouts in surprise.

"I don't know," I lie. "Can you play it again? I want to see if I can catch anything else," I add. This time, when the video gets to twenty-nine seconds, I slow. Instead of a white flash, I see a ghostly hand appear in a single frame. I can't actually see the whole hand. Just three blurry fingers. But it's enough proof for me. The thief walked into the exhibition room, grabbed the bible, and walked out, all within one-sixtieth of a second.

There is another slower out there.

CHAPTER 8

I'm stunned. There's another slower. And he or she is committing crimes. Are there more? Does anyone else know about this? I feel as if I'm discovering the tip of the iceberg in this whole mystery.

I look at Peyton, and speed time back up. I so want to talk with him about it, but I can't. He's my best friend and yet I can't trust him. It's all too weird. If he did believe me—that's a big if—then what if he told someone else and my secret got out? Would they use me for experiments? Dissect my body until they found the part of my brain that makes me like this? Or would they lock me away for being too dangerous?

My mind wanders again to the other slower. What else could he or she have stolen? It would be so easy to rob a bank or an armored car. You could wait until the door is open and slow time. Then you could walk in and take what you want before anyone knows what's happened. Even security cameras wouldn't catch more than a glimpse of the slower.

But if it's so easy to rob banks, why would the slower be

messing around with the Gutenberg Bible? I'm sure it's valuable and all, but it's not worth anything until you sell it. And I bet selling it without getting caught could be tricky. Plus, it's just more complicated than robbing a bank. Maybe the slower is religious and he wants to worship with a special bible? No, I bet it's actually pretty hard to read a five-hundred-year-old bible. I'm sure the pages are brittle and could easily break as you turn them.

The slower could just be interested in the historical importance of the Gutenberg Bibles. It is pretty cool that they were the first books printed using modern printing techniques. I mean, that's why everyone is making such a big deal about the bible being stolen in the first place.

My mind starts to wander across other crazy possibilities. If a slower stole a Gutenberg Bible, maybe the slower is responsible for other mysteries from the past few decades. Maybe he helped Elvis fake his death. Maybe he is Elvis in disguise. Or maybe he's the second JFK shooter on the grassy knoll. Actually …

"Hey, Peyton?" I ask. My words startle Peyton because, while my mind was wandering, he had been pondering the encryption method the museum uses on their login pages. "Isn't there a movie of the assassination of President Kennedy?" I ask.

"Huh?" says Peyton. "I thought we were talking about the Gutenberg Bible."

"We were," I say. "But I just started thinking about something else. Isn't there a movie of the JFK assassination?"

"Of course," says Peyton. "It's the Zapruder film. I read a book about that. This guy Zapruder just happened to be pointing a home movie camera at JFK when Oswald shot him in Dallas. JFK's limousine was driving through Dealey Plaza when Oswald shot at him three times. Two of the shots hit him in the head."

"Or maybe he didn't shoot him," I reply. "I remember seeing some stuff on TV that said Oswald didn't do it. It was the CIA or Cubans. And Vice President Johnson was in on it too, because he wanted to be president."

"Yeah, that's right," says Peyton. "Those weird conspiracy people think that the shots didn't come from Oswald. They came from the grassy knoll. That's a little hill in front of the limo."

"What do you think?" I ask.

"I think all of that conspiracy stuff is nuts," he responds. "I looked into it a bit. Oswald owned a rifle. He was an expert shooter. He tried to shoot an army general before he got to Kennedy. He just barely missed. And then after he killed JFK, he tried to escape, and killed a police officer to get away. If ever there was a guilty guy, it's him. Those conspiracy theories make about as much sense as claiming Elvis is alive, and he's working at a nearby McDonald's, and I'm his love child."

"But let's just have some fun," I say. "What happens if we watch the film of the JFK assassination?"

"We won't see anything new," Peyton replies. "That film's already been slowed down. I bet millions of people have analyzed each frame. They're all looking for evidence that Kennedy was really killed by Bigfoot or Elvis."

"Can we try?" I ask.

"Sure," says Peyton. He finds a site that presents a copy of the Zapruder film that's already been slowed down so people can watch it frame by frame. I push play, and we watch the horror unfold. There's JFK and his wife smiling in the limousine. Then, on the 314th frame, JFK gets shot in the head, with blood and brains flying everywhere. Real blood and brains, from real people. Not fake CGI images in a video game.

The Zapruder film is breathtakingly horrible to watch. And it's hard for me to breathe while I'm watching it. I'm a fan of horror movies and first-person shooter video games like *Warriors' Bloody Struggle 3*, but there's something uniquely horrific about watching a real death. I'm not as tough as I thought. Seeing it makes me want to throw up.

I turn my attention back to the Zapruder film as Peyton plays a slowed-down version. We watch as Kennedy grabs his neck as if he's choking on food. A few seconds later, as the second shot strikes, we both cringe as his head is almost blown off. But beyond the gruesome images, nothing else suspicious catches my eye.

"Let's watch it one more time," I say.

"Why?" Peyton replies. "Millions of people have seen this. Why do you think you'll see anything different?"

"Please, just do it one more time."

Peyton plays the slow version again and I slow time. It takes forever to get to the relevant part of the film. But there it is! On the 313th frame, there is a brief white flash near the back of Kennedy's convertible. The flash looks just like the flash I saw on the museum tape. It could be another slower. Or it could be just dust on the film, or a scratch. It's probably just dirt on the film. Or is it?

Adrenaline zaps through my body. A dread creeps over me as I begin to think about all of the crimes and terrible events throughout history that slowers could be responsible for. Killings, robberies, wars; a slower could be responsible for almost anything. Maybe a slower was involved in taking over the planes that flew into the World Trade Center on 9/11, or maybe a slower broke into the CDC and stole samples of the Ebola virus to release in Africa. Is there just one other slower, or are there several? If there are several, why are they doing evil things? What type of evil brotherhood am I part of? Does being a slower turn you evil? Or are there good slowers too? But wait a second. I don't even know that there was a slower in the Zapruder film. That flash might have been just something else.

Peyton packs up his bag and leaves. But before he goes, he helps me load onto my laptop computer the video-enhancing software that he had used for the Gutenberg video.

"That way, you can experiment on your own," he says. "But, Emit, stop watching the Zapruder film. There's nothing new there. And it's sick to watch."

"I know." I'm sure Peyton is right. The Zapruder film has

83

been looked at so many times, in so many ways, it's probably pointless to look at it further. I'll probably never know for sure whether a slower was involved with killing JFK.

I walk Peyton downstairs, still in a daze from realizing that there is at least one other slower and that I've seen evidence of at least one crime involving a slower, and maybe two. As I say goodbye to Peyton and close the front door, an idea occurs to me. Could you see a slower's face on video?

I decide to experiment. I lean my phone against my bedroom wall with the camera facing out and start a video. Then I quickly get out of the camera's view. I wait a few seconds and then start slowing. I stroll slowly through the camera's field of view, wait a few seconds, speed up time again, and end the video.

As expected, I'm barely visible. Played at one-quarter speed, there is a small white flash, as if there was a tiny bit of static. When I scroll through the video frame by frame, there's one frame where I can see a blur. That's me. It looks like a blur because the shutter of the phone's camera is open for what seems, in slowed time, to be many seconds. The blur is created by my walking in front of shutter while it's open. With this information, it will be much easier to spot a slower if there's one in the Zapruder film. Instead of looking for an actual person in the tape, I should be looking for a strangely shaped blur.

On my computer, I search for the Zapruder film in single frames. This isn't hard to find. There are several great websites devoted to it.

If my theory about the blurry static is correct, then when I go to the 313th frame, where I saw the flash, I should see the blurry image of the slower. Mr. Zapruder filmed his movie at twenty-four frames per second. If there really was a slower, the flash in the 313th frame should look like the blur in the video that I took of myself with my phone.

Maybe I'm completely wrong and Lee Harvey Oswald was the only shooter. Maybe the flash will turn out to be just a defect in the film, or the sun glinting off a car mirror, or a bird. However, my gut now tells me there is another slower involved.

I go quickly to the 313th frame, the one with the flash. There's just a white smudge a few feet from JFK's car. I move back to the 312th frame. The smudge isn't there. It's also not there in the 314th frame.

But a smudge doesn't prove anything. It could be just a smudge. I then remember the software that Peyton loaded on my computer for enhancing videos. I download the Zapruder film, start the video-enhancing software, and put the file with the Zapruder film into the software. The computer works away for several minutes. It must take a lot of processing time and power to enhance video.

Suddenly it's done. Excited and scared, I move to the 313th frame. What I see is no longer just a smudge. A few feet away from JFK's car, there's a blur that looks similar to the blur in the video I took of myself. I stare at it longer. I don't think I'm imagining it, but at one end of the blur is a shape that looks vaguely like a human head.

CHAPTER 9

I'm now convinced that a slower was involved in Kennedy's assassination. I can understand why nobody else has focused on this frame of the Zapruder film before. Even with the video-enhancing software, frame 313 just looks like there's some grease on the frame. It's like someone touched the film with an oily finger. And any other observer would assume that it's impossible for a person to get in and out of the camera's field of view in one twenty-fourth of a second. They would conclude that it's a smudge rather than anything real, because there was no trace of it on the frames before and after frame 313.

I know that frame 313 shows that there's a slower only because I know what to look for: the telltale blur of a slower moving through a slowed world. And I know that when the world is slowed, a slower can do a lot in one twenty-fourth of a second. So it makes sense that the slower would appear in only one frame. I save an image of frame 313 on my computer.

My mind bubbles with questions. Is it the same slower who stole the Gutenberg Bible and was involved in the JFK assassination? There were many decades between the events. If it's the same slower, he must be an old guy now.

Why do I keep thinking the slower is a guy? It could well be a woman.

Could a slower be involved in other mysteries too? I can't even imagine what those other mysteries could be. I grab my phone to start researching "unsolved historical mysteries." I scroll through so many stories I completely lose track of time, and soon my eyes start fading.

*

"Emit, I said WAKE UP!" yells my mother. I roll over and cover my ears with my pillow. "Emit!"

"I'm awake, I'm awake," I assure her.

"It's ten forty-five," she states matter-of-factly. "And church starts at eleven."

"Wait, seriously?" I jump out of bed and run downstairs. "You should have woken me up earlier!" I complain.

"I tried to," my mom retorts. "But you wouldn't wake up. It was like trying to wake an embalmed mummy. I also tried to remind you that Ellen is coming too. Uncle Ethan is bringing their whole family. Ellen is almost here."

I grab a bowl from the shelf, grab the box of Honey Bunches of Oats, and dump myself a heaping bowl of cereal. The milk comes next, poured until surface tension is all that's preventing a milk flood. My dad tried to sell me on unprocessed oats with organic prunes. Nope. Unfortunately, no time to enjoy my cereal now. I chug it.

Two minutes later, I dash back upstairs to my room. I quickly throw on a polo shirt and pair of khaki pants. I run across the hall to the bathroom and simultaneously pee and brush my teeth in ninety seconds. Any self-respecting guy should be able to get ready that fast. It maximizes sleep. I run downstairs, and greet Ellen, who has just arrived. "Hello, Emit," she responds. And then turns her back to me and starts looking at her phone.

Two hours later, Ellen and I wait for my family outside the church. Our conversation has been tense this morning. She won't say it, but I think that she's angry at me. Could it be because of the pranks? But I thought that she didn't know that I was responsible. The moments with her outside church are unpleasant, with none of the normal friendliness. My parents always spend at least ten minutes chatting with their friends after the service. Most Sundays, I end up waiting outside next to our car. If only I could drive home myself. In two years, when I'm sixteen, I'll be able to leave. That's only if I can work it out so my parents get me a car.

"Hi, Emit. Hi, Ellen." I smile at the sound of Mr. Zachs's deep voice.

"Oh, hi, Uncle Dimitri," I respond.

"Emit, where are your parents?" he asks.

"Still in church. Wait, here they are."

"Dimitri!" My mother runs up and gives Mr. Zachs a hug.

"Diana, how nice to see you," he says as he kisses each of her cheeks.

My dad walks up with Uncle Ethan and the rest of their

family. "Hi, Dimitri," he says. How are you?" Without waiting for an answer, my dad asks, "Uncle Dimitri, are you going to take Emit to lunch like usual? Can Ellen go too?"

"Of course." Mr. Zachs looks back at us and smiles.

"I'm sorry," says Ellen, "but I can't go. Can I have a rain check?"

"I'm sorry you can't join us, Ellen," says Mr. Zachs. "Next time."

"Pavana again?" I ask, and he nods.

"Thank you for taking him," my mom says, clasping her hands behind her back. "Emit loves it, and it gives us a little one-on-one time with Maddy."

"It's my pleasure," he responds. "And Pavana does have great pesto."

My parents smile.

As the rest of our family group goes off to their cars, Mr. Zachs and I walk to the other side of the parking lot. I smile when I spot his bright red sports car. It's parked on the far side of the parking lot so that nobody will park next to him and ding his car's side panels when they open their doors. He bought it about a year ago. He'd considered an Audi sedan, but I convinced him to get the Audi convertible. I smile whenever I see him drive: the ancient school principal driving in his hot set of wheels with intense old-man care at ten miles under the speed limit. I don't know how Mr. Zachs affords such nice cars. He also has a really nice house and a cabin on a lake in Vermont. I asked him one time, and he said that he has been fortunate with his investments.

"Emit, could you sit in the back seat today?" he asks.

"Yeah, sure." I jump in.

"Sorry, I've got a lot of school papers up here," he apologizes. "Believe it or not, they are somewhat organized in this pile."

"No, no. It's fine. There's more space back here, anyway," I reassure him.

The drive to Pavana takes about five minutes. Luckily, everything is really close by in our neighborhood. If there's no traffic, you can get around quickly. When we walk into the restaurant, a delicious aroma of pesto and marinara sauce engulfs me. We walk up to the counter and I order my usual. After Mr. Zachs pays, we sit down in a large booth in the corner of the dining room. I always like to sit here if it's open.

"So, how's your weekend been, Emit?" Mr. Zachs asks, trying to start a conversation.

"Good. Actually, great," I respond. "How about you?"

"Very good," he replies. "Have you thought any more about that textbook?" He sees the confused look on my face and elaborates. "The textbook that Ms. Beans mysteriously found in her car?" Mr. Zachs smiles and continues, "That could be a good topic for a mysterious short story. 'Textbook disappears then reappears in teacher's car.'" He chuckles. "I bet that she's just imagining things. She probably left it in there but made up a story so she wouldn't sound crazy."

"Yeah. Probably," I agree.

Mr. Zachs sees the guilty look on my face. "Is something wrong, Emit?"

"No, of course not," I answer quickly. "I'm just really, really hungry."

"Looks like you're in luck." He points behind me. I turn around and see a waiter carrying a bowl of my pesto tagliatelle and Mr. Zachs's favorite—spaghetti and meatballs. I lick my lips. As soon as the waiter sets down the plate, I start digging in to my lunch. After a few bites, I have a thought and momentarily stop eating.

"Have you ever seen the Zapruder film?" I inquire, trying to sound innocent. Mr. Zachs stops eating too and looks at me strangely.

"Yes ... Why?" he questions.

"I just had a few questions about the JFK assassination," I answer.

Mr. Zachs chuckles. "My little conspiracy theorist."

"I'm just—"

"Don't worry," he cuts me off. "I believe some conspiracy theories too. Some of them are true."

CHAPTER 10

"Uncle Dimitri, are they sure that Lee Harvey Oswald killed JFK?" I ask Mr. Zachs.

"There have been hundreds and hundreds of investigations that concluded Oswald was the shooter," Mr. Zachs replies. "But I guess anything is possible."

"What do you think?" I ask seriously.

"I don't know for sure," he responds, "but I think that Oswald was probably the shooter."

I consider telling him about my slowing and the blur with the head shape in the Zapruder film. Maybe I should tell somebody else about my present situation. I bet Mr. Zachs could give me some great advice. If I were to tell anyone, he would be that person. I have a great urge to tell someone; it's stressful holding this all by myself.

On the other hand, maybe he would think I'm crazy. And if I tell anyone, then he might tell others, and lots of people might find out. Then the value of my power would be much smaller. I decide not to tell him.

"I read an article about the smoke on the grassy knoll," I explain. "It's intriguing."

"Yeah," he agrees. "Trust me, millions of people believe in these theories. If you want to read more about the assassination, I could recommend a few books."

"Yeah, sure. That would be great," I thank him. We sit quietly for a while, enjoying our pasta.

"Speaking of conspiracy theories, Emit, have you ever heard about the assassination attempts on Hitler?" asks Mr. Zachs.

I look up. "No," I answer. "I thought he killed himself as Berlin was falling to the Allies?"

"He did," he says. "But before that, there were multiple failed attempts to kill him."

"Why didn't they succeed?" I ask.

"Nobody knows," he explains. "But by all accounts, Hitler was insanely lucky on several occasions. One time, a bomb in a briefcase that was planted near him was moved to under a heavy wood table at the last minute; the table shielded him from the blast. Another time, a sniper bullet was slightly redirected by a thick glass window and missed Hitler by a few inches. It was as if the universe itself was protecting him." He pauses. "I believe that something mysterious was happening. No one is that lucky. Hitler thought that the fates were protecting him for his divine mission."

"What do you think was protecting him?" I follow up.

"That's what I'm not sure about," answers Mr. Zachs. "I don't know any person that can always be in the right place at the right time, preventing every assassination attempt."

Suddenly it dawns on me that I do know such a person who could do a lot of stuff like that. It's me. Or any slower. Had the slower saved Hitler by moving the briefcase with the bomb under the table? Had the assassination bullet missed because of the glass window? Or had a slower nudged it off its path toward Hitler, just the way that I had nudged the soccer ball off its path when I was playing with Peyton?

This seems like a perfect example of a slower's powers. But that wouldn't be possible, would it? How would the slower know when the bullet or bomb was coming?

"Can you tell me anything else about the attempts to kill Hitler?" I ask Mr. Zachs. "I don't know anything about them, but they sound interesting."

"Well, I could show you an actual video from one of the assassination attempts," he says.

"Yeah! That would be great. There's really video? I didn't know they had video back then."

"It wasn't originally video," Mr. Zachs replies. "They are video transfers from black-and-white movies. Goebbels hired film crews and famous directors to follow Hitler around a lot, for propaganda purposes."

I get up and sit in the seat next to Mr. Zachs. He pulls up a YouTube video on his phone.

"Emit, this video could be a little violent," he warns.

"I'll be fine," I promise, thinking that it can't be worse than the flying body parts that I enjoy so much in *Warriors' Bloody Struggle 3*.

"OK." Mr. Zachs hits play and turns up the volume. At first, the scene appears to be a big event in a restaurant, normal except for the Nazi uniforms, that is. There's an empty lectern in the middle. I can hear many people speaking loudly in German.

"It's a Nazi party gathering in 1938 at the Munich Hofbräuhaus," Mr. Zachs explains. "Hitler is about to give a speech. It's an outtake from a Nazi propaganda film by Leni Riefenstahl."

Nothing interesting happens for over a minute. Suddenly a huge fireball erupts from the right side of the scene, from under a thick wood table. Many Germans are thrown across the room. There's a jumble of screams and moans of pain. Even the camera is thrown to the ground. Luckily, the camera is undamaged and keeps rolling.

A few seconds later, Nazi soldiers rush into the room. They search frantically for something. Shortly thereafter, an officer shouts in German. The soldiers rush over to where the officer is standing. They start separating bodies that are strewn on the ground. Finally, they lift up one man, helping him to his feet.

"*Alles gut, alles gut,*" Hitler yells to the other party members as his security force carries him away. Many of the soldiers visibly sigh in relief.

"If only Hitler had died that day," Mr. Zachs grumbles. "It would have saved millions of lives."

"He should have died," I conclude. "Everyone around him was killed."

"Yep," Mr. Zach agrees. "He was very lucky, and the world was very unlucky."

"Are there films of the other assassination attempts?" I ask.

"Let's see." Mr. Zachs backs out of the current video and looks for others.

"Do you see any good ones?" I ask impatiently, knowing that these videos might prove to me that there are other slowers.

"Yeah." He clicks on one. "This one looks good. It's from a newsreel. No sound."

Here the scene is from what looks like a big office. Hitler, in his military uniform, is posing for pictures with a short, stocky man in a dark pinstripe suit, surrounded by other officials and assistants. I see from the video's caption that this is a meeting between Hitler and the French prime minister, in Hitler's office in Munich, also in 1938. This time, we don't have to wait long for the action.

Instead of an explosion, a window shatters, showering the officials in glass. Again Nazi soldiers dash in. They surround the Führer, protecting him in case the attack continues. After making sure he isn't wounded, they usher him out of the room. The other people slowly get to their feet and resume their chattering.

"Did they ever catch the shooter?" I ask.

"I don't know. I'll check," he says. He does a quick Google search for Hitler's failed assassination attempts. He pulls up a Wikipedia page.

"See anything?" I ask.

"Nothing about the sniper." Mr. Zachs continues to scroll down the page. "Oh, here's something." He reads from the website. "'In 1938, an unknown sniper attempted to assassinate Hitler during a meeting between Hitler and the French prime minister Édouard Daladier. Though the identity of the shooter is unknown, many suspect that the assassin was a Russian agent. The agent was unsuccessful because the bullet ricocheted oddly off the thick triple-paned window. The only injuries as a result of the assassination attempt were cuts from shattered glass.'" He pauses. "That's all it says."

"That's interesting," I conclude. "I wonder who the shooter was?"

"Yeah, me too," he agrees. "Anyway, you should probably finish your lunch. Your dad wants me to drop you off at two and it's already one forty."

I resume eating in silence. Mr. Zachs and I finish our delicious meal.

"Thank you, Uncle Dimitri. That was great."

"Oh, no problem. I …" As he gets up, he loses his balance and leans awkwardly on the table with all of his weight, causing the table to tip toward him. Without even thinking about it, I start slowing. Time comes to a screeching halt.

Before I move, I try to remember exactly how I'm sitting. My legs are crossed, and my arms are resting in my lap. Now I can help Mr. Zachs.

The problem is, doing anything drastic, like removing all the dishes or straightening the table, will attract a lot of attention.

Maybe I will just drink the water in the glasses so Mr. Zachs doesn't get completely soaked. I would like to do more to help him, but I can't risk raising suspicions.

After sipping a few inches off each glass of water, I get back into my original position and return to normal time.

At the same time that Mr. Zachs falls back into his chair hard, every plate, glass, and piece of silverware slides off the table, many landing on Mr. Zachs's lap and feet. I hear a glass smash as it hits the ground.

"Are you OK?" I ask, worried.

"Yes, I'm OK," he responds. "Crap," he adds.

I nod in agreement. I can't help but start to smile at the sight of Mr. Zachs covered with food and dishes. He smiles too.

Two Pavana employees race over to our table.

"Are you OK, sir?" they ask Mr. Zachs.

"Yes, I'm fine," he replies. "I am so sorry."

"Oh, no. Don't worry about it," replies one of the employees. "It's all fine." They begin to clean up.

Once they clean up as much of the food from Mr. Zachs's lap as they can, they carefully help him up. We all groan as another glass falls and smashes on the ground.

Soon two other employees come over to clean up the glass and water on the floor. We offer to help, but they insist that we don't. They probably want us out of there. Mr. Zachs also tries to give Pavana money for the broken dishes, but the staff refuse. Finally we leave. I can tell Mr. Zachs feels terrible.

On the way home, he apologizes again for the mess. "I guess

I'm just too old and heavy and fat for the table," he jokes.

"Maybe on Sundays, we should go to some diet vegetarian restaurant instead of Pavana," I joke. He laughs heartily. In reality, Mr. Zachs is quite fit for an old man. Not extreme-athlete buff like Opa, but still in good shape. He must be eighty or so. I wonder what motivates him to stay in such good shape. In fact, I wonder a lot about him. When did he come to America? And how did he become so close with my family?

CHAPTER 11

When my alarm on my phone goes off on Monday at seven, I wake up with questions racing through my head. Who is the slower that killed Kennedy? Was there also a slower involved in saving Hitler over and over? What if there was? Was it the same person? Is there any link between Hitler and Kennedy? I recognize that these ideas are crazy. But I can't push the thoughts away.

Then a wonderful thought hits me. I can sleep for another fifty minutes. I could get up at 7:50, and then slow time while I'm taking a shower and getting dressed. That will still leave the normal ten minutes for breakfast before the bus comes at 8:10. Up to now, I have had fun with my slowing power. But now I have finally discovered a really essential use. I reset the alarm for 7:50.

When the alarm goes off again, I force myself to get up and move to the bathroom. I feel better, but it's still hard to get up. I turn on the shower; it's a white-tile traditional shower with a shower head over the tub and a shower curtain. I adjust the temperature until it's perfect. Opa's right when he says that the ideal shower brings you to your knees and scalds you. My dad installed a huge water heater, and he removed the flow restrictor on the shower head so that our shower is a deliciously hot waterfall.

I slow time. I move into the water, anticipating that fantastic feeling where the hot water hits you and warms you. With time slowed, I will now luxuriate in the water as long as I want.

Something's wrong. When I step into the slowed shower, I barely get wet. I'm in the shower, but I'm just a little damp. What the ...?

Then I figure out what's going on. When time slows, the flow of the shower water slows too, almost to a stop. So when I step into the shower, the only water that contacts me is the water that happens to be coming out of the shower head for the last half second or so. Even though our shower head puts out a waterfall, the number of drops that are floating there, from the shower head to the tub floor, amounts to a total of about half a cup.

What am I going to do? I wriggle around in the shower, trying to get in contact with every last floating drop. I'm barely damp. It's like I just sweated a bit. My dream of the perfect endless shower is dashed. And I haven't left enough time to take a normal shower. I'm afraid that today my personal hygiene is going to stink. I jump out of the shower and towel off.

I figure that I can at least brush my teeth with time slowed. I begin my brushing routine. I grab my toothbrush, slather on the toothpaste, and turn on the water handle to wet the brush. No water comes out. Is the water broken? Then I realize that, of course, no water will come out when time is slowed—at least not for a very long time.

I speed time back up, turn on the water, and rush through my brushing. By then it's 7:55. I run to my room. I hear my mom knock on my door. "Emit, honey, are you OK? You're late for breakfast. Don't miss the bus."

"Thanks, Diana," I respond. "I overslept. My alarm didn't go off. I'll be down in a second." I throw on my clothes, run my fingers through my slimy hair, and stumble down to the kitchen. Running by the mirror, an unkempt slob looks back at me. I grab a piece of my mom's toast from a plate on the table and run out the door just as the bus stops in front of my house.

I'm halfway down the driveway before I hear my mother yell, "Emit, you forgot your backpack." Crap! I motion to Mr. Sanders, the bus driver, that I will be back in a second, then run inside and grab my backpack.

"Have a good day, Emit!" yells my mother as I run back out the door. Mr. Sanders opens the bus's door as I get to the street. I dash up the three stairs, then sit down heavily in the front seat next to Peyton. We have to sit up there because freshmen are required to sit at the front of the bus. In fact, the grades are organized into distinct sections on the bus: freshmen at the front, sophomores behind us, then juniors, and seniors at the back. For a while, I thought this rule was totally unfair. You can't have any fun when you're sitting right next to Mr. Sanders. But then I saw that this rule is for our own protection. Another freshman learned the hard way that venturing into another grade's section is never a good idea. The freshman got a bruise on his arm for going into the senior's section of the bus.

When I get to school, the first thing I notice is the shouting. As Peyton and I step off the bus, I see a large group of students crowding around the front doors to the school. Many of them have phones up in the air, filming something in the center of the group. I assume there must be a fight going on. Although I like to think I always avoid confrontations, I do like to see who is involved. Peyton, on the other hand, is not so interested in seeing the fight.

"Emit, you know it's dangerous to get too close when people are going at it," he warns. "You could get hurt."

"Oh, come on, Peyton," I say. "We'll be fine." I continue to push toward the fight. I see Ellen's back.

"No! No! Stop!" she yells. She is anxiously bouncing from side to side and focusing on something on the ground. Actually, it's one person on the ground and one standing over him. I can't quite make out who it is …

I now see that the guy on the ground is Jake Judson. He's lying on his back. Dick Braun is standing over him with his left foot on Jake's chest, pinning him down. Dick Braun is not a good person to be angry at you. He's man-size, a lineman on the football team. His neck is thicker than my chest, and he's a foot taller.

"Let this be a lesson to you," Dick says, bending down and punching Jake in the upper arm.

"No! Stop!" screams Ellen again. A couple of Dick's big friends laugh and clap.

I smile. This has not been a very good few days for Jake. He's caught cheating on his test. He's caught cheating on Ellen—well, actually, I had fun framing him. So Ellen is bound to dump him. And now he has somehow incurred the wrath of Dick Braun.

"Let this be a lesson to you," Dick says again. "Don't ever go near Coco again. Stay." Arm punch. "Away." Arm punch. "From Coco."

"No!" pleads Ellen, moving toward Dick. "Don't hurt him. Please don't hurt him."

I feel my stress hormones surge. I caused this. Coco is Dick's girlfriend. When I framed Jake as a cheater, I also framed Coco as the girl he was cheating with. Dick Braun is not happy about Coco cheating on him with Jake.

I look at Jake on the floor, with Dick Braun using both Jake's chest as a doormat and his arm as a punching bag. He looks pitiful and confused. He is a scared fourteen-year-old. I see Ellen, worried but defiant.

I rush out of the crowd to Ellen's side. "Please stop!" I say to Dick. "This is wrong. There has been a misun—"

"Shut up!" Dick yells at me. "Shut up! Or I'll do the same to you." He punches Jake again in the arm.

I start slowing. I've never actually used my ability in a fight.

I could easily do some major damage to Dick Braun if he can't punch back or evade me. Even though he weighs fifty pounds more than me, he's a sitting duck when time slows.

I walk over to the frozen fight. I have to be careful not to accidentally brush into people. Even a light touch might knock them over when time speeds up again. What I see is not a fight; it's just Dick standing on top of Jake and punishing him and humiliating him. I start off with a soft jab to the senior's stomach; it's really nothing more than a firm tap with my fist. Because of the magnification of energy from slow motion to normal time, even a gentle touch when slowing should hurt a lot in regular time. If I really punch the senior hard, I could severely injure him. I decide to stick with soft taps.

Next, I kick him lightly in the left shin. Maybe that wasn't hard enough. I kick him a little harder in the same shin. Oops! That may have been too hard. I guess it doesn't matter; no one ever died from a kick to the shin.

The senior's body is already starting to slowly recoil from my very first punch to his stomach, but I finish my work with a firm push to his chest. This should make him tumble to the ground.

I return to roughly where I was before slowing, next to Ellen. I return time to normal. I had expected Dick to fall gently to the ground backward, like he tripped. But instead, he is blasted back by the force of my push. He lands in a heap five feet away. His left lower leg has a bend in it that lower legs don't usually have.

Everyone is silent and still.

The silence is broken as Mr. Davidson, the assistant principal, rushes up. "What is going on here?" Mr. Davidson runs over to Dick Braun on the ground. "Are you all right, son?"

The senior groans. "I think my leg is broken." From the bend of Dick's leg, we all see that his diagnosis is correct.

"You, what did you do?" Mr. Davidson says, glaring at Jake.

Jake stands up. "That guy was standing on top of me. He knocked me down. He was standing on top of me. He was punching me." Jake pulls up the arm of his T-shirt and points to the red mark. "And then he tripped. He just fell on the floor. I didn't do anything. He must have hurt his leg when he fell."

Kneeling beside Dick, Mr. Davidson looks suspiciously around at the crowd. "Did anyone see what happened? How did he break his leg? Who did it?" he asks.

Ellen steps forward. "That's right," she says. "Jake didn't do anything." She kneels next to Jake. "Dick was attacking Jake. Dick just fell down by himself."

As the school police officer arrives, attention switches back to helping the injured student. As an ambulance is called, the bell for first period rings, and we disperse for class. About twenty-five minutes into the class, I look out the window and see two EMTs pushing a rolling stretcher with Dick Braun on it to their ambulance, which is parked in front of the school. A man who must be Dick's father is walking on one side of Dick. Coco is walking on the other side, repeatedly trying to hold his hand. But Dick keeps jerking it away from her. Coco is crying.

I'm surprised that my little kick during slow time broke Dick's leg. I grossly underestimated the power differential between slow time and normal time. I need to be more careful.

The rest of the day is normal, except for excited chatter about the morning's fight. After the last period, I walk down the hallway to the school exit and notice a couple senior guys behind me. Alarm bells go off in my ahead. They are the guys who were cheering on Dick this morning when he was standing on Jake. I glance over my shoulder to see if they're following me or just walking to their bus.

I turn a corner and they turn too. I stop and they stop. They're acting casual, talking quietly to themselves, but they're slowly gaining on me. I look around for some of my friends who could back me up, but I don't see anyone; by now the hall is empty.

This isn't looking good. I don't even know why they're following me. I assume it has something to do with the fight this morning, but they can't know that I did anything. Can they?

I feel a tap on my shoulder just as I near the doors leading outside.

"Hello, freshman."

I turn, then gulp as I see the two students.

"Or should we call you a piece of crap?"

"Umm … hi," I respond with a shy smile, trying to look as innocent as possible. The tallest senior, who seems at least eight feet tall, grabs my arm and pushes me into the boys bathroom.

"My name's John Grybowski, and this is Buster Jones. We're so happy to meet you. We know what you did this morning."

"No," I reply shakily. "I was just in the crowd watching Dick beat up Ja … um … that kid. Dick was awesome."

"Don't lie to us," warns John, the tallest of the two. "I saw you walk up to Dick. I saw you smile after Dick went down."

"No, I was just …"

"STOP LYING!" grunts Buster. "I saw you. John saw you."

"Well," I start, "I'm not lying to you. The boy that Dick was beating up, he's Jake. I know him. I didn't want him to get beat up. I smiled because I was happy to see that he was OK. That's all. I didn't do anything."

John stares right at me.

"You're lying," Buster says. "You did something. I don't know what. You went up to Dick. Then you did a quick move. And suddenly Dick was on the ground with his leg busted. It was some secret karate move."

I realize that when I speeded time back up, I must have not been in quite the same place as I was when I slowed time. So when time resumed, I appeared to jerk.

Buster moves toward me and punches me in the stomach. I groan and sink to the bathroom floor. I struggle for a breath but find none.

John laughs as I lie on the ground, the same laugh that I remember from when Dick was hitting Jake.

Buster leans over me. "What's up, tough guy? Can't breathe, karate kid?" He punches me hard in the right arm. They both continue to laugh as I try to roll away from them.

"Can't get away from us that easy," says John. John punches me on the left arm. Buster punches me again on the right arm.

Suddenly John stops. "I just had a great idea. This guy seems thirsty. He needs some water. There's some water right here in the toilet. I think he'd like a swirly."

They pick me up and carry me into a doorless stall, then drop me on my knees and force my head over the toilet.

"This is for messing with Dick," Buster says, as he forces my head into the toilet water. He holds me down as John flushes the toilet. I kick and flail around as I struggle for air. John is merciless though. He keeps me under the water for what seems like hours. When he finally pulls me out, I sag to the floor. Dark spots swim before my eyes. The two guys laugh as I cough up water.

"You're just lucky," Buster says. "You're just lucky that we didn't give you a brown swirly."

"Pick him up," John says. Once they have me fully upright, John walks behind me.

"What are you doing?" I shout desperately. "Please, no!" John suddenly wraps his elbow around my neck, almost tightly enough to choke me.

"Give him a few more punches." My tormentors start to punch me in the arms again, but I barely feel the blows. All I'm focused on is the arm around my neck. I try to pry John's hands off my throat, but I can't get a good hold. He laughs and then tightens his grip.

I scream and everything slows, but John's neck lock is still tight. I need to get air before I pass out. I elbow him gently in the stomach, then return to normal time. The gentle elbow during slow time is so powerful when speeded up that John recoils from my hit. He loosens his grip and I get a breath of fresh air.

I start slowing again. After a few seconds, I am able to wriggle out of the hold John has on my neck. Now I can make them all pay for the pain they've put me through. First, John. I grab him from behind under the arms. I start to drag him. He's heavy, but I can just barely do it. I try to remember to move him slowly and carefully. Although I'm furious at him, I've got to be extremely careful to avoid abrupt movements that would injure him when time returns to normal speed.

I drag him out of the bathroom, down the senior hallway, and into the cafeteria. I am glad to see that over a hundred students are still hanging out in there; after school, people are allowed to use it as a study hall and a safe place to hang out.

Unlike in the pro football game, I can move John safely because he was standing still when I slowed time. So there's no momentum that will be continued when time speeds up again.

I drag him into a corner and push him upright against the walls. I pull down his pants, keeping his underwear in place. I slide his pants off one leg and then the other, careful to keep him standing. Now it will look as if he just wandered into the cafeteria without his pants.

I go back to the bathroom and do the same for Buster,

dragging him into the cafeteria and setting him up right next to John. Buster is easier because he's smaller. Then I return to the empty hall, speed up time, and wander into the back of the cafeteria.

I can't wait to see how the two try to explain their situation. They'll know that I was somehow involved, but they won't have a clue what I did, and they certainly won't be able to explain it.

CHAPTER 12

At first John and Buster look confused. They blink a few times and look around. John looks startled. Buster looks as if he's in a dream. I almost feel sorry for the guys. But not really.

Silence spreads over the cafeteria. People start pointing and turning in their seats. They notice that John and Buster snuck into the cafeteria without pants.

For the first time, John looks down and realizes that he's only wearing underwear. Buster looks at John, and then looks down at himself. They look out at the students with surprise, and the students respond with their own expressions of surprise.

A single giggle escapes from the crowd. Gradually a few more are heard. And then it all breaks out; a wave of laughter roars across the cafeteria. Students pull their phones out of their pockets or purses, or wherever they've been keeping them all day, and start filming. These two tough guys just stay in the same position, displaying the same confused expression. I laugh along, mostly just because of their dumbfounded looks.

Finally the teacher monitoring the cafeteria hurries over

to the two of them and pulls them out. After a few minutes, the cafeteria begins to quiet. Everyone starts to chatter and to admire the videos on their phones. I smile. I've finally caused Buster and John enough embarrassment to make up for the pain of the swirly and banged-up arms.

Now, half an hour after the final bell, I finally walk along the hallway toward the school's front doors. Peyton comes up to me. "What happened to you?" he says. "You look horrible."

I suddenly realize that I must look like a mess. I reach up to my hair. It's wet and messy from the swirly. I touch my neck. Ouch! It's bruised from when John did the neck hold. And my arms hurt too from being hit. I look at them, and they are starting to sport large, dark bruises.

"Two seniors beat me up in the bathroom," I say. "It was John and Buster. I was able to run away from them after a while. That was really scary."

"Are they the guys who streaked the cafeteria?" he asks. "I was in the cafeteria, waiting for you. I looked up, and there were two seniors there without pants on."

"Really?" I fake surprise. "Maybe it was them. Maybe they were taking a naked victory lap after punching me in the bathroom. Senior prank."

After we get to my house, I say goodbye to Peyton, and he walks across the street to his house. When I step through our front door, my mom sees me and my bruises. "Emit, are you OK?" she says. "What happened to my baby? You're all black and blue." I explain the incident at school. "You're sure you're

OK?" she asks, and gives me a hug. "Let me give you some ice."

As she returns with a ziplock bag of ice, she asks, "Emit, would you do me a favor?"

I look up the stairs then back down at my mom. "Yeah, sure. But I need to do my homework in a minute."

"OK, thanks. I just need you to help me move some pictures and frames from my car into the house. I was getting some things framed."

"All right." I put down my ice and follow my mom outside and to her car. I wait while she grabs her keys and unlocks the car door.

"The pictures are in the back. Please be careful not to bang them. There's some new fancy frames with glass." I grab a bunch of picture frames and stacked photographs, and carry them inside. I end up having to go back for two more loads.

When I get back inside for the third time, I find my mom staring at one of the pictures, an old photo of me.

"What are you looking at, Mom?" I ask.

"This is a picture of you when you were three years old," she replies. I look down at the photograph, a picture of a little me with dark hair, sitting next to my mother.

"Mom, I've seen that picture of me a lot before. But I didn't know I was three in that picture. I thought I was much older in it. I look at least five." She studies the picture for a few more seconds.

"Believe it or not," she states, "you were three."

"How do you know?" I ask. "You could be mistaking this

picture for another one when I was older."

"No, I'm sure about this one. I remember taking this picture on your third birthday." I take a closer look at the picture. I'm standing beside a birthday cake with three candles in it. Behind me are my parents and both sets of my grandparents. I also see Mr. Zachs in the background of the photo. I'm reminded that my parents knew him even back then. The strangest thing is how old I look.

"I look so much older than normal," I comment.

"Yep," she agrees. "For some reason, you've always looked much older than your age. And it's become even more noticeable as you've grown older."

"That's really weird," I say. "I wonder why. Maybe I have some mysterious illness where I age faster than everyone else."

"Emit, I've never told you this, but at your fourth-birthday checkup, we asked the pediatrician about it," she says. "He said it's just genetics and it's nothing to worry about. You just happen to look older at a younger age."

"Yeah, or maybe I'm a superhero. Superman's got the strength. Spider-Man can sling webs. I can get old fast."

"Sorry, buddy," jokes my mom. "You're probably not a superhero."

"You don't know that," I reply, thinking about my slowing ability. "I could be the next superhero. Not Superman. Not Spider-Man. No. From the planet Decrepit, it's Oldman. Able to get three years older in a single year."

"Well," my mom replies, "I happen to know you came from

my belly, not from another planet. You're not Superman."

"Then how else can you explain why I look old faster?"

"Well …" She thinks for a minute. "It's a total mystery. Just one of those things that makes you you."

My mind wanders, and a strange idea begins to form.

"Emit, you're daydreaming again," my mom says with a smile.

"Sorry, mom."

"That reminds me so much of when you were little," she continues. "You would get this distant look, and you would stop paying attention. We all would notice. Dad and I would call it your trance."

"I haven't changed at all," I say. "That's just like my daydream trances at school."

"You always have daydreamed a lot. Even when you were a little kid, you would go into this daydream mode, where it's like you're off in another world. Sometimes it's hard to snap you out of it. It's the same thing you do now at school. When you were little, we were worried about the daydreaming. We asked the doctor about that too, just like the aging. He sent you for a lot of tests. But he couldn't find anything. He said that you were fine. He said that some kids just daydream a lot."

She then pauses before she continues. "I always wondered whether the daydreaming might have something to do with why you look old. I thought maybe there's some hormone that makes you daydream. And the hormone also makes you age faster. But the doctor said that he had never heard of anything like that. All of your levels for growth hormones were normal. I looked around in medical journals, and I couldn't find anything either." She smiles. "It's just one of the things that makes you special."

I suddenly look up at the ceiling as mom's musings trigger a strange realization: maybe I look older than other fourteen-year-olds because I *am* older.

CHAPTER 13

I should have thought of this sooner. But in the excitement of learning about my power in the last few weeks, I hadn't made the obvious connection between slowing and my physical condition. It all comes to me now in a flood. When I slow time, it slows only for other people, but not for me. If I slow time for half an hour, then I'm still going about life during that half hour, while other people experience only a few seconds. But that means that when time slows, other people hardly age at all, but I keep on getting older.

But there's a problem with this. I've only known how to slow time for a few weeks. I have probably slowed time for a total of a few hours. That would mean that I should be a few hours older than other people. But I look years older than other people.

"Emit," I hear my mom say from a long way off. "Emit, you're daydreaming again."

"Sorry, Mom. I guess I really do that a lot."

"Yeah," says my mom. "The trances were never a big deal. But there was one thing that made us worry. When you came out of your daydreams, you almost always would have a spasm. You would always jerk your body. And you would often have a headache."

"I know all about the headaches," I say. "But you never told me about the spasms."

"Dad and I talked about it a lot when you were little. But after a while, we didn't want to embarrass you. But we all would notice it. We would ask you if you were OK, whether the jerking and spasm hurt. But you wouldn't know what we were talking about. We had to work hard to get Maddy not to tease you. We had lots of discussions with her about accepting people who are different and special."

"Wow, Mom. I didn't know I was so weird."

"So we finally took you to the doctor about that, when you were five," she says. "That was a year or so after they did all the tests about the aging and the daydreaming." I notice her eyes becoming moist. She pauses, and I can tell that she is wrestling with whether to tell me more. Finally she continues. "I've never told you this before. In my medical practice, I see lots of people wheeled into the operating room whose problems started with headaches and fainting spells." Her tears really start flowing. "I hate to dump this on you. But I was worried that you had brain cancer."

"Mom!" I say. "You're too much of a worrier."

"Or maybe you were having little strokes that caused you to go into the little trances and have the headaches and spasms. Or maybe it was epilepsy, or a brain embolism, or little seizures.

We were all so worried. We ended up having you see a lot of specialists. But they didn't find anything."

A smile breaks through Mom's tears. "You were probably too young to remember, but that was the big joke around here for a while: 'They did an MRI of Emit's brain, but they didn't find anything.'"

Mom keeps talking, as if a dam has released a torrent. "But we still worry. Your symptoms have stayed the same. The trances. The headaches. The spasms. Just because they didn't find anything bad doesn't mean that something bad isn't there. Maybe it's just hiding, and growing."

She gets up, sits next to me, and gives me a huge hug. I hug her back. "Please, Mom. Please don't worry."

As I'm sitting there hugging my mom, with my head resting on her shoulder, something suddenly clicks inside of me. Trances. Headaches. When do I slow time? When my mind wanders. What happens when I slow time a lot? I get a headache.

So maybe when my mind has wandered before, and I have zoned out, this has caused me to slow time, but without noticing it. Maybe I've slowed time since I was a little kid. Maybe I've gotten so used to it that I don't realize that I'm doing it. Even when time has slowed, I've kept daydreaming while my mind wanders. I just sit there and zone out while time changes from normal time to slowed time.

But could I really have slowed time without noticing it? Maybe I could, now that I think about it. In Ms. Beans's class, I start daydreaming, and the class seems to go by with excruciating slowness. I sit there and almost nap, waiting and waiting and waiting for it be over. It's torture. It seems like it will never end. But maybe that's because time is slowed to a crawl. My daydreaming is what I do to get through it. Maybe the class doesn't just seem horribly slow, with the seconds seeming like minutes. It really *is* horribly slow, and the seconds really *are* minutes. The other kids suffer sixty minutes of Ms. Beans. I have to endure hours of her.

Could I really not notice that time has slowed? It seems impossible. But my mom has told me about patients at the hospital who get used to just about everything. They adapt to amputations, to becoming paraplegics, to going blind. She says that after a while, they hardly realize that their legs are gone, and they can't walk. They stop focusing on how they can't see. Mom says this is especially true for people who were born that way. It's all they have known. They don't have any other reality. This is their normal.

Maybe it's the same with me. Maybe I've always slowed time, ever since I was born. So I've gotten used to it. And I don't think about it. I don't recognize it.

I notice that I'm still hugging my mom. I turn my head to the left as I suddenly realize that my headaches are another piece of the puzzle. I have seen recently that slowing causes headaches. When I do it for even an hour or so during a day, then my head really starts to hurt. What if I was slowing time for hours without knowing it? I think back and remember that I would often get a headache after I daydreamed. Maybe I was getting headaches because I was slowing for hours without noticing. Who knows how long I slowed time when I daydreamed? It could have been hours and hours. No wonder I was getting so many headaches. I was slowing time so much it was amazing that my head didn't explode.

My mind stops wandering down these strange avenues. I focus again on the feel of the hug from my mom. What worry I must have put her through over the years. She really is a great mom.

"Emit, are you OK? Emit! Emit!"

"I'm fine, Mom," I respond. "What's wrong?"

"Didn't you feel it?" Mom says.

"Feel what?" I say.

"Your head and body," she says. "Your head and body just had a huge spasm."

"What?" I say. "There was no spasm. I was just sitting here giving you a hug."

"No, Emit. You suddenly jerked your head to the side. You banged my nose. It was a violent spasm." I look at her. Her hand is to her nose. Blood starts to trickle from under her hand, down across her upper lip.

Stepping quickly to the counter, I get her a wad of paper towels. I help her press them to her nose.

"This is the first time that I have ever been holding you when you had a spasm," she says. "It's really strong." She pauses. "It's really scary. Your body just instantly seizes up into a new position."

But I know that I didn't jerk like that. I think back. All that happened right before my mom got her bloody nose was that while I was hugging her, I had been thinking about all the stuff that she had been telling me. Then what had I done? I had slowly turned my head to the left.

Suddenly I understood. While hugging my mom, my mind had wandered. Without knowing it, I had slowed time.

The spasms that people saw when I was a kid were the aftermath of my unconscious slowing. When I daydreamed as a kid, and slowed time, I inevitably was in a slightly different position when time returned to normal. Even though I was mostly just sitting there when time slowed, I didn't stay completely in the same position. The same thing happens when I daydream in Ms. Beans's class. To the people who are with me, they see an instant change in position. To them, it looks like a spasm. No wonder they call me Herky-Jerky. I now also understand why I never realized that I was jerking or having a spasm; why I thought the kids were just making stuff up and being mean. It's because I wasn't really jerking. It was an illusion created by the slowing process.

So I'm older than other people my age. But how much older than other people who were born the same time as me? I could estimate that. I had reached puberty about three years before other kids my age, and I looked about three years older. So in my first fourteen years, I must have slowed time about three years of it. That seems like a lot. But it makes sense. Every afternoon at school, I must daydream and slow time for several hours without noticing it. No wonder school has always seemed to go on forever. It does.

My mom, noticing my silence, asks, "Emit, are you all right? What are you thinking about?"

"Just thinking about how cool it would be if I could slow time … uh … during my daydreams," I reply.

"Yes," she agrees. "Hey, you know what would be even better? Being able to fly."

"Are you sure you're OK?" I ask. "Your nose, I mean."

"Yes, I'm fine," she says, blowing her nose again into the paper towel. My thoughts wander to how I have bloodied my mother by accident.

"Emit," my mom continues, "there's one other thing that I wanted to talk with you about."

"Yes, Mom?"

"I've never told you this. That's because I didn't want you to worry."

"What, Mom?"

"We always wrestled with your ADHD and your sleep disorder. But I never let your doctors dose you up on ADHD drugs. I never told you why."

"Why, Mom?"

"It's because I don't think your ADHD is normal ADHD. I don't think your sleep problems are normal sleep problems."

"Why? What are they, Mom?"

"I don't know exactly. But I just have a gut feeling that the ADHD and sleep stuff is connected to your headaches and seizures. It just has to be. Your brain is your brain. You get frequent little seizures and bad headaches. It's got to be connected to your ADHD and sleeping. But the doctors could never figure out the connection. But there has to be a connection. The seizures and headaches just have to be causing the ADHD and sleep problems."

"But what does that have to do with the ADHD medications?" I ask. "Why can't I take them? They might help?"

"I was taught in med school that a main rule for patient care is to do no harm. You don't have normal ADHD. So I'm worried about using normal ADHD drugs."

My mom continues talking, but I'm no longer listening. It instantly becomes clear. My mom is right. My ADHD is connected to my headaches and spasms. So is my sleep problem. But they're all connected in a way that's different than she thinks. What do I do when I slow time without knowing it? For a lot of it, I probably nap. Hours of secret napping each day. No wonder I can't sleep through the night. I've already slept for hours during the day.

It explains why I wake up in the middle of the night after four hours of sleep, feeling fully rested. It's because I've already had another three hours during the day, when time was slowed.

It explains why I feel exhausted in the middle of the afternoon. By then, I've already been up for three hours more than everybody else.

My sleep cycle is all messed up. A normal human is designed for a twenty-four-hour cycle of waking and sleeping. That's how humans have evolved. But I don't get to enjoy a twenty-four-hour cycle. My day has twenty-seven hours if you include the three hours when time is slowed. No wonder I can't sleep like a normal person. My time is always thrown off. I'm always jet-lagged.

Now that I think about it, it also explains my ADHD. Because my sleep is constantly messed up, it's no wonder that it's hard to concentrate. I'm glad I didn't take the meds. There's nothing wrong with me.

Suddenly I realize my mom has said something while I was thinking.

"Excuse me?"

"I was just saying that many people in your dad's family look older than their age too. It must just be genetics."

My stomach drops.

"Who?" I almost whisper.

"Oh, I don't remember exactly. I just remember him saying something about it."

"Oh," I try to sound uninterested.

"Oh," she says, suddenly remembering something. "Your dad said it had something to do with Germany."

"When did dad's family originally come from Germany?" I ask.

"The end of World War Two," she says.

A thought pops into my mind.

"One minute," I explain as I run upstairs. "I'll be right back."

"OK." My mom, confused, opens the newspaper.

Upstairs I sit down in my swivel chair and open my laptop. I try to remember the name of that video that Mr. Zachs had shown me before he spilled the drinks on himself in Pavana. I know it was about a Hitler assassination attempt, but I can't remember the name. I decide to just text Mr. Zachs.

I grab my phone and finger type my message: *Hi Uncle Dimitri, I was wondering if you could send me the link to that video you showed me in Pavana. Just curious. Thanks!*

I sit back in my chair and wait for a reply. Unfortunately, like most older people, Uncle Dimitri feels like he always has to respond with a call instead of just texting back. My phone rings, and I answer it.

Uncle Dimitri gets right to the point. "So, I saw your text. You want the link to that video?"

"Yes!" I say with a bit too much enthusiasm. "I mean, yeah, sure. That would be great."

"OK, do you want the one with the explosion or the sniper?"

I think for a minute. "The explosion," I say finally.

"All right, I'll send you the link now. Say hello to your mom and dad for me," he says.

It takes only a few seconds for the link to pop up in my messages. I click it and am redirected to the YouTube page. When the video is loaded, I click play. The familiar film shows a room full of people in old-fashioned clothes. After about a minute, a large explosion erupts from the right side of the room. Then the soldiers enter and find Hitler. Yep, this is the video I saw before.

I restart the video at the beginning. This time, I focus less on the overall scene and more on the details. I see Hitler on the left side of the room. He is surrounded by several admiring officers who seem to be hanging on to his every word. I scan to the right of the screen, where the explosion will occur. As I watch, the bomb explodes. But wait, what was that! I scroll back through the video. A few seconds before the explosion, a black briefcase suddenly appears beneath a thick wood table. Does that briefcase contain the bomb? It must; Mr. Zachs said that the force of the bomb's explosion had been moderated by a wood table. But where did that briefcase come from?

I start the video over. As I scan the room, I see a gray-haired man carrying the briefcase enter from an entrance at the left. He stands casually among the group listening to Hitler. Then, about ten seconds before the explosion, the man glances around nervously, and moves into a clump of people behind Hitler. Then he can be seen slowly exiting the door on the left. He must have left the briefcase in the tangle of feet of the people behind Hitler. Then, about five seconds before the explosion, a faint outline of what must be the briefcase can be seen in the shadows under the wood table on the right. The explosion then erupts from under the table.

It must have been a slower that transported the bomb from behind Hitler, where it could have killed him, to across the room, under the wood table. But who is the slower? It could be anyone in the room. Even Hitler, for that matter. Or maybe the slower is the same one involved with the Gutenberg Bible theft?

If so, he couldn't have been older than ten or fifteen at the time of the Hitler assassination attempts.

I play the video again and see three boys that look to be in their early teens. Each is dressed in some weird Nazi Boy Scout uniform. I search around on the web. I learn that this is the uniform of the Hitler Youth, a group that was like Boy Scouts, except for Nazis. I have no idea why the boys are there, but there they are.

I watch the video three more times, focusing entirely on one boy during each review. The first boy looks completely normal—a clean-cut blond boy who seems to exemplify the ideal Hitler Youth. Throughout the video, until the explosion, he is politely chatting with some older people who I assume are his parents. It's possible that the boy had slowed time during the conversation and moved the bomb away from Hitler. But it would be extremely difficult to smoothly transition from talking to slowing and back again without the slightest disruption in his position. At the end of the video, the area where the family was sitting is covered in rubble. They may not have survived.

I rewind the video and focus on the second boy. He has dark hair, looks a little older than the first boy, and is politely standing next to a man in uniform. At one point, the boy leaves the officer's side and goes into another room. Fortunately for him, he is in the other room when the bomb explodes. He returns after the explosion and is visible at the end of the video as the soldiers scramble to find Hitler.

I rewatch the video, this time concentrating on the third

boy. This one also has dark hair, and he spends the entire video standing and looking at people. He's observant, like that's his job. His eyes dart around the room constantly. I wait to see a sudden disruption in his posture or position, the telltale sign of a slower, but nothing happens. His every movement looks fluid.

I rewatch the video, focusing intently again on the third boy. If the boy did slow time, I should see a sudden jerk or glitch in his movement when he returns time to normal and isn't in the exact same position. But nothing happens.

It suddenly dawns on me. The Nazis were not stupid. They may have tried to protect the real slower with a decoy. Certainly, the slowing ability would have been useful for the Nazis, for protecting Hitler if nothing else, and they would have planted a decoy to take the fall in case an enemy discovered the slower's existence.

I focus again on the second boy. He awkwardly stands next to the officer. This time, I notice that when the gray-haired man with the briefcase enters the room, the boy looks up and exchanges a glance with the officer. A few seconds later, as the gray-haired man with the briefcase disappears into the clump of people behind Hitler, the boy's hand twitches: it instantly goes from a fist to an open hand. The boy then leaves the room. At the exact time as the twitch, the faint outline of the briefcase appears under the wood table. It's him! The twitch was when he moved the briefcase. I pause the video and stare at the monitor for a while. Though this is an old film, I can see his facial features very clearly. He's a handsome boy, young and innocent—except that he's dressed in the Nazi Hitler Youth uniform. Also, he has a metal badge with the letters "SS" pinned to the left front of his collar. The two other boys do not have this pin. I stare at the picture. It's strange, but there is something familiar about the boy.

CHAPTER 14

After dinner, I do homework in my room. I can't concentrate. I puzzle over the video and the German boy. He looked familiar. I wonder if he is someone famous that I've seen in a textbook or on TV. Was it a young Arnold Schwarzenegger? Did Elvis grow up in Germany?

I grab my phone and call Peyton. "Hi, Peyton. It's me."

"What's up?" he replies.

"I've been looking at some old Nazi movies on YouTube where they tried to kill Hitler, and something's bugging me," I reply.

"Wow, Emit, you've become quite the Sherlock Holmes conspiracy guy," Peyton says. "First it was the Gutenberg Bible. Then it was the Kennedy assassination. Now it's the Nazis. Have you figured out the link? I get it now. Johannes Gutenberg was a time-traveling Nazi who killed Kennedy."

"I know it sounds silly," I respond with a smile. "But all three things are really interesting to me. I don't know why I'm so obsessed. It's like I have a personal connection."

"I understand," says Peyton. "I'm kind of the same way with playing *Warriors' Bloody Struggle 3*. To each their own."

"Could I get your help?" I ask. "There's a boy in the Nazi video. He looks familiar, but I can't figure out why. I'm texting you a screenshot." As I say this, I text Peyton a still image of the boy's face from the video.

"Hmmm," Peyton says. After a silence, he says, "He does kind of look familiar. I don't know why either. Let me think about it, and I'll try to figure out why."

★

At school the next day, with my mind trying to recall where I've seen the boy, I have trouble focusing. My math teacher, Mr. Binion, asks twice why I'm daydreaming in class even more than usual. The second time, he asks whether I'm sick, and I say, "No, just trying to figure out this equation."

"I'm sure that's the reason," he says, and goes back to teaching.

When the bell rings to mark the end of fifth period, I go to my locker to switch books. I'm still zoning out, thinking about the other slower. I do not see the foot stretched out in front of me until I've fallen in the middle of the hallway. Laughter erupts behind me. I groan as I look up at two cackling seniors. The leg that tripped me is attached to John. Standing beside him is Buster. They seem displeased at their humiliation in the cafeteria.

"I thought you learned your lesson, John," I say as I struggle to stand up. He stops laughing and shoves me down again. This time, I don't bother trying to stand up.

"Let's carry him to the restroom," suggests John as he spots Ms. Beans far down the hall. Buster grabs me under one arm, and John grabs me under the other. They pick me up and begin to walk me down the hall toward the boys bathroom. I know not to struggle. That could end with me getting hurt before I have a chance to slow. Slowing now would be almost impossible with Buster and John holding me so tightly. I decide just to wait for the right moment to fight back.

When we get into the bathroom, they drop me roughly to the floor. Buster kicks me hard in the right arm. It hurts even worse because of the bruises from yesterday. I really hurt, and I can't manage to slow and try to escape.

"Pick him up again," says John, annoyed. "I didn't tell you to drop him."

"Sorry," Buster mutters as he and John lift me up again.

John motions to the first stall, and his henchman carries me over and stands me in front of the toilet. Suddenly a kick to the back of my right knee brings me down into a kneel. John grabs the back of my head and forces it into the toilet water. I try to pull my head out, but Buster leans on me with all of his weight. Suddenly I hear a whoosh and the water begins to swirl. He's flushing the toilet with my head still in the water, just like the other day. The pressure is intense. It feels like I am at the bottom of a waterfall with the water battering my head.

When the flush finally finishes, my head is yanked out of

the water. Buster leans over me and whispers into my ear. "We know what you did."

I almost groan out loud. "You don't know anything," I bluff, trying to buy myself time.

"Emit," Buster starts, "one second, we were punching you and giving you swirlies. The next, you were gone and our pants were—" he clears his throat "—um, removed." They both eye me suspiciously and nod in agreement.

I try to think of a good excuse but John beats me to it.

"We think you're working with satanic magic," he says in absolute seriousness.

I almost laugh out loud with his stupidity. He thinks I'm working with the Devil! "Why do you say that?" I ask with feigned sincerity.

"Don't lie to us," John warns sternly. This time, I can't hold my laughter in.

"It's not funny," John yells. He kicks me in the leg. Pain shoots through me. The seniors haul me up and pin me against the wall of the stall, one on each side of me. I try to speak, but my leg hurts so much that no sound comes out of my mouth.

Suddenly the bathroom door opens.

"Oh, crap!" John yells. He shushes Buster and me, and peers around the wall of the stall.

"John!" someone calls from the door to the bathroom. The seniors sigh in relief. John exits the stall and high-fives the tall senior who has just entered the bathroom.

"Trey!" says John.

"What are you guys doing?" inquires Trey.

"We were, uh …" John starts. Trey sees me with Buster still pinning me against the wall.

"What the heck!"

"Trey, it's nothing. No big deal."

"Then what's going on?" Trey asks again. John, at a loss for words, just gestures at me. Trey walks over to where Buster is holding me against the wall and asks, "What did you do, freshman?"

I ponder the best way to answer for a moment, but when nothing clever pops in my mind, I decide to go with the truth. "They think I'm working with the Devil."

Trey looks at me seriously for a second, then bursts out laughing.

"The Devil?" Trey chokes. I crack a smile. Trey seems like a good guy. Maybe he'll sort this out. I suddenly realize I missed something Trey has said to me.

"What's your name?" Trey asks.

"Emit."

"Well, Emit. Are you working with the Devil or not?" John and Buster look very embarrassed.

"Buster, let Emit go," Trey says. Buster looks over at John. Thank goodness for high school hierarchies. John nods and Buster releases me. I drop to the floor.

I slowly rise to my feet and walk toward the door, slowly at first and then more quickly. As an afterthought, I slow. One after the other, I take John's and Buster's iPhones out of their pockets and dump them in the toilet. After I've completely dried off the water, I check the phones. Both dead. I replace them in their pockets, smooth my wet hair with my fingers, and resume normal time.

CHAPTER 15

As I walk toward the freshman hallway, I start having regrets—not regrets about ruining the seniors' phones, but regrets about not having done something worse. I should have at least repaid what they did yesterday by giving them a few bruises. They certainly deserve it, and more. I fight my urge for further revenge, and I continue down the hallway.

As I'm crossing a busy intersection in the hallway, I look back over my left shoulder once again at the bathroom of my torment. Oof! While I'm looking back, someone slams into me from the front right, where I'm not looking. Defending myself, I grab my attacker, falling on top of him and slamming him onto the floor. Lying there, I almost hope that it was John who attacked me so that I have some excuse for inflicting further vengeance.

Full of anger, I grab the perpetrator's head and turn him over.

"Emit?" inquires a high-pitched voice. I recognize that voice. Then I recognize the face.

"Peyton!"

He struggles to get up, but falters and drops back to the ground. He clutches his nose tightly. I stand and help him up.

"Emit, I think you broke my nose," he says. "Why did you grab me and slam me on the ground? I was standing in the hall, and then, next thing I know, you bumped into my back, and then you grabbed me and body-slammed me on the floor."

I sigh. "I'm sorry I banged into you, Peyton. I was distracted. I thought you were someone else. Here, let me see your nose."

Gingerly he opens his hand so I can see. Other than a little water from his nostrils on his upper lip, his nose looks fine. But I decide to play with him a bit.

"Oh no!" I exclaim in fake disgust.

Peyton gasps. "Is it bad? How bad is it?"

I wince. "It's pretty bad."

He groans. "Do you think we should call a teacher?"

This time, I can't help but smile at the serious expression on his face.

"What are you smiling about?" he asks.

"Nothing," I respond. He looks at me and starts to smile.

"My nose is completely fine, isn't it?"

I pause, then smile and nod.

"I knew it all along," he claims. "I was just playing with you."

"I'm sure you were," I say. Together we walk toward the freshman hall. We arrive at my class first. I say goodbye and turn to enter my classroom.

But just as I step toward the door, Peyton calls my name.

I turn around. "Yes, Peyton?"

He looks to see if anyone is listening, then says quickly, "Emit, do you want to come by my house later? I have a new piece of software that I think you'd like to see."

"Sure," I reply, curious.

"All right." Peyton proceeds a few more feet down the hallway, then turns around. "It's about that Gutenberg Bible thing that we looked at, and the Nazi boy. Maybe we could play some soccer too?"

"OK, thanks! Can't wait." I duck into my class.

"Where were you?" asks Mr. Derren, our history teacher.

"I was … uh … in the bathroom," I respond.

"Mm-hmm, sure you were. Do you have a bathroom pass?" he says, knowing that I don't.

I think for a second and then nod. "Yes."

"Well, can I see it?" he asks.

"Sure. I reach into my pocket, then slow. While Mr. Derren is frozen, I walk to his desk, and in the top desk drawer, I find a stack of his bathroom passes. I quickly fill one out and forge Ms. Beans's signature.

I practiced forging her signature one day during a particularly boring class. It turns out to be a useful skill today. I'd better make sure it's perfect so that Mr. Derren doesn't get suspicious.

When I'm content with the signature, I stick the pass in my pocket and return to my original position by the door. I return to normal time.

"Well, Emit, can I see your pass, please?" Mr. Derren repeats.

"Yes, sure." I pull it out and hand it over. He puts on his reading glasses and peers at the pass. It's nerve-racking, watching him analyze it.

After what I'm certain is too much time to spend looking at a bathroom pass, Mr. Derren finally takes off his reading glasses and puts the pass into one of his desk drawers.

"Thank you, Emit. Now go sit down. We're working on page two hundred and sixty-one in our textbook." I breathe a sigh of relief and go to my seat.

*

"Hey, Emit. I'm glad you came over." Peyton smiles at me as he opens his front door. He has a deep, dark bruise under his left eye.

"Peyton. Wow! Gosh. I'm so sorry I gave you a black eye."

"That's OK," he replies. "I guess I look like quite a tough guy. I told my mom I slipped in the bathroom at school."

"Peyton, I'm so sorry." There's an awkward pause.

"Thanks for inviting me," I continue. "Now, what do you want to show me?"

"Oh, right." He clears his throat. "Come upstairs; it's on my computer."

In his room, Peyton gestures for me to take a seat in the chair in front of his desk.

"It's fine. It's your chair," I insist.

"Well, you're the guest," he explains. "And I like standing up." If I'm not mistaken, he looks kind of afraid of me.

I raise my hands in surrender as he pulls up a program on his computer.

"What is this?" I ask as the computer screen fills with computer-animated faces. On the left side of the screen are numbers starting at 5 and going to 100.

"This is a cool website called the Aging Simulator," he explains. "You put in a picture of a child, and it supposedly creates a picture of what the kid would look like when they grow up."

"What do you mean, you put in?" I ask.

"You just enter a picture of someone into the website and tell the computer an estimate of how old they are in the picture. You then specify how old you want the program to make the person. The website does the rest," explains Peyton.

"How does it do it?" I lean in toward the computer.

"It was initially a program developed for the police," Peyton begins. "It helps them find kidnapped kids by predicting what they will look like at different times after their disappearance. It works by running a person's face through a complicated algorithm that, in simple terms, uses established cranial development patterns to predict future facial structure." He sees the confused look on my face and tries again. "In even simpler terms, the program determines the yearly growth and change in an average face after studying tens of thousands of examples; then it estimates what the designated kid's face will look like based on those patterns."

"That makes sense," I say slowly.

"Good," he responds, obviously enjoying showing me cool things on his computer. "But that is really an oversimplified explanation. Luckily, you don't have to worry about the learning algorithm or statistical estimation; all you have to worry about is providing the clearest picture you can of the face."

"Enough with the techie talk, Mr. Computer Genius. Can you show me what you have in mind?"

"All right, but first, do you have a better picture of the kid?"

I look at him blankly.

"The kid you saw in the Nazi video. You texted me a screenshot last night."

"I don't know," I say.

"Can you pull up the video of the boy?" Peyton asks.

"Sure." I quickly find the video and pause on a good picture of the boy's face.

Peyton saves the picture to his desktop, then uploads it into the aging program. "Here we go. Now, how long ago was this? World War Two ended in 1945, right?" He sets the aging simulator and presses play. We watch the face change year by year, getting older as the year moves to the present.

At the end of the simulation, I sit in shocked silence.

"No, it can't be," I say.

CHAPTER 16

Appearing on the screen is a likeness that looks a lot like my father. The resemblance is not perfect. Most importantly, the image looks ten or so years older than my dad appears now.

"How accurate is this?" I choke.

Peyton, not understanding my agitation, answers, "I've tried it on several pictures of kids that are adults now, and it is not perfect, but it's pretty good. The only exception is when the person has gained or lost an unusual amount of weight as they got older. That can change their appearance a lot."

I groan. "This can't be true. This can't be true."

"I don't understand," worries Peyton. "What's wrong?"

I sit in silence, trying to figure out what this all means.

"It's ..." The words freeze in my throat. We both stare at the face.

"Hey, Emit," Peyton says. "I just noticed something. That picture kinda looks like your dad, except that it's older. It looks like what your dad will look like when he's old."

"You're right it does," I respond. "But that's silly. My dad was born long after World War Two, and he's never been to Germany."

"Do you have any older relatives who lived in Germany?" Peyton asks.

"Well, my grandfather lived in Germany," I say. "You know, Opa. You've met him at my house."

"I thought of that," says Peyton. "Well, Opa doesn't look anything like the aged picture. He's way wrinklier than the picture. Twenty years older than the picture. Do you have any other uncles who are younger than Opa?"

Peyton keeps talking, but I don't hear him. Opa looks older than he should for the same reason that I look older than I should. We are both slowers.

That night, after returning from Peyton's house, I immediately go to the computer in my room. I then pull up the aging simulator's website, and I load a copy of the aged face that Peyton had created from the simulator. I age the picture even more, year by year. After twenty years of aging, the resemblance is unmistakable. It is a picture of Opa. Opa now looks exactly like the Nazi boy should look twenty years from now.

*

Five days later, I'm listening to the end of a church sermon.

"… and God said to Moses, 'Thou shalt not kill!'" preaches our pastor, Dr. Jefferson. "When God said this, Moses shrank back in fear and said, 'What if I have already taken a life?' To that, God responds, 'Then you shall repay your sins.'"

The church erupts in "amen" as the pastor steps off the

pulpit. When the crowd quiets down, she adds, "Go in peace."

I am the first one out the door. I have learned from experience that you shouldn't mess around with church lines. If you are caught in the middle of one, it could easily take five minutes to get out of the door.

Also, I'm looking forward to going to Pavana with Mr. Zachs. Hopefully, this time, he won't spill drinks all over himself. If it had happened to me, I wouldn't go to Pavana for months so that the waiters would forget about me.

A few minutes later, I spot Mr. Zachs coming out of the church doors. It took him long enough. He must have been trapped in the lines. Like most old people, he always loves to chat with other adults after church. My parents do it too. Small talk is such a waste of time.

"Uncle Dimitri! Uncle Dimitri!" I call to him. He looks around for a moment, then spots me.

"Emit, how are you?" he approaches and gives me a big hug.

"Good, good," I breath as I'm pressed up against his strong shoulders.

He pulls back, looks at me for a minute, then asks, "You don't want to go to Pavana, do you?"

"Of course I want to go. I was hoping you would ask."

"Good, me too," he agrees. "Let's see if I can go the entire meal without spilling anything on myself."

At Pavana, we order our usual favorites and sit at our usual table. While we wait for our food, I suddenly notice that the pinky finger on his left hand has a red scar. "How did you get that?"

"An unfortunate encounter with a lawnmower a few years ago. I'm lucky that it didn't get cut off."

I inspect it briefly, then tell him, "My grandfather got an insect bite on his left pinky when he was a kid. It got infected and he eventually had to have it removed. Now he ..." It suddenly dawns on me.

"What is it, Emit?" Mr. Zachs inquires.

I look over at him, then pull out my phone. "I need to look at that video of the bombing again."

"Why?" he asks suspiciously. I look up from my phone at him.

"I had a thought." I pull up the YouTube app and search for the video. It's the first one to come up. I click it and begin to watch.

The slower stands next to the officer in front of the camera. Could this really be my grandfather? As the video runs, I search his face for a clue. Toward the end of the video, when the bomb is about to detonate, he stands and walks out of the room. When he is about halfway to the doorway, his body twitches.

My heart skips a beat. The twitch. That is exactly how it should appear on camera when you slow and then don't return to your original position perfectly before returning to normal time.

But the thing that really shocks me is his hand. After the twitch, as the slower continues toward the door that leads out of the room, I get a perfect view of his left hand. Or, more specifically, his pinky finger. Or, more specifically still, the absence of a pinky finger.

Just like Opa, the boy's pinky finger is severed right above the bottom joint. There is no longer any doubt in my mind. My grandfather is the slower.

He saved Hitler's life. Why in the world would he do that? So many deaths could have been avoided if Hitler had died before the war in 1938.

After a quick lunch, Mr. Zachs drives me home. I notice him looking at me curiously several times during the ride home. I know I haven't been paying much attention to him, I've been too focused on my discovery about Opa. When we pull into my driveway, I thank him for the great lunch and head inside.

My objective now is to do some background research on Opa. I guess that he'll only be honest with me if I have some great evidence about his slowing ability and motivations. I start compiling a computer folder of materials on Opa. I name it the Opa folder.

To start, I take a screenshot of the picture of the Nazi boy without the pinky finger. I upload the picture into a photo-editing app and clean it up. The details become clearer and the picture becomes sharper and more focused. I don't want any debate about who this is. I add it to the folder.

Next, I take a screenshot of the aged picture of the boy from the aging-simulation software, aged twenty years extra—the picture that looks just like Opa. I save this screenshot to the same folder.

I think again of the video of the Gutenberg Bible theft. I

remember that the blurred image was not of a complete hand, but only of three blurry fingers. The first time I saw the hand, I thought that the missing finger was just a visual effect from the high-speed movement of the slower.

I pull up the film of the Gutenberg Bible burglary and watch it again after slowing time. As before, right before the bible disappears, I spot the ghostly three-fingered hand reaching toward it. The image is not a video effect. The pinky's simply not there.

I take another screenshot of the ghostly hand with the missing finger and add it to the folder, which now contains the images of the slower from the Nazi video, original and aged, and from the Gutenberg theft. I'll be ready to confront Opa next time I see him. Luckily, we're going to my grandparents' house for dinner in about a week. That will give me some time to think through what I'm going to say to him.

I lie down on my bed and sigh. Not only is Opa a slower, he saved Hitler's life and stole the Gutenberg Bible. Could it get any worse?

Well, yes, it could. I break out in a cold sweat.

I get up, go again to my computer. I add to the folder the blurred image of the slower's head from the Zapruder movie of the Kennedy assassination. But it's not enough for me to make a connection, thankfully. I can't handle any more.

As I ponder my grandfather's crimes, I drift into a fitful sleep. I dream of Opa running from people, trying to escape capture. I can't tell if the people chasing him are good or bad.

And even in my dream, I feel confused about whether I should be rooting for Opa or against him. He's done terrible things, but he's my grandfather. Then, somehow, I become Opa in the dream. It makes perfect sense in the dream, in the way that in dreams, the nonsensical always makes sense.

I wake with a jolt. There was some sort of time warp in the dream. As I lie there emerging from my grogginess, it occurs to me that slowing time could produce a time warp.

By comparing how much time passes for me when I'm on slow time to how much time has actually passed in the real non-slow world, I've estimated that I can slow time to about one-thousandth of regular time. If I can run ten miles per hour on slow time (that's at a very fast six-minute mile pace), that means that I would actually be moving at close to ten thousand miles per hour. The speed of light is 186,000 miles per second, so I'm still pretty far off. But if someone could slow time enough, or if someone could move in a jet or something that is much faster than I run, then they might be able to get very close to the speed of light. Reaching the speed of light would actually warp time. That is mind-blowing!

A physics thought occurs to me. Einstein's theory of relativity. $E=MC^2$. I never really understood it from physics class, but I remember that the faster something goes, the greater the mass it has. Doesn't that mean that, at ten thousand miles per hour, I would have a very high mass, in the thousands of pounds? That mass would prove very powerful if I were to hit something, or someone, while moving at that speed. It could certainly kill someone. I understand now why, when I gave Dick Braun a little kick when I was slowed, I broke his leg. I understand now why Mean Jim Keen tore his ACL at the Giants game when I moved his leg a few inches.

I turn over again in my bed, unable to get back to sleep. Speaking of power, my slowing powers are getting stronger. In the beginning, when I was just learning to slow time, I could hold it consciously for only about three minutes. Now, after all the practice, I can hold slow time for an hour or more.

I can also bring time to an even slower pace. Though I never measured how much I could slow time in the beginning, I know I can make time even slower now. In the beginning, even when I slowed things as much as I could, things continued to move substantially. I could see slow movements in people—in their lips while talking, their hands while waving, their legs while running. Cars and bikes also seemed to slowly inch forward. But now, if I really concentrate and slow things as much as possible, I see much less movement, or maybe no movement.

It strikes me that Opa must have achieved this level of slowing ability at an early age. Otherwise, the slowing in the video of the bombing of Hitler would have revealed him; he had been able to slow time so substantially that he was able to move the bomb between two frames, without being seen in either frame.

Even though it's the middle of the night, I decide to get up and conduct my baseball experiment again. In the beginning, when I was a novice slower, I threw a baseball at a stack of cereal boxes while slowing and discovered that the baseball crashed through the boxes and dented the wood fence behind.

I slow time, grab a baseball and some empty cereal boxes, and return to the same spot in the backyard where I had done the test before. A security lamp for the neighbors behind our house provides just enough light to see. As before, I set up the boxes three deep against the wood fence. After I slow time, I throw the baseball at the boxes and return to normal time while the ball is in the air. Before, the ball had forced a rough hole through the boxes. Now a clean hole the size of a baseball has been cleanly burned through the boxes. Before, the wood fence had been dented. Now a hole the size of a baseball pierces the fence too. The baseball has moved as fast as a bullet and created a similar hole in the boxes and fence, except the hole is much bigger than a bullet. More like a cannon ball. In just a few weeks, my ability has become much stronger. If I continue to improve at this pace, my power could be unstoppable in a year.

As I walk back to the house in the dark yard, I imagine how strong Opa's slowing ability is after eighty years. I need to talk to him. When I get back to my room, I go to my computer. I print out all of the images in the Opa folder on my computer. I then place them in a manila folder, which I put in my backpack.

CHAPTER 17

"Hey, Dad!" my father exclaims as we walk into Opa and Oma's house, a sprawling home with a single level. With a brick exterior, the house has an elegant long hallway that extends from the front entrance to the back, with rooms off each side. The house looks a hundred years old. But it's not. When Opa moved here to be with us, he had it built. It's a new house, but he built it to look old.

"How ya doing, Rob?" Opa replies gruffly. He reaches up from his wheelchair and gives Dad a hug.

"Diana!" Oma wraps her arms around my mother. I stand awkwardly to the side and watch Opa closely. I try to spot any jerky movements that would suggest he's slowing. Unfortunately, I don't see anything.

"Emit!" Oma rushes over to me and wraps me up in her arms. I pat her back, trying to act loving, but feeling awkward in her arms. When she finally let's go, she invites us all into the kitchen.

"Oma, how's the mold problem?" my mom asks.

"What mold problem?" asks my dad.

"Oma told me last week that they're having a problem where, once a day or so, their house fills with a strong smell of moldy garbage," Mom responds.

"It's not so bad," says Oma. "The house just smells moldy for a bit. But each time, the smell goes away after an hour or so. Maybe our noses get used to it. We just want to make sure there's not something bad, like a plumbing leak."

Opa cuts in, "Well, we just put a pizza in the oven. It should be ready in half an hour."

"Yessss!" Maddy exclaims. "We haven't eaten in forever. I'm starving. Thanks, Opa!"

"Oh, you're welcome, sweetie," he responds as he hugs her. I roll my eyes. Maddy always sucks up to our grandparents. She thinks that they'll give her anything she wants if she does. She's right. She is very close with Opa and Oma, especially Opa. It might seem weird for me to say that, given that Opa often does nice things for me, like taking me to pro sports, but there's something that just makes Maddy and Opa closer.

Since I was six or seven, Maddy and Opa have had a very strong bond. Oh, sure, he's always nice and polite to me, but with Maddy, it's been something different. I used to think it had something to do with what I said or how I looked. What else is a seven-year-old supposed to think when his grandfather clearly prefers his sister? But now, with my recent revelations about Opa being the other slower, I'm beginning to understand the real reason. I think Opa sees something of himself in me, and he doesn't like it.

I'm not sure whether Opa knows I have the same slowing ability as him. But regardless, I do look a lot like he did when he was a kid. And I probably have a lot of the same peculiar traits: the trouble sleeping, the unusual aging. He must have suspected I was a slower too. But why wouldn't that have brought us closer?

Maybe Opa is keeping his distance from me for my own good. Maybe he guesses I'm a slower too and hopes I won't recognize my own powers. Maybe he thinks that's better for me, given all of the trouble he's encountered in his own life.

Well, keeping his distance hasn't worked. I clutch the strap of my backpack, which I have on my right shoulder. I know my abilities, and with the pictures I have in my backpack, I know Opa is a slower too.

A tap on my arm brings me back from my thoughts. I notice that Opa is no longer in our group.

"Emit," starts my mom, "didn't you hear what Opa said? He wants you to meet him in his library."

"Why?" I ask.

"I'm not sure. But it sounds like he wants to give you something. Maybe it's a present!"

"All right." I make my way down the hallway to Opa's library. This is where he keeps all of his valuable books.

Just before I walk into the library, I pause, and a tingle runs down my spine. I suddenly feel like someone's watching me, but as I look around, I see no one.

Quickly the tingle disappears, and I try to shrug off my nervousness about approaching Opa. I knock on the library door.

"Emit, is that you?"

I open the door and am surprised to see Opa painting a portrait on a large canvas. I step closer and try to identify the portrait's subject. After a minute of silence, Opa speaks up.

"Emit, I've got a book for you that I think you'll really enjoy."

"Thanks," I answer mindlessly as I concentrate on the portrait.

"It's about Germany during World War Two," he explains. Now I perk up.

"Wait, weren't you a Hitler Youth?" I recall.

"Yes … unfortunately," he adds after a moment of thought. "I was forced into it by those horrible people."

"That must have been tough," I say. I want to cry in immense relief. I suddenly realize how much I was holding back when I learned he saved Hitler's life, wondering if he shared all the same disgusting values. I try to think about what it would be like if I were suddenly forced into an army to fight for a cause I hated.

"Yes, it was tough," Opa sighs. After a silent moment, he shakes his head. "Well, here's the book I was talking about."

"Thanks, Opa." On the cover of the book, I can't help but notice the faded swastika.

After a pause, I gather my courage and say, "Opa, I have a serious question to ask you."

He sits up straighter. "Yes, Emit. What is it?"

I take a deep breath. "Opa, can you slow time?"

He looks at me for a moment to make sure I'm serious. Then he breaks into a hearty laugh. "Yes, of course. I can also fly and shoot spiderwebs out of my hands." He laughs again.

"Opa, I'm serious," I say in a stern voice. "Please don't lie to me."

"Why would I lie to you?" he responds, now in a scolding tone. "And why in the world would you think I can slow time?"

"Because," I reply confidently, "I have a lot of evidence that says that you can."

"What evidence?" he says, but with a nervous look.

"I have it in here," I tap my backpack that is still slung over my shoulder.

"I have no idea what you're talking about, but please show me what you have," he says. "There must be some mistake."

I take my backpack off, unzip it, and pull out the folder of evidence. I put it down on the table in the center of the room. Opa rolls over in his wheelchair and opens it. I suddenly get the tingle-on-my-neck feeling again. Only this time, it is a thousand times stronger. I look around for someone watching me but see no one. Opa jerks slightly. When I look down again, the folder and the evidence are gone.

CHAPTER 18

I stare at the place where the folder used to be. My mouth opens slightly.

"What evidence?" asks Opa with an innocent expression.

"It was right here," I mutter. "I put it in here before …" I look up and see the smile on Opa's face. "You took it," I insist, realizing he must have slowed time and taken the folder. It is probably hidden in some drawer, if not burned or ripped to pieces.

"Oh no," he responds, putting his hands up as if being arrested. "You must have misplaced it."

My mouth presses into a hard line. "You know I can print out all of that stuff again. And what you just did just gives me more proof." I walk toward the door and turn. "Opa, I also know you saved Hitler's life and recently stole a Gutenberg Bible from a Russian museum. Did you kill JFK too?"

Now it's Opa's turn to look surprised.

I leave the room, slamming the door behind me, and walk to the living room. I sit down heavily on the couch and wait for dinner.

At dinner, I sit on the opposite side of the table from Opa and try not to make eye contact with him. My insides are in turmoil. I only participate in the conversation when it is absolutely necessary. The entire situation feels surreal. My grandfather and I have the ability to slow time. He's used his powers to do bad stuff. I figured it out. And now we've become something like enemies.

After dinner, I complain to my mom that I have a stomachache. I beg her to take me home early. Around eight, we politely thank Oma and Opa for having us over and we leave.

During the drive home, I finally start to breathe normally again. I can't believe that Opa took that folder of evidence. I realize I was accusing him of some terrible things, but he's still my grandfather. I guess I'd hoped that when I confronted him, he would somehow explain things in a way that made sense to me. I wanted to understand why he did what he did. But instead, I realize that after taking my evidence folder and denying everything, I can't trust him.

I also realize that the tingling feeling that I feel on the back of my neck must be related to slowing. I felt it at the exact moment Opa slowed time and stole the folder. I imagine Opa slowing and then rolling around in his wheelchair, wreaking havoc. The image is funny. But what's not funny is the atrocities he's committed. What am I going to do?

*

The next day, Monday, I ride the bus to school like normal. I'm surprised to see John, one of the bullies who gave me the swirly, sitting alone halfway back on the bus. I've never seen him on the bus before. He's staring deeply into his phone, and he doesn't notice me.

"What is he doing here?" I whisper to Peyton, who is seated beside me near the front. "He's one of the guys who beat me up in the bathroom last week."

"I think he's on the bus now because his family moved," says Peyton. "I heard one of his parents lost their job and they couldn't afford to stay in their house. They've moved into some apartment near us."

"Oh," I respond. "Well, now I almost feel bad for him, even after what he did to me. I wonder if he was taking out his worries on me," I say.

"No, John has always …" Peyton trails off as we realize that John has turned his head upon hearing his name. When he sees me, a smile breaks out on his face. I can see him considering whether to walk up to where we're sitting. Ugh, a fight is the last thing I need today. Luckily, after a few seconds, John looks back down at his phone.

"Oh, crap!" I whisper to Peyton. "Now we have to ride the bus with him every day. That sucks."

"Yeah," he grimaces. I sit back and think about my horrible luck.

When we get to school, I get off the bus quickly with Peyton. John sweeps past us. As he goes by, he smirks and mouths the words, "I'm gonna get you." Ugh. I need to end this conflict with him as soon as possible. I have enough real worries on my mind; I certainly don't need to be constantly fighting with him. Unfortunately, scaring off John may require more than just pulling his pants down.

After fifth period that day, I put my books in my locker, then immediately slow time. I run over to the senior hallway and find John amid a crowd of frozen seniors. Once I get to him, I look around for something to use as a blindfold. My eyes fall on a black sweater wrapped around a girl's waist.

"Sorry," I mutter as I pull it off her and tie it around John's eyes. Then, I grab John from the back, under his arms, and drag him to the closest janitor's closet. There, I set him down, make sure the sweater is tied tightly over his eyes, and return to normal time.

John jerks up and yells when he realizes he's suddenly sitting somewhere blindfolded. "John!" I whisper, covering my mouth with my hands to mask my voice. He stops moving. "Your days of bullying are over. You will no longer pick on kids younger than you. I will be watching, and if it happens again, you'll find yourself in a much more dangerous and painful situation than you are now."

"OK, OK," he stammers, clearly bewildered by finding himself vulnerable in the dark. "Is that—are you Emit?" he stammers.

I pause. "Yes, and I will never be your victim again." With that, I grab his right hand and slowly pull his pinky finger back farther than it should go. I hear the crack of the bone breaking.

I had hoped my show of strength would subdue him, but instead, it seemed to rile him up. "Ahhh!" he screams in pain. And then, in anger he growls, "I'll make you wish you hadn't done that!"

John groans as he grabs his broken finger with his other hand.

"Enough with the threats too," I growl loudly.

John chuckles, still full of anger. "You know I can do damage with my left hand too."

I ignore him and continue in a loud whisper in his ear. "John, if you ever, and I mean ever, whether it's tomorrow or in thirty years, hurt another person, it will be more than just your finger that gets broken. Am I clear?"

He laughs. "Sure, Bruce Wayne."

I slap him in the face. "John, I'm not kidding."

Suddenly he quiets, then smiles. He yells, "Teacher, teacher, please help me. Please! He's hurting me!"

"You shouldn't have done that," I whisper.

I hear footsteps and then, from thirty or so feet away in the hallway, "Where are you? Who is it? Are you OK?"

I whisper in John's ear, "Well, it looks like our time together has come to an end. Remember today, and remember that it will be much worse if you ever hurt someone again." I punch him in the face, right in the nose. His nose starts to bleed. As he starts to squirm, I slow again. I open the door and slip out. At the thought of John sitting bloody in the closet, I smile as

I stroll past the frozen students and teachers, and walk to the bathroom about a hundred feet away. Entering it, I see seven people using the facilities between classes. I know several of them. While time is still slowed, I enter a stall with a door, and use water and toilet paper to clean off John's blood from my hand; my hand got a bit bloody when I punched John in the face. I then resume normal time and flush the toilet. I leave the stall and begin talking with the others in the bathroom. When we all leave the bathroom, we hear yelling from down the hall. I recognize John's voice. But nobody will suspect me. I have the perfect alibi. While John was being attacked in the janitor's closet, I was in the bathroom. Seven people saw me there. Dang, I'm clever.

*

That night, I lie in bed. I think of my Opa, my kind grandfather, who does so many things for my family, Maddy, and me. This is the Opa who takes me to football games. This is the Opa whom we see often at our house and his. This is the Opa who raised my dad, and who helped Dad develop into a fine person. This is the Opa who was an innocent little kid.

But then I think of the Opa that I have begun to know only recently. This is the evil Opa, the Nazi Opa who protected Hitler. This is the Opa who stole the Gutenberg Bible. This is the Opa who seems to have helped kill President Kennedy. How can these be the same person?

Opa must have started out as a good little kid. How did he become a person who would do such bad things? Maybe it was just the time and place where he grew up. Normal people in Germany in the 1930s got swept up in the Nazi mania and did horrible things. A lot of normal people in Germany ended up helping out with the Holocaust and murdering millions of people.

In my darkened bedroom, I go over to my computer and turn it on. Still on the screen is the screenshot of Opa in his Nazi Youth uniform from the video when he saved Hitler. I zoom in on his face. An innocent face peers back at me, wearing a dark tie with a swastika pattern. What was going on in that head? Could it be something with the slowing power that turned Opa bad? Maybe there was something different in Opa's brain that allowed him to slow time, but maybe the difference in his brain also caused him to be cruel and violent. Maybe the slowing skill had bad side effects. Maybe the slowing skill results from a brain condition that is like the injuries that American football players suffer; among the symptoms that often appear after the players retire from playing are anger and aggression.

Or maybe Opa's brain is normal, but the slowing ability creates opportunities for cruel behavior that are difficult to resist. What a thrill it must have been to be asked for help by the leader of your country. How hard it would have been for a teenage Opa to decline the request. How thrilling to be able to use your skills to protect your nation's Führer. Unfortunately, Opa's efforts led to the deaths of millions of people; if Hitler had been assassinated before the war, the Holocaust might never have happened.

How exciting it must have been to evade the protections around the Gutenberg Bible. Nobody before had been able to steal the book. What an exciting challenge!

How thrilling to attempt to assassinate the president, the leader of the free world—to penetrate the intensive security surrounding JFK and succeed without a trace, misdirecting the blame onto the hapless Lee Harvey Oswald.

So maybe Opa does bad things because doing bad things is a much more exciting way to use slowing skills than doing good. What good things could you do with the slowing ability? Not very much. It's hard to think of good things that you could do as a slower. Good is boring.

Using slowing to do bad things is much more exciting. It is much easier to think of bad things. Is the slowing power like a drug for Opa? The slowing skill gives Opa great power over others. And power is intoxicating. But this drug has a huge side effect: it harmed countless innocent people.

I continue to stare at Opa's young Nazi face on the computer screen. Suddenly I notice on the screen a transparent image of another face—my own reflection. I shudder. I suddenly realize that I've succumbed to the same slower's disease as Opa, doing many bad things. I see all the bad things that I have done streaming fast before my brain as if I'm watching a speeded up YouTube video. I shudder again. I started relatively small. I stole Ms. Beans's book. I broke into her car and stole her miniature Rubik's cube. I didn't even think about this being criminal. It seemed fun. I did it because I could.

I'm also a liar. I was dishonest to Ms. Beans and Mr. Zachs about what had happened. I misled them and confused them. I think back to Ms. Beans's angry and bewildered expression when her book suddenly disappeared from her desk and then appeared in her car. I think of my false denials of responsibility to her and Mr. Zachs. I didn't think about the dishonesty being wrong. It was fun. I did it because I could.

But then I quickly escalated. I altered the outcome of an important professional football game, stealing the win for the Giants. In order to ensure the win, I destroyed Mean Jim Keen's knee and ended his season and maybe his career. I also destroyed the hopes of all Keen's teammates on the Cardinals, and of all of the Cardinals fans. Because of me, Keen has lost his livelihood, and he will never be able to pick up his children in the same way, if at all. Why did I do it? Because I could; it was exciting and fun.

I see now that I'm jealous that Ellen is going out with Jake Judson. I miss the attention that Ellen now gives to Jake rather than me. So what do I do? I frame Jake for cheating on her with Coco. I forge a letter from Coco to Jake, and I even, while time is slowed, press Coco's lips against the letter to leave a lipstick mark. Why did I do it? It was fun. And I'm clever. And it's fun to use my slowing power.

Thoughts about what I've done continue streaming through my brain. Now I see myself break Dick Braun's leg. And I picture Dick hobbling around the school for two months in a cast, missing the whole football season. Why did I do it? I didn't really mean to; I didn't think my kick would break his leg. But I kicked him because I'm just a little freshman, and it was fun to win a fight against a big senior. When I think back on it, I have to admit that I enjoyed seeing his leg lying broken on the floor of the school hallway at that impossible angle. That's sick. What's wrong with me?

Now I see myself stealing the video game from Gamestop. I didn't need to do that. I did it for convenience. I stole it because I could, and it was fun.

The video in my brain fast-forwards to how I punished John and Buster by taking their pants off in the cafeteria. John and Buster did bad things to me in the bathroom, but I'm no better than them, because I did bad things to them right back. Why did I do it? It was fun to humiliate them, to make them suffer. What's wrong with me?

My mental video moves forward to my most recent incident with John. I kidnapped him from the hallway. I blindfolded him and dragged him into a closet. While I threatened him, I smashed him in the face and broke his finger. I tortured him. I'm a torturer. And I enjoyed it—the power and getting away with it. I enjoyed seeing him suffer.

Earlier I had recognized how evil Opa had become. I was deeply puzzled about how my kind grandfather could have gotten that way. He was kind Opa to me, but he had another life as a murderer without morals. Now I can see why. The puzzle is solved. It's happened to me too. Was it something about my brain being defective? Did whatever physical traits that permitted me to slow time also make me a sociopath?

No. Opa and I are normal people. We have the normal ability to be good and nice. And we also have the normal ability, like everyone else, to do bad things. Just look what lots of normal Germans ended up doing in World War II. It's power that causes normal people to do bad things. That's why Germans did terrible things in World War II: they had the power to do them. They had the largest economy in Europe and the best military. They had complete power over other countries. They had complete power over vulnerable groups such as Jews, gypsies, and gay people.

It takes a lot of energy and thought to use power for good. Doing good is hard. Doing bad is easy. Hurting people is easy. Killing people is easy. In fact, doing bad is so easy that good people sometimes do it by accident while trying to do good. Look at all the well-meaning presidents who have blundered— Herbert Hoover, George W. Bush. Think of all of the millions of people that have died in unnecessary wars that were started by well-meaning leaders who thought they were doing good. Doing bad is quick. You don't need to be careful. Go ahead. Don't think. The result will probably be bad. If you want, you can carefully plan bad things. But you can do bad with little thought too.

It's not so much that power corrupts. It's that it's fun to use power. And it's much easier to use power to do bad than to do good. Or to use the power without being careful, which often leads to bad results. People are lazy. So people do bad things with power, rather than good things. Or they use the power carelessly. It's a much easier way to use your power.

This is exactly how I ended up doing bad things. When I learned that I had the slowing power, I wanted to use it. I did use it, but without thinking through the impacts on other people. I didn't start out trying to hurt people, but I didn't concern myself with the impacts on people; I didn't care. But as I got used to my power, I began to enjoy the power that I had over people. And I could get away with it. It's fun being Superman.

Except I'm not Superman. I'm more like the Joker. He uses his power to have fun by harming people. He's much more creative and ambitious in the bad things he does. He blows up Gotham City. I break a teenager's pinky finger.

Opa must have felt like this too, when he was a boy. The excitement of discovering his slowing power. The thrill of using it at first for modest things. The thirst for bigger thrills from bigger uses. The excitement of using the power to help Hitler, of changing history. The need for even greater thrills and risks. The excitement of the Kennedy assassination. Like a drug addict, needing ever bigger doses of excitement. The excitement of stealing the Gutenberg Bible. The excitement of many other things that I don't know about.

It's so easy to do bad things. If I keep on, I'll probably get better at it. And like Opa, I'll need to keep doing ever more ambitious bad things to get the same excitement. I'm on exactly the same path as Opa was at my age. A few more years of this, and I'll be just like him. Unless I get off this path.

I need to get off this path—I NEED TO GET OFF THIS PATH. I must not be like Opa. I must not hurt people for kicks. Opa and I are thrill addicts. We're power addicts. Our slower power is like a drug that provides the thrills and power that satisfy our addiction. I must not let an addiction control me.

*

"Emit, we're going to Opa and Oma's house tonight," my mom informs me the next Saturday.

"What?" I say in exasperation. "We were just there last weekend!"

"Why does that matter? You should enjoy spending time with your grandparents," she insists.

"I do, I do. I just …" I pause as I think back to the last confrontation with Opa. "I just have a lot of homework to do this weekend, and it's stressing me out."

My mom frowns. "Well … how about you just do your homework there?"

"No, I need …" I sigh, realizing I'll never win this battle. "Fine," I say.

"Good, I'm glad you're happy to go. We leave in twenty minutes." She looks at her watch again. "Maddy! Rob! It's time to go."

"Already?" my dad yells back. "I thought we were leaving at five."

My mom crosses her arms. "Really, honey. You're as bad as your son," she says with a wink in my direction.

A half an hour later, Oma greets us. "Hello, Friends!" Maddy giggles. This family joke never seems to get old for them.

Suddenly Opa appears in the doorway and rolls his wheelchair out onto the porch. "Hello, Diana," he says as he grabs my mom's arm, pulls her down to him, and kisses her on the cheek. He turns his chair around and leads her inside, and we follow after them.

"Maddy," says Oma. "Would you be a doll and grab my knitting from the bedroom upstairs? I have a present for you."

After a minute, Maddy comes back down with a big smile on her face. She sprints over to Oma and gives her a hug.

"Thank you for the sweater," she says. "I love it!" Maddy unfolds the sweater and shows it to us. It is solid red with the exception of a green Christmas tree knitted on the front.

"Did you make one for Emit?" my mom inquires. Is she kidding? I would never wear a Christmas tree sweater.

"I'm working on it now," Oma answers. "But it's different." Thank God. "I'm making something special for Emit."

"Thanks," I say, trying to be polite even though I really don't want a new sweater. "I can't wait."

"Opa helped me with the design," Oma informs me. "Thank him too."

"That's so nice of you both," says my mom. She turns to Opa. "I'm …" She stops. "Wait, where did he go?" I also turn and see that Opa has disappeared. I immediately slow time.

Where is he? Why would he leave in the middle of a family conversation?

While time is slowed, I head to the master bedroom. I check

both the closets and the bathroom, but Opa isn't there. I'm about to leave when a thought pops into my head. There may be more evidence of Opa's slowing in here.

I turn to Opa's desk and gently open the top drawer. Nothing but pens, notepads, paper clips, and other random office junk. Next, I open the bottom drawer. Still nothing compelling, except a picture of a swastika. It isn't exactly evidence, but it is strange for someone to keep this in a desk.

I head to Opa's closet. I search all of the drawers, even the ones full of old-man underwear. I'm pretty disgusted, but still I see nothing. I'm beginning to get discouraged, realizing Opa could store things anywhere, even outside of the house. Or worse, maybe he burns or destroys all evidence of his activities, so I couldn't possibly find anything. But I press on.

After leaving the closet, I turn to Opa and Oma's bathroom. I search through the drawers, cabinets, and even check behind the toilet. Still nothing. I'm heading back to the bedroom when something catches my eye. There's a sticky note attached to the wall next to Opa's sink, and on it are written the numbers "1-7-3." The numbers may be the code for something, but I don't see a safe or anything requiring a punch code. I put the sticky note in my pocket in case it comes in handy in the future.

Next, I head down the hall to Opa's library. That is where he originally stole my evidence. Maybe he hid it somewhere in there, or maybe there is other evidence concealed among all of his books.

Upon entering the door to the library, I carefully look

around for Opa. Good! He isn't here. However, I do notice that a small safe is sitting on Opa's desk. I haven't seen that before. I pull the sticky note out of my pocket as I scurry over to the safe and enter the numbers 1-7-3. The lock clicks loudly. I hold my breath as I slowly open the door of the safe. I look inside and … nothing is there. I search inside and even check for fake walls. But there's nothing. No evidence that Opa was a Nazi, presidential assassin, or bible thief.

In frustration, I push the safe and other stacks of papers off Opa's desk. The safe lands with a thud on the floor. But then I notice, taped to the safe's inside ceiling, another yellow sticky note. I pull it out and read the numbers "4-2-3." What's this? A safe that contains the code to another safe? I sigh. This could go on and on.

I sit dumbfounded on the floor for a few minutes. I don't want to play some elaborate game of treasure hunt with Opa, who is obviously clever and doesn't mind deceiving his own grandson. I decide just to return to my original position with the family in the other room and return time to normal. I'll just print out my previous evidence again. Somehow I'll confront Opa in a way that he can't deny what he's done.

I stand up and walk toward the door. At the door, I turn off the light. Who am I kidding? It actually is fun to try to outfox Opa. I'm not going to let him get the best of me. He thinks he's so smart and can manipulate me. Let's see if I can turn the tables on him. Maybe I can catch him in a mistake. I look back into the library, at the bookcase on the far wall that extends from floor to ceiling. That's when I notice a sliver of light at the bottom of the bookcase.

I stare at the light for a few seconds before I register what I'm seeing. I quietly walk back into the room and to the bookcase. I get on my knees and peak into the crack under the bookcase. I can't see anything except light. But light doesn't normally come from under a bookcase.

I think about all the spy movies I've seen where the spy has to push a certain section of a bookcase or wall for the secret door to be revealed. I check the entire bookcase, and the wall beside it, from floor to ceiling. I can't find anything out of the ordinary.

I sit back against the wall, pondering what to do next. My eyes fall on the piano in the corner of the library, and I'm suddenly reminded of the scene from the Batman movie *The Dark Knight*, where Alfred enters the bat cave by playing a certain set of chords on the piano. Well, it's worth a try.

I pull up the cover from Opa's old Steinway and admire the keys for a moment. Then I quietly play the lowest two-note combination by using the pointer fingers on my left and right hands to play the two keys on the far left of the keyboard. I realize I have unlimited time to try as many chords as I want. Moving my right hand up one note at a time, I play a chord with the lowest and third-from-lowest note. I slide my right hand over again and combine the fourth-from-lowest note with the lowest note played by my left hand. I continue this way until I've played all possible two-note chords that include the lowest note. When I'm finished, I move my left hand up one, to the second-lowest note.

I continue for quite some time, playing every possible two-note chord on the piano. About twenty minutes later, when I finish the last highest two-note chord, I mutter to myself. "Crap!" I had hoped that would be the solution to opening the wall. Out of ideas, I amble over to the wall and lean against it. To humor myself, I knock on the wall. "Knock, knock," I say.

"Who's there?" says an automated female voice from inside the wall. I jump back in surprise.

Without thinking, I answer, "Ummm … Emit?"

"Emit who?" continues the machine, which sounds a lot like the computerized voices from Apple Siri or Amazon Alexa.

"Emit Friend," I play along. After a long pause, I add, "May I come in?"

"You may, if you tell me the code."

"What code?" I inquire.

"The safe code," she continues in the robotic voice. My mind momentarily goes blank as I try to think of a code that would create safety.

"Please?" I joke.

"Yes, that is correct. Please come in."

"Really?" I ask excitedly.

"No!" the voice seems to rise in volume. "Tell me the safe code or you can't come in."

"OK, OK." I sit down in silence. What is the safe code? It sounds like some sort of nuclear bomb code or something.

Surely Opa doesn't have some sort of dangerous device, does he?

With newfound interest, I stand up and knock on the wall again. "Knock, knock."

"Who's there?" responds the AI voice.

"It's still Emit."

"Do we really have to go through this again?" she responds sarcastically.

"No," I mumble. "But I need to get into that room. Right now!"

"I don't care how urgent it is," states the voice. "You're not getting into this room without the safe code."

I sigh in frustration. Suddenly I'm puzzled. "Wait, how can you even talk to me when I'm slowing time?" I ask the AI voice. "You shouldn't be able to hear me or respond to me."

"No." She pauses for a moment as if she's thinking of a suitable answer. "My builder designed me to interact with humans at the same speed they interact with me. Much like he designed me not to let you in unless you can give me the safe code."

I scratch my head. But what does the voice or Opa need with safety? Then I realize what the safe code is!

"Wait, you mean the safe code from the safe?" I inquire.

"What else would a safe code be?" she responds sarcastically. I fish the yellow sticky note from my pocket.

"The code is four two three," I read, and place the sticky note back in my pocket.

"Thank you," responds the voice.

The bookcase pivots to the left, revealing a room behind the bookcase.

CHAPTER 19

I cover my eyes with my hands as a bright light shines into my face. When I realize the lights are not dimming, I slowly lower my hands and force my eyes to adjust. Finally my pupils constrict enough for me to see. I am surprised to see many shelves stacked with books, framed pictures, documents, and random memorabilia. I look around the room. It's a modest space—about the size of my bedroom. I can't believe I never noticed from outside the house that there was an extra space here. I'm also astonished that I never before noticed the light emitting from under the false wall. It must be that it's normally off. I got lucky that Opa must have left the light on accidentally. In my defense, I never would have suspected my grandparents of having a hidden room.

The room is organized into two parts. The left part has a black rubber floor, and it is crammed with exercise equipment. There's a low rack of dumbbell weights. A horizontal bar is suspended approximately five feet off the ground. A ramp offers wheelchair access to a treadmill. Next to the treadmill sits a recumbent bicycle. A pair of aluminum crutches leans against the far left wall. The wall is completely covered by full-length mirrors.

Why is this workout room here? Who uses this? It can't be my million-year-old grandfather in a wheelchair.

But then I see the drying sweat on the rubber floor. I notice the pungent smell of recent sweat and exercise. Then I see that the exercise equipment is all wheelchair accessible, from the recumbent bicycle to the free weights. I see that the horizontal bar is at the perfect height for Opa to reach up, grasp the bar, and pull himself out of the wheelchair for pullups. But when would he use it? We often visit Opa and Oma, and we have never seen him work out. He never mentions working out. Oma never says anything about him working out. He can't be the one working out; he's over eighty years old, and looks even older.

My mind returns to the smell. Boy, it stinks in here.

My eyes shift to the right part of the room. The walls on the room's right part are covered by three bookcases arranged in a U-shape, with one on the left, one in the center, and one on the right. The shelves are filled mainly with documents and books. Many of the documents are in file folders, each with a year printed on the front. I immediately notice that the documents and books are chronologically ordered. The shelf on the left contains materials from around World War II, the center shelf contains documents from the 60s and 70s, and the bookshelf on the right holds reports and other things from the 80s until the present.

Although my first instinct is to go to the most recent events, I instead force myself to start at the oldest documents. I walk over to the left bookshelf and immerse myself in Opa's history.

Inside the first file folder that I open is a black-and-white picture of Hitler and a teenager I recognize as Opa. The two are standing, straight-faced, in a bunker. Opa looks older than he did in the video of the assassination attempt, so I assume this picture was taken closer to the end of the war. Hitler looks tired and tense. Perhaps this picture was taken in the Führerbunker in Berlin where Hitler died.

The bookshelf also contains a dozen art pamphlets from the 1940s and 1950s. The pamphlets contain black-and-white pictures of paintings and sculptures. I'm certainly no art expert, but a few of the paintings and sculptures look familiar. Why would Opa have art pamphlets hidden in a secret room?

After a few more minutes of flipping through the pamphlets, I turn to the rest of the left bookshelf. On the top shelf, I see a white bedsheet covering something. I reach up and gently pull on the cloth to reveal two beautiful paintings. One is a black-and-white drawing of ballerinas. The ballerina in the center is in the middle of a dance, toes pointed and arms in the air. Why would Opa have a picture of ballerinas in his closet? The artist must be famous. The artist did an amazing job of capturing the dancers' expressions and the shadows on their bodies as they dance. It almost feels like I'm in the same room. I look for the artist's signature and can barely make out the word "Degas" in cursive letters in the corner of the drawing. Wow! I've heard of Degas, from when my parents dragged me to art museums when we took trips to New York. He's really famous.

The second painting is a portrait of a man who is dressed in a loose white shirt and a black beret. Based on his clothing, he doesn't look rich or like royalty. However, there is something striking about his face, a sadness emerging from the dark shadows. It looks like something I would see in a museum. Again I look for a signature. I can barely make out the word "Raphael." Raphael is really famous too. Why would Opa have such expensive paintings hidden here?

Suddenly I recall something. I pull the pamphlets off the shelf and flip through them again. Sure enough, the two paintings are there, in the pamphlet, along with about fifty others. I flip to the first page of the pamphlet and read inside the cover flap: "*Berühmte Gemälde im Zweiten Weltkrieg gestohlen.*" It's definitely in German, which I can't understand.

I pull my phone out of my pocket and push the button to turn it on. To my frustration, it takes almost a minute to turn on. Then I remember that I'm still slowing time. The phone is responding normally, just slower in this time. But after a minute of struggling to slide the bar at the bottom of the screen over to unlock the phone, I finally succeed. I open the phone and go to Google Translate. I type in the German words and select German to English. After a few minutes, the English translation appears on the screen: "Famous paintings stolen during World War II."

Of course, that's what the paintings are. I remember reading about all of the art that the Nazis had stolen from the Jews during World War II. They had taken thousands of pieces, many of which have never been found or returned. Amazingly, some of the stolen pieces still hang in museums and private collections today, even with irrefutable evidence of their theft. The ones in the pamphlet must have been some of the most famous stolen ones. Given his ability to protect Hitler, I assume Opa probably held an important position in the Nazi army. This would have given him access to the stolen art. He could have stolen the pieces he liked while slowing time, or considering how rampant the theft was, he may not have even needed to slow time.

I look again at the two paintings themselves and then at their pictures in the pamphlet. In the pamphlet, the pictures are next to each other. The caption under each has two lines. The first line is the artist's name and the name of the painting. The second line for both is "*Ruth und David Schapiro, 1943, Auschwitz gest.*" I don't need to be fluent in German to see that this lists the paintings' original owners, and where they died.

I turn off my phone and continue my examination of the closet. The center shelf contains material from the 60s and 70s, but most of it seems to be about the JFK assassination. There are magazines and books about the event, various black-and-white photographs, and a file folder with the word "Classified" stamped in red across the front. There is even a pistol in a glass case. It's a German Luger, the famous German military handgun from World War II.

I pick up the stack of photographs and begin flipping through them. There are several pictures of Kennedy himself and pictures taken in Dealey Plaza in Dallas during the minutes surrounding the assassination. There are also about a dozen pictures of men I don't recognize. With their slicked hair and slightly showy suits, they look like characters from *The Godfather*. And they all look sinister.

Also on the shelf is a silver frame with a picture of Oma and a little boy that I recognize as my dad. I shiver as I remember that my father is somehow related to all of this, even if it is just through his relation to Opa.

A little plaque with the name "Werner von Braun" catches my attention. Next to the plaque is a picture frame holding a picture of a man (who I assume is von Braun) walking across a street. There's a second picture too, with the same man holding a model airplane and standing next to another man that I recognize. I think for a minute. Oh yes! That's Walt Disney.

Now I'm curious. I pull out my phone again and do a Google search for "Werner von Braun." After waiting a few more minutes, several pages come up. I click on the Wikipedia entry and learn that von Braun was a rocket scientist who was a member of both the Nazi Party and the SS. He invented the V-2 rocket for the Nazis, but then was moved to America after World War II. In America, he developed the Saturn V rocket that launched Apollo 11—the famous spaceflight that first landed people on the moon. Von Braun was almost awarded the Presidential Medal of Freedom by President Ford. But his Nazi past made that just too awkward politically.

Why would Opa be interested in Werner von Braun, I wonder? I guess it's the Nazi connection.

I return my phone to my pocket and go back to the bookshelf. I see a folder marked "Investments." I open it. It is a stack of financial statements. I don't have time to look at it. I grab one from the middle of the stack, fold it, and stuff it in my pocket. I'll look at it later.

Looking around further, the book entitled *JFK Assassination: Facts and Theories* catches my eye. After perusing the table of contents, I decide to take a closer look at the chapter on "Possible Assassins." I soon become completely absorbed in the reading.

About halfway through the chapter, I pause when I hear a strange sound. I think it's laughter.

"Is that you?" I ask the AI machine.

"No," it responds. "I think that's my maker."

"Who?" Then the realization hits me. "Opa," I whisper. I turn and see him in the opening to the room.

CHAPTER 20

"Hello, Emit," Opa says with a steely smile. "I haven't seen you in—" he thinks for a minute "—a few seconds." I realize that ever since I had left the family, I had been on slow time. Now Opa is here with me, also in slow time.

"I knew it," I say. "You can slow time."

"Of course," he responds. "I'm surprised it took so long for you to figure that out. I'm even more surprised that it took you so long to figure out your own slowing powers. Fourteen is a little old for that. I figured out I could slow when I was seven."

"But wait," I say. "When I slow time, can you follow me into slowed time?"

"Yes," he says. "It's easy with a little practice. Haven't you felt that delicious tingle in your back when I slow? Well, when you feel that, you can practice so that you can quickly slow too and join me in slow time. It just takes a little practice. I call it simul-slowing. I can teach you sometime."

"But I've slowed time a couple times with you there, and you didn't join me in slowed time," I say. "Instead, you were just frozen like everyone else. That happened when you almost hit me with the car, and when you took me to the football game."

"With the car, I didn't have time to react and join you in slow time," Opa says. "At the football game, I did join you. You just didn't know it, because I was faking that I was frozen. I'm surprised that you didn't notice. It's really hard to fake being frozen in time. I was afraid I would giggle while you were staring at me. And when you came back from the field, I forgot to put my head in the same position as before, and I was afraid you were going to notice."

"So you were watching me when I went on the field and messed with the players while they were frozen?" I ask.

"Yup," Opa says. "Seeing you doing that, it reminded me of when I was just learning about slowing and figuring out what I could do."

"You also simul-slowed already one time without knowing it," adds Opa. "Remember at the Giants game, right at the end, when time slowed? That wasn't you who slowed time. I did it. But you somehow slowed yourself down too. You've got a real talent for it. With a little practice, you'll catch on fast."

"OK. I see," I say. "I remember feeling the tingle in my back right before the game slowed that second time. That was you slowing it, not me?"

"Yes, but enough about the past," Opa says, with sudden, abrupt energy. "Welcome to my special room. It took me months to build it, when I was much younger." He smiles and continues. "Actually, it took me about thirty seconds. I did it all when time was slowed. You can't imagine how careful I had to be to get all the materials and equipment in here without Oma noticing. Pretty clever, eh? I also got quite good with carpentry tools. It looks nice, doesn't it? Many hours working in here by myself, sawing wood and pounding nails. It's the miracle of slowing that Oma didn't hear me, although she was sitting nearby. She would just tell me about that strange scratching noise that would happen some evenings for a couple seconds. I told her I'd hear it too. I told her maybe it was the sound of a tree branch cracking."

Opa looks straight at me again. "You're not supposed to be here, Emit. Why did you break in?"

"What do you expect, Opa?" I ask. "Did you think I would quit digging just because you stole my folder? Don't you know that I now know everything that you've done?"

Opa begins laughing. "Oh, you don't know anything. And even if you did, it wouldn't matter. No one would believe you if you told them," Opa says with a smug look.

"I …" I start.

Opa cuts me off. "What would you possibly tell someone? 'My grandfather can slow time and killed JFK fifty years ago. Also, he saved Hitler's life and steals things. You have to arrest him.'" He laughs again.

I think for a moment about how to respond. "Then I'll have to stop you myself," I finally say.

He chuckles, his eyes gleaming. "Though I'm very excited to see that you've learned how to use your abilities, how would you possibly stop me?"

"You're in a wheelchair," I say. "Obviously, I'm much stronger than you."

Opa rolls toward me in his wheelchair. "Believe me, Emit. There is no way I would let you touch me, much less capture me."

"I think I could touch you," I assure him.

"Just try," he responds coldly, with the same smug look on his face.

I take a few steps toward him and reach for his hand, but he disappears. I almost fall forward in surprise.

"I told you," Opa says from behind me. "Don't underestimate me, Emit."

"How, how'd you do that?" I stutter.

"You think I haven't learned a few tricks in all my years of practicing with this power? Believe me, I can do a lot more than you think. I can do a lot more than you. You've only seen the tip of the iceberg."

I look at him in silence. "Did you just teleport?"

"No, Emit. I didn't teleport."

"You must have," I insist. "You were in front of me and then immediately behind me. And I've already slowed time, so you couldn't have slowed it and moved."

"Well," he says. "What appears to happen and what really happens are usually two different things." He pauses. "To appear to teleport, as you say, all I have to do is slow down time more than you've slowed it, and change my location. During the time when I've slowed time further, I can move while you are frozen so that you can't detect that I'm moving. Then I restore time to the rate that you have slowed it. To you, I appear to disappear and suddenly appear somewhere else."

"But, how did you slow time more than me?" I ask, confused. "I can only slow to one speed."

He pauses and looks around. "Well, I guess I should start at the beginning and explain how our abilities really work."

I nod, still a little fearful. "Please do."

"OK, where should I start?" Opa asks rhetorically. "I guess I'll start with our unusual bodies."

"My body is normal," I claim defensively. I'm confused about why Opa has stopped confronting me and is now giving me a lesson in the science of slowing.

"No, your body is not normal. It's not," he says. "And I'll explain how. Human cells are in a constant state of motion. Our blood is always in circulation; our nerves are always electrically charged."

"OK …" I say skeptically. It feels like I'm in science class.

"But our bodies, yours and mine, are—" he pauses "—a bit different. Our cells can move more than others. A lot more. In fact, our cells can vibrate about one thousand times faster than the cells in a normal person. So, yes, our cells are different."

"But what does that have to do with our ability to slow time? Those two things don't seem to have anything to do with each other."

"Oh, believe me, they do," he assures me. "And here's why.

I'm sure you've heard of the great physicist Albert Einstein."

"Of course," I say impatiently.

"It's a pity he was a Jew," Opa says.

"That's not right," I respond, shocked. "There's nothing wrong with being Jewish."

"Oh, you misunderstand me. I have nothing against Jews. I meant only that it was a pity that Einstein's people had such troubles in Germany, when I was growing up there." He pauses and stares at me. "Have you heard of his laws of relativity?"

"Yes, E=MC2, right?"

"That is one of Einstein's theories, but E=MC2 is not one of his laws of relativity. Instead, the laws of relativity have to do with space–time, gravity, and the constant speed of light. What is especially important for us is the constant speed of light in a vacuum."

"OK …"

Opa continues. "Consider this example and remember that the speed of light is always a constant one hundred and eighty-six thousand miles per second. It never changes."

"Got it," I assure him.

"Now, imagine two boys are riding in separate spaceships, and the spaceships are hovering above the ground, say one hundred feet in the air. To start, the spaceships are next to each other, at a starting line. Also, imagine that there is a huge mirror on the ground below them. Both spaceships have large lights underneath them. Now, when they are at the starting line, the lights shine down to the mirror, and then the light is reflected back to the spaceship. Both boys can see the reflection at the same time because the light travels at the same speed down to the mirror and then is reflected at the same speed back up to the boys."

"Weird example, but OK," I nod.

"Suddenly the race starts," he continues. "One spaceship heads off at a very, very fast speed. But the other one doesn't move, it just continues hovering still above the mirror. The still spaceship's light still shines down to the mirror and is reflected back just as it was before. But think about the moving spaceship. The moving spaceship's light still shines down to the mirror and is reflected back, but because the spaceship is moving, for the reflection of the light to reach the boy, it has to travel in a V-shaped path."

Opa illustrates with his hand. The light shines from the spaceship straight down to the mirror, but the spaceship moves on, so the light is reflected back at a diagonal to meet the spaceship. He pauses so the idea can sink in. "Now, whose light travelled farther in this situation?"

"The moving spaceship's light," I answer.

"That's right. The light travels a shorter distance when it travels straight down and straight up to the still spaceship than when it travels straight down and then at a diagonal up to meet the moving spaceship. Also, remember that light always travels at the same speed. So if light travels at the same speed but travels a greater distance, then it will take the boy in the fast spaceship longer to see the light."

"Ok, that makes sense," I say slowly.

"Consequently, the faster the moving spaceship travels, the farther the light will have to go to bounce back up to the ship, and the longer it will take for the boy to observe the light," Opa continues. "So the faster the traveler, the longer the time to see the light. And because it takes him longer to see it, it appears to him that the light is moving slower. Similarly, anything else he observes would appear to be slower, because every image we see travels at the constant speed of light. So for a person moving faster, the world seems to go by slower."

"OK, that's really confusing," I shake my head.

"Maybe I should have used a different example," Opa apologizes. "But trust me, time is slowed to a faster observer. It's all summed up in Einstein's famous time dilation effect. You and I are living proof the time dilation effect actually exists."

I start to put the pieces together. "So because our cells move faster, time slows down for us?"

"Exactly!" Opa says triumphantly.

I think about it for another minute. "Then why is time not slowed for us all the time? Most of the time, I'm in normal time."

"I've wondered that too, but never found a complete answer," Opa replies. "My best guess is that our brains can control the speed of our cells."

"OK," I nod. "So how can you slow time at different rates?"

"I've just learned that I can slow more or less, depending on how much I concentrate on it." He pauses for a minute and then continues. "It's like walking. I can't tell you exactly how I do it, but I've just done it enough and practiced enough that it's automatic for me."

My attention suddenly shifts to the left side of the room. "Opa, why is all that workout equipment there?"

"I'm surprised that's not obvious to you, Emit," Opa says.

I think for a moment. Then it hits me. "You use it, Opa?" I say.

"Of course, Emit," he says. "Don't you see why?"

I look back blankly. I don't see why an eighty-something-year-old man, who looks even older and uses a wheelchair, would have a room filled with a stationary bike, treadmill, and weight-lifting equipment.

"Emit, look in the mirror," he says, pointing at the mirror to the left. "How old are you?"

"You know that," I say. "I'm fourteen."

"How old do you look?" he continues.

"I know, older," I say. "I look maybe seventeen. I've figured it out that I age faster than a normal person because I live so many more hours when time is slowed."

Opa stares intently at me. "What are you doing about it?"

"What am I doing about what?" I answer.

"You're aging faster than everyone else," he says. "Which means that you are getting weaker and more fragile faster than everyone else. Which means that you are going to die sooner than everyone else. What are you doing to protect yourself?"

While he is saying this, he unbuttons his shirt, pulls it over his head, and drops it in his lap. I see Opa's wrinkled face and head atop the lean, strong body of a fit young athlete. Wow, he has ripped arms. He's in way better shape than me. Way stronger.

"Emit, do you think that this happens by itself?"

"I thought you just had a fast metabolism and natural muscles," I say.

"Of course not," he says. "It takes lots of hard work. I slow time every morning for a couple hours, come in here, and use the wheelchair treadmill and ride the recumbent stationary bike. My knees have too much arthritis to walk. But I can manage the recumbent bike just fine. I just use the crutches to get myself from the wheelchair to the bike."

"Does Oma know you can slow?" I ask.

"I've never told her," he says. "I want to protect her. I don't want her worrying about me."

"How do you explain to Oma why you're sweaty and stinky in the morning?" I ask.

"She thinks that I have an allergy to coffee that makes me sweat and turns my skin red," he says. "Then, after dinner in the evening, I come here again and do more aerobics and also lift weights. In the evening, Oma thinks I'm sweaty because I'm allergic to the Diet Coke that I always have with dinner."

"Emit, you need to start a workout program too. If you don't, you'll die early. Your body is wearing out much faster than for a normal person. You've got to make up for that by staying fitter than a normal person. I know it's a lot of work, but it's the only way."

Now I get it. This explains the puzzle of Opa's appearance: that he looks wrinkly and ancient, but he has the body and brains of a young athlete. It's the combined effects of slowing and fitness fanaticism.

"Opa," I ask, "does this room explain what Oma was saying about your house having a mold problem?"

"It's a little embarrassing, isn't it?" replies Opa with a smile. "She thinks that we have a mold problem. But it's really just her smelling me and my pain cave. You've noticed the smell in here? This is what it smells like when you work out in a tiny room for several hours each day with bad ventilation. Whenever I leave the room, a cloud of this pleasant odor follows me into the house before I can close the door again. It takes a while to dissipate."

Even though I am disgusted that my grandfather may have been a murderous Nazi, I can't help grinning as I imagine Oma mistaking her husband's aroma for a serious mold infestation.

After a pause, Opa leans toward me, and the smile drains from his face. "Emit, I can teach you how to use your slowing power to the fullest. If you want to learn, I can teach you quite a lot about your abilities."

"Why would you do that?" I ask, surprised.

He chuckles, then rolls closer to me. "Emit, if you and I work together, we could do great things. Important things."

I stare at him suspiciously. "Opa, I love you. But you're a

Nazi and a murderer. You're like some cliché villain out of a bad James Bond novel. Except you're not fiction. You really did these awful crimes."

"That's all in my past, from when I was young—younger than you. I'm different now. I've grown up. You've got to see me as I am, not as I was."

"You're my Opa, and I've loved you as long as I can remember," I say. "But ..."

Opa interrupts. "We could have an important impact on the world. We could do a lot of good. I've thought about it a lot. We could plan carefully and we could act precisely. We could take power away from tyrants and really make the world a better place. Let's do it together. I need your help. I can't do it by myself." He reaches out his hand toward me.

I freeze, looking at him and his outstretched hand. I want to shake it; I consider it. But then I remember all of the things that Opa has been a part of.

"Opa, I can't join you. You've killed people and done horrible things."

Opa looks at me; his eyes are full of sorrow, filling with tears. "Yes, Emit. I have done things that might seem terrible, but they were always for the greater good. And what you don't understand is that I haven't always had a choice."

"People always have choices, Opa," I say. "I'm sorry, I can't help you."

"Emit, if you had been in my place, you would have done the same thing."

"No, I would not," I say. "I would not."

"Emit, you don't know the situation. You don't know the facts. You don't know what was going on. Things were going on that were much different than you think. You will understand once I tell you. When I explain to you, you will see that I had some very hard choices. You will see that I made the right choices."

I see my Opa with red eyes, and tears on his cheeks. His eyes and cheeks look like mine, except older and sadder. I wish that I could work with him. It would be fun to follow him. I wish that I could trust him. But he has been involved in too many awful things. I can't trust that he has changed. As I fight tears, I say, "I'm sorry, Opa. I cannot help you."

Suddenly his gaze grows stern. "I see," he says. "Please think about it. You really need to join me. Trust me, if you don't join me, you will regret it for the rest of your life."

He disappears. Instantly I am sitting on the floor in the library with my back to the bookcase that hides the entrance to Opa's secret room. Or I think it does. Opa must have slowed time further and moved me there while I was frozen. Then he must have left the room, and restored time to the rate that I had slowed it. To me, he would have seemed to disappear.

I stand up and move to the wall next to the bookcase. As before, I knock on the wall and say, "Knock, knock." Nothing happens. No AI voice. Nothing. I try again. Nothing. I reach into my pocket for the yellow sticky note with the number. It's gone.

"Hi, Emit." I turn toward the door and see Opa in his wheelchair, smiling at me from the door. "Is everything OK? I heard some knocking from in here."

"You know perfectly well why I'm here," I say. "We were in your secret room, talking about your horrible past."

Opa looks blankly at me. "What secret room? What horrible past?"

CHAPTER 21

A few hours later, we say our goodbyes and head home. Because I spent so much time slowing today, I'm completely exhausted and have a huge headache. I immediately fall asleep in the car. When we get home, I have barely enough energy to pull myself up the stairs and into my bed.

The next morning, like every Sunday morning, we go to church. I try to listen to the sermon to avoid thinking about Opa. The pastor is emphasizing how the line between good and bad is often very blurry. People often do bad things that are motivated by good. As an example, she reports a recent news story about a man who robbed a bank because he was about to lose the house where he and his wife were raising their four kids. She then explains that many good deeds are motivated by self-interest. When people do something good, they sometimes expect to get something in return. Or they strive to establish a generous reputation so they look good to others. My thoughts drift to Opa. Opa said he didn't always have a choice when he committed his evil acts. Is there any possible justification for what he did?

No. What he did was too horrible.

After church I go with Mr. Zachs to lunch. But unlike most Sundays, we don't go to Pavana. Instead, we try out a new Indian restaurant near my house. It's an all-you-can-eat buffet, which is perfect for me. I definitely prefer quantity over quality when it comes to food.

"Hello, gentlemen," says the hostess as we walk in. "Please follow me." She leads us to a booth near the back.

After finding our seat, we get in line for the buffet. When it's my turn, I put a huge helping of rice on my plate. Then I scoop chicken curry on top and finish it off with a few red tandoori chicken drumsticks that smell amazing.

"Looks great," Mr. Zachs comments as I sit down, "but there's not much green on that plate."

"I know, I know," I reply as I look down at his food, which is a big bowl of vegetarian soup made of spinach and tofu. That's the one dish on the buffet that I don't care for. It's stinky green glop. "How can you eat that when there is so much delicious food right next to it?"

"Willpower," he answers as he takes a bite. "The most important thing. The doctors tell me that I have to eat healthy and lose weight."

I try to eat my meal without revealing my great enjoyment. But that's tricky, because it tastes so good. Mr. Zachs looks a bit forlorn with his bowl of green gruel.

After a few minutes, Mr. Zachs perks up.

"Emit, have you heard about President Brown's State of

the Union Address?"

"Oh, yeah," I say. "But I can't remember the details. What's going on with it?"

"It's in a couple weeks, on Tuesday, February fourth." Mr. Zachs continues. "The administration has announced that he'll be discussing specific plans for fighting terrorism. That includes fighting domestic terrorism by neo-Nazis. He'll also talk about a new treaty with Russia."

"What treaty?" I inquire.

"Oh, I think it's something to do with oil prices. Nothing you'd be interested in."

"Yeah, but the terrorism plans sound interesting. What's he going to do?"

"Well, I doubt if he'll be that specific. He can't be, you know, or he'll alert the terrorists themselves."

I nod in agreement.

"But I think all of the recent terrorist activity merits some sort of government response," Mr. Zachs continues. "It will be interesting to see what he says."

"Wait, what did you say about a Nazi thing?" I ask, my thoughts drifting back to Opa.

"Oh, I'm surprised you haven't heard about it," Mr. Zachs says. "Apparently, there's a resurgence of Nazi hate speech on the internet, and then there was that school shooting where the kid was motivated by neo-Nazi hate material that he read on the internet. It's crazy, right? I mean, it's been over seventy years since World War Two, and we still have Nazis."

I nod in agreement. "Haven't these people figured out how wrong they are?"

"Guess not," Mr. Zachs replies. "But Brown is advocating for new laws that will allow people to be arrested for preaching Nazi beliefs or displaying Nazi symbolism. He wants a constitutional amendment too. These activities would normally be protected under the First Amendment as free speech. But I think the school shooting is changing public attitudes about that. In a lot of other countries, like England and Germany, such awful racist hate speech can be a crime. And a lot of people are hoping that Congress and the courts will allow it to be punished here too. You know, there is often a tension between protecting our constitutional rights and protecting our safety. If we let people spout off hateful speech, we run the risk that people will be motivated by that speech to commit awful crimes. Or if we don't protect people's privacy at all, that's what the Fourth Amendment protects, then we risk giving the government too much power to dig into our personal lives. It's a tricky situation, and I don't think there's a clear answer."

"On this issue, I'm with Brown," I say. "How could I be otherwise, with my mom telling me how wonderful Brown is since I was a kid?"

Mr. Zachs smiles and continues. "Anyway, Brown is hoping to harness people's sympathy about the recent shooting, and probably their fear of future ones, to push a new bill through Congress. He also wants the constitutional amendments, so there's no chance that the Supreme Court will strike it down as unconstitutional."

"Hmm," I respond, "that seems like he's taking advantage of the situation." I flash back to the sermon, about the blurry line between good and bad.

"A little bit," he agrees. "But I do think it's an important law. As a Russian, I despise Nazis."

I think about Opa's attempt to persuade me to join him. "Uncle Dmitri, I've always thought of Nazis as utterly evil. But why did so many normal people follow them in Germany?"

"That's a hard question to ask a Russian who lived during that terrible time when the Nazis were simply awful to us, and many others. To me, the Nazis will always be the face of utter evil. But I can tell you how normal Germans lost their way and started following them.

"In the early 1930s, the Western world's economy was at an all-time low. In America, we, of course, called that the Great Depression. In 1933, Hitler and the Nazi Party came to power. They created many new jobs and started building projects to bring Germany out of the slump. So the depression ended in Germany before it ended in the rest of the Western world.

"But unfortunately, the Germans resented the outcome of World War One," Mr. Zachs continues. "The Treaty of Versailles was quite harsh to Germany. The country lost control of a lot of its land. It had severe restrictions placed on its military. It was required to pay a lot of money as reparations. This contributed to hard times in Germany. Hitler then exploited the situation by blaming the hard times on the Jewish people.

"So, under Hitler, the Nazis started passing laws to punish the Jews," he says. "They started off with laws that restricted the kinds of jobs they could hold and the schools they could attend, but the laws progressively got more restrictive and anti-Semitic. Eventually, the laws required them to live in certain places and mandated that they forfeit certain belongings to non-Jews. Hitler was getting away with it while he invaded Poland, France, and Czechoslovakia. But then he made a big blunder when he tried to invade Mother Russia. We pushed him back off our land, and then kept pushing."

"You also got a bit of help from the US and Britain," I add with a smile.

"It was mainly us." He grins.

"So, you think that what attracted Germans to Hitler was that he brought Germany out of the economic depression?" I ask.

He thinks for a moment. "Well, the Nazis made several scientific advancements during the war, like in rocketry, but I'm not sure I'd attribute that to Hitler."

"OK." We return to silence and finish our meal.

"Emit, why are you asking about Hitler and the Nazis?" Mr. Zachs then asks.

"Oh, um, we were learning about World War Two in history class," I say quickly.

"I'm glad that you're learning about it," he says. "It was certainly an important time in history. I hope we'll always remember the importance of shutting down tyrannical psychopaths as soon as they come to power."

"No doubt," I agree. We sink back into another silence.

This time, I start the conversation. "So, what was it like for you during World War Two?"

"Well, I was only eight in 1939, when World War Two started. In the fall of 1941, I turned ten, just after Germany betrayed Russia and invaded us during the summer. Germany was advancing quickly, deep into Russia. Russia was very desperate at that point to do anything to protect the motherland. I was forced into the military when I was ten. They needed more soldiers, even ones that were children. I quickly went into the front lines. I stayed in the Russian military for four years. I was in Berlin when Germany surrendered."

"I never knew that," I respond. "You never told me you actually fought in World War Two."

"I didn't see why it was important," he responds.

"I thought you'd just had a boring life, but it turns out you were a soldier. Actually, a child soldier."

Mr. Zachs shrugs. "Believe me, I wish I'd had a boring life. I have seen many things that I'd rather not remember."

"Oh, right. I'm sure." I pause, still in disbelief. "Um, Uncle Dimitri, have you ever killed anyone?"

He hesitates. "Yes," he replies. "Yes. I'm sad to say, more than one. I wish I didn't have a life like that, but I did. It was kill or be killed, even when I was just a child. I was very lucky that I wasn't killed. You don't know how ruthless you can be until you don't have any choice."

"Can you tell me about what happened in one of them? I can't imagine how horrible that must be."

"Sure." He takes a deep breath. "Here's one that I remember very clearly, the first one. It was in October of 1941, just after my squad had been sent in to fight. We were ordered to attack this little town near Prokhorovka; the Germans had just occupied it as they were moving toward Moscow. Some German troops were holed up there. We were told to kill them."

"You were only ten?"

"Childhood is a luxury," he says. "In the war, you did not have that luxury. You grow up instantly when the bullets and bombs come whizzing at you, and you see your friends torn apart."

"What happened in the town, Uncle Dimitri?"

"From the second that we walked into the town, we knew something was off. There were no people in the streets. There was only silence. It was a ghost town."

"Somehow the Germans knew we were coming. They had placed a sniper on a nearby hillside to greet us."

"Oh no," I whisper.

"The first bullet hit my lieutenant, whom we called 'Vezuchiy.' That means 'Lucky' in English. He wasn't very lucky that day." Mr. Zachs's face contorts, and his eyes became moist.

"What happened next?" I ask. "Please tell me."

Mr. Zachs takes a deep breath and collects himself. "Sorry," he says. "It's a bit hard for me when I think about this."

After a further pause, he continues. "The next person to get hit was a private named Vladimir. He died instantly. Shot in the head. By this time, the rest of the squad realized that a sniper had spotted us. We quickly ducked behind a building that offered protection and started to discuss a plan to eliminate the sniper. Unfortunately, while we were scheming, the German snuck around to the other side of the village. From his new post, he could see us clearly again.

"When the sniper opened fire for the second time, I was sure I was going to die." Mr. Zachs grabs his napkin and twists it in his hands. His mouth opens and closes, like he wants to say more but can't find the words. He finally collects himself. "I remember thinking, 'I'm only ten years old. I can't die yet.' Somehow none of the bullets hit me. Several more members of my squad weren't so lucky."

I can see tears in his eyes, and I don't know how to feel or what to say.

"Three of them fell in a slow sequence of bullets. Thud." He slams his hand on the table. "Another thud." He slams his hand again, and I imagine the bodies falling. "A final thud. Three of us dead. There were no screams of death. Only thuds and then silence. The sniper was too good." He grits his teeth against his anguish at reliving this awful time. "The blood … I can't quite describe …"

"What did you do?" I ask. "How did you get away?"

"The rest of us just fled for the forest that surrounded the town. Not surprisingly, we got separated. Eventually, I found myself running through the thick foliage alone. I ran for what felt like hours. But it was probably really only a couple minutes. I was too afraid to look back.

"Then I crashed into a small clearing, and there was the German sniper, standing there, his back to me and his rifle hanging on his sling on his shoulder. He turned toward me. He was older than me, but not much; he looked about sixteen. He was a boy too. Blond and blue-eyed, he was wearing the uniform of the Hitler Youth. He must have learned how to hunt from his father.

"For a moment, we stared at each other. Then he reached for his Luger. I didn't think about grabbing my gun. I probably wouldn't have had time anyway. So I just ran straight at him. Just before my ten-year-old body slammed straight into him, there was a loud bang. My arm hurt." Mr. Zachs pauses, rolls up his left sleeve, and shows me a scar on his upper arm.

"After I tackled him, I can't remember exactly what happened. Somehow he slipped and fell backward. I was much smaller than him, but somehow I knocked him over. When he fell, he dropped his pistol. I dived for the gun and grabbed the grip. As I lifted the gun and began to point it at him, the German grabbed the gun's barrel. We each tried to pull the gun away from the other. Then I looked him in the eye, and he looked back at me, and I remembered to pull the trigger." His hands have twisted the paper napkin into a spiral. "I was so terrified. I was purely fighting out of fear, not bravery." Mr. Zachs stares into space. "I kept pulling and pulling until bangs turned into clicks. I was covered in blood: my blood from my arm, and the German's blood. I crumpled to the ground next to the German boy. I curled up in a ball. I closed my eyes and shook and sobbed." As eighty-year-old Mr. Zachs remembers his ten-year-old self, tears flow down his cheeks.

"Did you ever find the rest of your squad? Were they OK?" I ask, too eagerly.

"I hiked back to our barracks, using only my compass and my map. When I finally got back, I was told that I was the only member of my squad that survived. Others had been killed by the sniper or had run into some other Germans in the forest."

"Wow, that's awful," I say. "That happened to you when you were only ten years old?"

Mr. Zachs nods. "Yes. Most ten-year-olds today have things quite differently. But it was another time.

"Oh, there's one other thing that I forgot to tell you about my terrible adventure in the forest," Mr. Zachs continues. "As I lay on the ground next to the German boy I had shot, the boy moaned. As I shook and sobbed, I turned toward him; his face was about a foot from mine. His open blue eyes looked skyward, and blood flowed from the corner of his mouth, down across a metal SS pin that was attached to his collar. He said quietly, 'Langsamer. Langsamer. Warum hast du mich verloren?' Then, as he continued to look skyward, he was silent and still."

"That's so weird," I say. "That's so scary. Was he talking to you? What was the boy saying? What's the translation?"

"Ever since then, I've been puzzled about those words," Mr.

Zachs responds. "My German isn't great, but I've checked with native German speakers, and the translation is something like 'Slow person, slow person, why have you forsaken me?' I have no idea what it means. I remember from Sunday school that it's similar to what Jesus says to God when he's dying on the cross. But here, the dying boy said it to this slow person, whoever that is. Maybe I misheard it. But I don't think so. I was right next to him."

CHAPTER 22

"Thanks for meeting me," I say as Opa rolls toward me. We're in a quiet area on the west side of Central Park. My mother has dropped me off in Manhattan on Saturday morning to have quality time with my grandfather while she sees college friends in Brooklyn. We're taking this small trip because it's winter break weekend; school is on break the following Monday through Wednesday. It's hard to believe it's still January. It's sunny and sixty degrees. In the flower beds, confused daffodil buds are beginning to open.

"I assume that you have reconsidered my proposal," he replies with a confident smile.

"Possibly," I respond. "But can you tell me a bit more about your plans?"

"Not so fast," Opa chuckles. "I'll tell you more when I know you're joining me."

I should have known I couldn't easily trick Opa like that.

"Emit, consider something for a minute," Opa continues. "We can work together, and we move a thousand times faster than anyone else. So we are much stronger than anyone else. We can do anything. No one could stop us. We could do so many important things. We could do so much good. We could help so many people."

"I know, Opa," I respond, trying to sound genuine. "I've been thinking a lot about that. I'm just struggling with what we would do. I don't want to do evil things. I want to do good. I also know there's a blurry line between good and evil."

"Ah, yes, there is, my boy," Opa nods encouragingly. "I only want to do good too. We have great power. And with it comes great responsibility to do good."

"What?" I say. "I don't think you're worthy enough to think you're like Spider-Man. You've done so many horrible things, Opa. You've protected Hitler. You've assassinated a president. You've stolen things, big things. You haven't used your slowing power for good. You're the villain, not the hero."

"Emit, it makes me so sad to hear you say that. It's the last thing that I would ever want, to have you think of me that way."

"Well, what am I supposed to think?" I ask. "You're a murderer, and if you hadn't protected your friend Adolph, six million innocent Jews wouldn't have died."

"Emit, I only did it because I had to. I did it to protect my family. I did it to protect my comrades in the army. I did it to protect you."

"What do you mean?" I say.

"I didn't want to help the Führer. But I had to."

"You didn't have to," I say. "You always have a choice."

"No," he says. "They put my parents and whole family in Dachau, living at the commandant's guesthouse there. Emit, that's your great-grandparents. They told me that if I didn't help them, then my family would instantly be moved to the gas chambers. I would be shot too. I had to help them. I had no choice. If I hadn't helped them, my family would be dead. I would be dead. You wouldn't exist. It was an awful choice to have to make. But I did the right thing. I did the only thing I could do. You would have done the same thing."

I look him in the eye. "I don't believe you, Opa," I say. "You enjoyed your work."

"That's not so, Emit. I detested a lot of my work. But I had to do it, for my family."

"I don't believe you, Opa," I repeat. "How would they have even known that you were a slower unless you volunteered?"

"I didn't want them to know. But they found out when I made a blunder. I slowed time but then moved around, and then I forgot to move back to my original position before I returned time to normal. They saw me magically move thirty feet across a conference hall. They were smart to figure it out."

He's so sincere, I conclude. He's either telling the truth, or he's an amazing liar.

"The only part of my work that I did enjoy was when I was asked to help protect the normal low-level soldiers," he continues. "There was a lot of that work. Slowing time before the soldiers made an especially dangerous assault, so that I could cross enemy lines and disable the enemy's weapons.

Or slowing time and carrying one of our snipers through the enemy to place him in a perfect spot for an ambush."

"I got quite a reputation among the foot soldiers. I was called the 'Langsamer,' the soldier's savior. *Langsamer* means 'slower.'"

My thoughts immediately return to Mr. Zachs's deadly encounter with the German sniper. Did Opa put the sniper in position to kill Mr. Zachs's comrades? Was the dying German sniper talking about Opa when he said, "Slower, why have you forsaken me?"

I glare at Opa. "Maybe you did some of it to help the common soldier. But you did a lot of other really bad stuff for the thrill. You did it for the power. If you really had been forced to help Hitler, then you wouldn't have continued on with your awful work after the war. Nobody was forcing you to kill Kennedy, but you did it. Nobody was forcing you to steal the Gutenberg Bible, but you did it."

"That's wrong, Emit," Opa says quietly. "I had no choice there either. I don't want to burden you with the details. In fact, I can't tell you the details. If I told you, then you would be in the same danger that I am always in. Many of the Nazis who knew about my slowing power survived the war. They sold the information to the highest bidders. The highest bidders were in organized crime. President Kennedy was cracking down on organized crime. Bobby Kennedy was the president's brother, and he was attorney general. His mission especially was to fight the mafia and put crime bosses in jail.

"So organized crime wanted President Kennedy dead," Opa

continues. "They said that I had to help them, or they would kill me and my family. They wanted the Gutenberg Bible so they could sell it. They said that I had to help them there too, or they would kill me and my family. I stole the Gutenberg Bible, but I didn't get a penny from it."

Opa looks me directly in the eye. "At the time of the Kennedy assassination, the people they were threatening included your father. At the time of the stealing of the Gutenberg Bible, that included you. I did it for my family. I did it to save my son, your dad. I did it to save you. I love you, Emit. I couldn't let them hurt you."

"Emit, now I'm free of all that. Finally now, I can do what I want to do, rather than what I'm forced to do. They've released me, Emit. The group that was forcing me has released me." He looks down as his eyes glisten with tears. "We had an agreement that they would release me from threats if I got them the Gutenberg Bible. I never stole anything for myself. I never got to keep anything I stole. I never would have wanted to keep anything that I stole. I only stole because I had to. I did it to save my family. I did what they asked. I did that, Emit." He rolls up to me, takes my hand, and looks me in the eyes. "But now I don't have to do it anymore. I'm free, Emit. Finally I can use my power for good. Finally I can start trying to make up for the bad things that I did, that I was forced to do."

I stare at Opa. I want to believe Opa. I want to love him. He's my Opa. He's the Opa that held me as a baby, that smiled at me, that talked baby talk to me, that helped me blow out candles at my birthday party every year. Was he really innocent, committing horrible crimes only because of threats? If he was under duress, was that an excuse? Or is this all a lie? Maybe he wasn't threatened at all. Maybe he was an enthusiastic Nazi? Maybe he committed all these crimes because he enjoyed it. I certainly savored the thrill of using my slowing power to do bad things. Maybe he stole the Gutenberg Bible on his own and sold it because he wanted the money. But he told me that he never got any money from stealing the Gutenberg Bible.

Was he lying about why he did the bad things? Opa wouldn't lie to me, would he? I'm his grandson. I'm his family. Opa wouldn't lie to me. No, he would not. He looked me in the eye and told me that he never stole things for his own benefit. He promised me that he did dreadful things only because he was threatened with dreadful things. I want to believe him. I need to believe him. He's my Opa.

But I frown as I realize that, even if he's telling the truth, it doesn't make sense. Is it an excuse to murder innocent people in cold blood just because someone threatens you and your family? I'm not so sure. That is the excuse that lots of Nazis gave for helping with the Holocaust. This is all very confusing. And he's my Opa. This is too much to figure out right now. "Opa, what are you going to do to make up for all of the horrible things you've done?"

"I'm still working it out, Emit. We can work it out together. I need your help to decide how we can do the most good."

I force a smile at Opa. "I'm still pretty new to slowing time,"

I say. "My abilities are much weaker than yours."

"That's true," Opa agrees. "We'll just have to give you a bit of training."

"Um, thanks," I reply. "That would be great."

"OK, well, let me teach you a few things," he begins. "Some of these tricks I've learned over the years. Others I've always wanted to try. Let's start with how to simul-slow. That means simultaneous slowing. Remember we talked about that before? I'll slow first. Then you slow the instant you feel that tingle on the back of your neck that you are probably familiar with."

"I remember you said that that tingle means that someone around you is slowing," I say. "OK, let me try it."

Opa disappears. I immediately feel the tingling sensation on my upper back and neck. Opa must have slowed time and then moved somewhere else. To me in normal time, it seemed that he disappeared.

I slow time too. After everyone around me freezes, I turn around searching for Opa, to see where he has moved while he was slowing time without me. I finally see him sleeping in his wheelchair next to a tree, fifty feet away.

I groan and decide to wake him up.

"Opa," I whisper gently as I pat him lightly on the shoulder. "Opa," I say a little louder. "Opa!" I finally yell.

His head pops up and he blinks quickly. "Ah, yes, sorry. Central Park is just so beautiful this time of year."

"Sure," I agree. For a minute, we sit there in silence and take in the beauty all around us. It's strange in the slowed world. Everything looks beautiful, as it would in normal time. But everything is still and quiet. I have never realized how important sound is to my perception of a place.

"So I guess it worked," Opa finally states.

"Yep," I agree again. "But it didn't happen immediately."

"How long did it take?" he asks curiously.

"Probably three seconds passed after you disappeared from your original location until I was able to slow," I answer honestly. "But I guess that was a long time for you."

"Yes, it was over half an hour. That's why I fell asleep," he explains. "But don't worry about the lag. You'll get faster as we practice more."

"Wait," I say. "How did you learn how to simul-slow? You can only simul-slow with another slower. You're teaching me how to do this. That means you must have simul-slowed before, with someone else. Who was it?"

"My grandfather," Opa says. "He was a slower too.

"My dad's not a slower?" I ask. "Anyone in my dad's generation?"

"No," Opa says. "And I would know, because I've gotten really good at telling from the tingle when someone's slowing. I think the genetics for slowing must skip a generation."

"All right. What's next?" I ask eagerly.

"Patience, patience," Opa says. "We're going to keep practicing that until we're perfectly in sync." I groan. "Believe me, it will be great when we can meet each other in slow time. I did it with my grandfather a lot."

"Fine," I grumble.

So we practice simul-slowing again and again. Finally, after what feels like hours, Opa calls for a break.

"My brain hurts so badly," I say as we sit down next to a large tree. "Do you have any water?" I ask as I rub my temples. "That would really help."

"You'll have to get used to the pressure in your brain. That comes with slowing for a long time or, as you get further in your training, slowing time too much. I'll get you some water. Be right back." Opa turns his chair and disappears. He reappears a half second later with a bottle of water in his right hand. I'm getting used to how a slower can seem to disappear and then instantly reappear somewhere else; they slow time, change positions, and then restore normal time. He pushes himself closer to me. He slowly pulls himself out of the chair and onto the ground beside me.

"Opa," I begin, "how did you end up in the wheelchair? You know, Mom and Dad never told us anything but that you got arthritis in your knees, after you fell down the stairs. Is that right? What really happened?"

"Well, Emit, do you want the truth, or do you want an exciting explanation?"

"The truth," I respond, puzzled.

"OK. Yes, I fell down the stairs when I was thirty-one."

"Oh, you're right. That's not exciting," I agree. "But why couldn't you have slowed time to save yourself?"

"I was drunk. Being drunk made me fall down the stairs.

And being drunk slowed my reactions so that I didn't slow before my knees hit the bottom of the stairs. The trauma to my knees caused me to get the arthritis ten years later."

"You were drunk? But you never drink any alcohol now. Just Diet Cokes."

"I learned my lesson there. After my accident, I experimented some more. I found out that alcohol hinders your ability to slow reliably. Even a small amount of alcohol makes slowing erratic."

"Oh, right. I see." I pause. "Opa, what story would you have told me if I'd asked for the exciting explanation?"

"I probably would have told you something about a failed assassination attempt," he says. "It would have been much more exciting."

I laugh.

"Well, are you ready for another lesson?" Opa asks.

I groan. "Yes, I think so, but this is hard work."

"It is," Opa agrees. "I tell you what, why don't you pick something you'd like to learn about?"

"OK, sure," I reply, suddenly with much more energy. I think back to John and my troubles at school with defending myself from bad people, with keeping myself safe. "I'd like to know the best techniques for fighting."

"Yes, good choice. But I'm guessing that you're asking the wrong question. The question should not be how to fight. The question should be how to avoid a fight." Opa looks at me and smiles. "Our slowing skill is perfect for allowing us to avoid a fight. And that should be your assumption about how you respond to aggression. I can't begin to count the number of times that I have avoided a fight by slowing time and simply slipping away. I do it in a way that doesn't arouse suspicion. I can teach you that. But I don't get hurt, and the other person doesn't get hurt. It's the best way."

"Opa, I would love to learn those techniques. But can we learn them later? I know it's wrong, but I'm just really curious about the best way to use our slowing powers in a fight."

"OK," responds Opa. "Are you wondering how to fight someone but keep them alive, or kill someone?" Opa replies.

I look at Opa in disbelief. He is a completely different person than who I thought he was a few months ago. He talks about killing so matter-of-factly.

"I'd like to know how to fight someone, but I don't want them to know that I've been on slow time," I say. "I just want it to seem like I've won the fight."

"I see," he responds. "Well, there are three techniques that I've found to be the most effective when fighting. Obviously, you don't want to use a weapon. It will look like the blood came out of nowhere."

"Right," I agree.

"So the easiest thing to do is to punch them in the chest when you're on slow time. But you can't punch too hard; just touch them lightly with your fist. If you punch at all hard, the person will fly across the room in normal time. It can also shatter their ribcage, or worse."

"Yes, I know that."

"There are some details about how to punch. You need to slow time when your fist is near or touching your opponent and then return time to normal in that same position. That way it will look like you hit them, and not like they just fell back for no reason."

"OK, I've got that." I smile. "That's great. What's next?"

"Patience, young Padawan," Opa quotes Obi Wan Kenobi from *Star Wars*. He's really up on his popular culture.

"I'm getting to the second technique," he says. "Emit, I have to say that this is so fun for me to talk with you about slowing, and teach you. It's lonely being a slower and not being able to talk about it."

"Yeah," I say. "I feel exactly the same way, and I've only been slowing for a few months, and you've being doing it for half a century."

"Emit, we are going to have such a great time together." Opa smiles. Suddenly his eyes get red. "I wish I could have done this years ago. I'm old now. I don't know how much time I still have."

"Don't worry about that, Opa," I say. "You're in great shape. You're so careful. I'm sure you'll be around a long time."

"Yup, totally right," Opa says with a sniffle. He perks up. "OK, back to the lesson. In slow time, focus on their windpipe." Opa makes a motion of karate-chopping his throat. "Again, you can't do this too hard or it can definitely kill someone. Just do it very lightly. The nice thing about this technique is you can do it subtly. You don't need to do the same thing as punching;

there's no need to slow time just before touching the opponent and then return time to normal in the same position. Simply slow at any time and give them a pleasant little touch to their neck. When time speeds back up, they will just start coughing. They won't know why they are coughing. They'll just feel like something got caught in their throat."

"Wow, that's great," I say.

"It makes your opponent seem pathetic, like they're too scared to fight you," Opa says. "Imagine, in the middle of a fight, if you just started coughing and couldn't fight anymore."

"Yes, it will look like they wimped out!" I say.

"Exactly. That's a good one to use when you want to embarrass your opponent as well as win a fight."

"OK, what's the last technique?" I ask eagerly.

"Drumroll please," Opa demands. "This technique is more of a defensive one," Opa starts.

"Wait, why would I want to be defensive when I could take down anyone with my slowing ability?" I ask.

"Emit, you have to learn. Sometimes winning doesn't matter, all you want to do is not lose. Sometimes the best thing to do is dispel conflict." I can't help but think back to the assassination attempts against Hitler. Opa never killed or even attacked the would-be assassins. He just made sure they never succeeded.

"OK." I pause. "So how do you do that?"

"Well, you have to be quick on your feet. Every time the person starts to punch or kick you, slow time. Then, when they're frozen, imagine where their punch or kick will land.

Move just slightly out of their aim and return time to normal. You can't move too much, or you'll look twitchy to your opponent, and it will be obvious something strange is going on. But if you just move slightly, to the side or backward, so that the impact doesn't hit you square on, your opponent will exhaust himself attacking you, and you'll never get hurt."

"OK, that's clever," I agree. "Hey, can we practice?" I look around to see if there's anyone that might want to fight me.

"Well, first, do you want to know the most effective method for killing someone on slow time?" Opa asks.

I look at him in disbelief again. Just as I'm beginning to believe in Opa, he says something that causes me again to doubt him. "No, I don't want to know how to kill someone," I say.

"Why?" Opa asks innocently. "You're going to have to do it sometime."

I stare at him in shock. I collect myself. "What do you mean?" I say. "Why would I ever have to kill somebody? I thought that we were going to do good things. I want to save people. I don't want to kill them."

"Emit, it doesn't work that way. Fighting for good is still a fight. People get hurt. People die. The bad people will be trying to hurt you. They will be trying to kill you. I know that because I had to be on that side. In a battle, the good guys need to kill too. In the US, everybody loves the Greatest Generation that helped win World War Two. That Greatest Generation were not pacifists. Oh no. They were killers. They killed millions of German soldiers and Japanese soldiers.

"The Greatest Generation also killed millions of innocent women and children in firebombings of German cities and Japanese cities. The Germans did bad things. They incinerated the innocent in the ovens of Auschwitz. The Greatest Generation incinerated the innocent in their beds with fire from the air. They turned whole cities into crematoriums—Hamburg, Dresden, Tokyo, Hiroshima, Nagasaki. But the victors got to decide who were the Greatest Generation and who were the war criminals. The Germans lost, so the leaders who were hanged for war crimes were Germans. If we had won, the war criminals who would have been swinging from ropes would have been Truman and Churchill."

CHAPTER 23

Opa leads me to the center of the Great Lawn in Central Park.

"Another important principle," he begins, "is variation in time change, or how much you slow time."

"The thing you did in the closet," I continue.

"Yes. I'm going to teach you how to do it."

"Really? You'll teach me?" I ask. "Yes! Let's do it," I say.

"First, focus on the normal slowing that you do," he says. "That will allow me to teach you how to control the sensation."

"OK, so I should tell you what it feels like?" I ask.

"Yes."

"OK," I say. "Let me quickly slow so I can remember how it feels."

"Of course."

I quickly slow, concentrate on what I'm feeling, then return back to Opa in normal time.

"What do you feel when you slow?" he asks.

"Well, the instant I slow, I feel a sudden calm, like a relaxing feeling," I explain.

"Do you feel anything else?" Opa inquires. "Try to think beyond that, to anything deeper that you feel."

"OK. Ummm … one minute." I slow again, then return to Opa.

"OK. This time, I noticed that there is a pressure in my chest. It's very subtle, but it feels like something is pushing down on me."

Opa smiles. "OK, that's good. But is there anything else? Try it a few more times and focus on that feeling of pressure."

"OK, I'll see you in a few—" I slow without waiting for an answer. Over the next several minutes (or seconds in real time), I slow, then return to real time. Then I slow again, and return. As I do this over and over, all I feel is the sinking feeling in my chest. Finally, as a headache develops, I decide to stop and return to Opa to update him on my progress.

"Hello," greets Opa as I reappear after what feels like only a second or two to him.

"Hi," I say as I catch my breath.

"How did it go? Did you notice anything else?"

"Not really," I respond softly. "And unfortunately, my headache also got worse."

He thinks for a moment. "I might have something for that." Opa reaches behind him into his backpack that's hanging off the rear of his wheelchair. After a bit of rustling around, he pulls out a clean red apple.

"An apple? For a headache?" I ask skeptically.

"Yes. Surprisingly, apples really do help with headaches. I

guess 'an apple a day keeps the doctor away' works for slowers."

"Great." I take a bite out of the apple and sit down. We sit for a few minutes in an uncomfortable silence.

"Opa," I say after a while. "Can you tell me really why you killed Kennedy? I know you said it was threats from the mafia. But was there more to it than that?"

"Ah, good question," says Opa as he leans back in his chair. "Have you ever heard of Operation Paperclip?"

"No," I answer honestly. "Never heard of it."

"Well, Paperclip was a secret program after World War Two that brought high-value Germans and their families to America. Several Nazi scientists were included in the program, over a thousand of them, in fact. Famous scientists, like Werner von Braun, who developed the rockets that launched the Apollo 11 mission—the first spaceflight that landed men on the moon. From my time with Hitler, I knew a lot of them. They were frequently reporting to Hitler and the people around him. I would see them frequently as they came and went. Many of the scientists were quite brilliant and had developed new weapons technology. They weren't dedicated Nazis. They were scientists, doing science. They didn't focus on how their work would be used. It was the same way that Americans who invented the atomic bomb didn't focus much on what the bomb meant. The German scientists were kind people. They were normal people with normal families. In Germany, I think they saw something of their own children when they saw me.

"Anyway, the US wanted to make sure the scientists didn't

end up in the Soviet Union. Even though the American ......
the Soviets were technically on the same side during World
War Two, they started hating each other right at the end. The
Cold War started even before World War Two ended."

"OK …" I say, impatient to hear his answer. "But what does
this have to do with you?"

"The American CIA," he says. "Or actually, it was the
predecessor to the CIA. They had to hide what they were
doing. You see, the American president Truman had explicitly
prohibited any former Nazis from immigrating to the US. So
the CIA had to go behind his back to get the scientists; that was
because many of the great German scientists had been members
of the Nazi Party. The CIA had to protect their identities, so the
CIA created false identities for the scientists."

"What did the scientists do in America?" I ask. "Just sit
around in witness protection for the rest of their lives?"

"Quite the opposite," Opa responds. "The scientists went to
work and made many important discoveries for the American
government. Several were involved in the development of
ballistic missiles and rockets. Some actually went on to become
top officials in the NASA space program."

"OK, that seems strange that we had Nazi scientists working
for the US government," I say. "But that still doesn't explain
anything about you or Kennedy."

"Well, the identities of some of the scientists leaked out
over time. But many managed to keep their pasts secret. That
is, until their true identities got to Kennedy. Now, Eisenhower,

the president before Kennedy, had publicly claimed he supported the program. But Kennedy was appalled that the US had prioritized scientific advancement over punishing those he thought were true war criminals. He was preparing to expose the identities of so many of the scientists that had lived peacefully here for years. It would have ruined them and their families. There were going to be war crimes trials, like right after the war. There would have been more executions."

"So you killed him?" I ask.

"I did," Opa nods. "I told you before that the people from organized crime wanted Kennedy dead. They were putting huge pressure on me to do it. Threats against me. Threats against my family. But it was the right thing to do anyway. I couldn't let Kennedy murder my friends. It was the right thing to do. I did it in self-defense of my friends."

"And Oswald?" I ask.

"Oswald was exactly what he said he was—a patsy." Opa shakes his head. "Poor guy."

We sit in silence for a few minutes. I try to process Opa's proud admission that he is a cold-blooded presidential assassin. Overwhelmed, I give up. It's too much. Finally I speak. "Opa, what should we do now?"

"How does your head feel?" he asks. "Is it feeling better from the apples?"

"Yeah, it is," I say. "That's a great trick."

"Let's keep working on variable slowing, or how much you slow," Opa responds.

"Right, let's go," I say. I'm excited to turn the conversation away from assassinations.

"I want you to focus on that feeling of pressure, and experiment with what you can do to make it stronger or lighter."

"All right." I walk into the field and start the process of slowing over and over again. Slow, stop, take a deep breath. Slow, stop, hold my breath. Slow, stop, close my eyes. Slow, stop, cover my ears. Slow, stop, stick my tongue out. Slow, stop, pinch myself. Slow, stop, close my eyes. Slow, stop, crack my knuckles. Slow, stop …

After about half an hour, I stop and report back to Opa.

"I'm back!" I announce approaching Opa as he sits in the shade of a tree.

"Ah! Have you discovered anything interesting?"

"No, not really," I respond. "Well, I guess I figured out a lot of things that don't work," I add with a smile.

"It's always good to look on the bright side." Opa smiles. "But I must admit, I didn't expect you to succeed."

"What? Why?"

"Because I left out one key piece of advice," he answers.

"What is it?" I ask.

"Well, as you've probably guessed by now, variable slowing is not about closing your eyes or pinching yourself as you slow, even though you may have tried both of those things."

I smile. "Yep."

"Well, believe me, I tried all those things too when I was trying to figure out how to control my gift."

"Well, how did you eventually do it?" I ask.

"It's all about the brain," he points to his head. "But I can't tell you exactly how to do it. It's not that I won't. I can't. You have to figure it out yourself. I'm just going to say that it's something in your head."

"Well, that really narrows it down," I say sarcastically. "Isn't everything really in your head?"

"Don't be so philosophical, Emit." Opa grins. "Just focus on a sensation in your head. Once you feel it, you'll learn to control it. Then you can slow at different speeds."

"OK, but I'm getting tired. I don't think I can keep trying for much longer."

"Emit, this is important." Opa pauses. "It's possibly the most important skill in slowing. You must keep trying."

"OK," I say reluctantly, wanting to do something exciting. I immediately start slowing. This time, instead of focusing on my chest or trying different gestures, I close my eyes and focus on the way my head feels as I slow, and then as I return to real time. Slow and return. Slow and return …

I can't feel anything for the longest time; there is only the calm, relaxed feeling I'm accustomed to. Then, gradually, I start to feel another sensation. Almost unnoticeable, the new feeling is like pressure under my skull in the back of my head. It's almost as if there's a bubble there. As I continue practicing, the feeling of the bubble becomes more and more noticeable.

I start moving my head ever so slightly, and it feels as if the bubble moves. It moves slightly down as I tilt my head up and moves slightly up as tilt my head down. It takes only the slightest movements of my head. I keep tilting, up and down, getting the feel of moving the bubble and …

I gasp as a deafening boom rings around me. I look around to see what made the loud noise and am startled to see Opa sitting behind me in his wheelchair.

"Congratulations," he says. "You figured it out."

"I don't think so," I say in response. "I just heard a loud boom."

"Emit, that was a sonic boom," Opa explains. "It happens when you slow enough that your movements in slow time are faster than the speed of sound."

I look around frantically, expecting to see terrified people in the park running from the huge boom.

"Don't worry," says Opa. "The people in regular time can't hear the boom. I don't quite understand the physics of it, but only the slower can hear it. Otherwise, I'd be frightening my neighborhood all of the time."

"I can't believe I did that. I slowed that much that I set off a sonic boom?" I ask, confused.

"Yes," says Opa. "You get the boom after slowing down a lot and then returning to normal time."

"I think I'm getting the hang of controlling the slowing," I say. "There is this feeling in the back of my head, like a bubble; I was just moving it up and down."

"Yes. That's how you control variable slowing. Obviously, you had to figure out that feeling for yourself. I wasn't even sure it would be the same feeling for both of us. I'm glad to know it is."

"Wow!" I exclaim. "This is so cool."

"Well, let's get on with it." Opa begins to roll away.

"Wait, where are you going?" I ask without following.

"It's time for us to get started," he explains impatiently. "We don't have much time."

"Get started on what?" I ask.

"I'll fill you in later, but we only have a few days. We have a big project that we need to do now. It will do a lot of good. It will really help people. But we need to start it now. I need your help. We can only do it together."

"What is it, Opa? I need to know."

"I'm sorry, Emit. I can't tell you yet. I know that's hard for you, but there are good reasons that I can't tell you yet. You've got to trust me."

"But I don't know if I can trust you yet," I say. "I feel like I have whiplash. Until a few days ago, I thought you were evil; you killed a president and helped a genocidal Nazi. Then, wham! You sent my heart in the other direction. You explained that you weren't really at fault and you had no choice. But I don't know what to trust. I'm not there yet. It's too fast. I'm going now." I start to walk away.

"Emit, wait."

I stop, still with my back to him.

"You've got to trust me. You've got to trust me now. I wish there was more time, but there's not. We have to act now. It can't wait." I can feel him rolling his wheelchair toward me. "I promise you that I'm a good person. The things that I did that seem horrible, there were good reasons for them. I've already explained that to you, in a quick way. I had to do them. I had no choice. They were the right things to do."

I turn to him. "But—" I say.

"You've got to trust me," Opa interrupts. "I'll prove to you that I deserve your trust, over the next months and years. I wish I had more time to prove it to you now. I wish I had more time to prove to you that you can love me. I wish that I had more time to prove to you that you can respect me. I wish that I had more time to prove to you that you can trust me. But I don't have more time. We need to act now. There's no time to wait. There's too much at stake. We can do so much good. But we have to do it now."

Opa looks at me with hope. He looks at me with love. I feel love for him flowing back into me. A warmth spreads through me. I know that I can love Opa. A smile grows in me. As I look at him, I see how wonderful he is. He has been through so much, even as a kid. He was just in the wrong place at the wrong time. Others used his powers for evil. But he's not evil himself. He did his best in horrible circumstances. I feel my heart decide that I'm proud to be his grandson. I smile as I feel giddy with happiness and pride at Opa. I'm so proud that I can work with him. I'm so proud that I'm a slower like him. I'm so proud that we can use our slowing powers together. I'm so proud that we can do so much good. We really will make the world better.

But wait, am I just seeing him as I wish he were rather than as he really is? Maybe, at least according to my brain. But I can feel my brain being pushed aside by my heart. My heart is telling me that Opa is my grandfather, the man whom I have admired since I was born. He's my family. I love him with unconditional love.

He's worthy of my love. He's worthy of my trust; you have to trust your family.

He's worthy of my respect. He's had to make so many hard choices. And he's always made them selflessly. He always looked out for his family. When he's helped bad people, he had no choice. When he killed, he had no choice, and he thought he was doing the right thing. When he stole, he only did it because he had to. The bad people made him steal. He never kept the things he stole. He was forced to steal them for other people.

My mind suddenly moves back to Opa's secret room. I see the top shelves. I see the white sheet covering the two paintings. These are paintings that Opa stole from Jews who died in Auschwitz. My smile fades. The happy warmth cools. My brain regains control from my heart. My eyes clear as I see who Opa is rather than who my heart wishes he were. Opa didn't have to steal those paintings. He didn't have to *keep* those paintings. He didn't have to do any of the countless other evil things.

I look into Opa's loving, hopeful eyes. "Opa," I say. "I'm sorry, but I can't help you." I pull out my phone and text my mom to take me home.

CHAPTER 24

"Seriously?" asks Peyton, sitting at his computer in his room after dinner on the following Monday, the first day of the three-day winter break.

"What's the problem?" I ask.

"You want me to hack your grandfather's computer and access his stock portfolio?" Peyton asks again.

"Yep."

"Why don't you just ask him?"

"Ummm." I pause. "I just can't," I respond.

Peyton takes a deep breath. "All right, let's try it."

I smile. "Thanks."

"No problem." He leans toward his computer and begins typing. "Command," he mutters, "prompt. Trojan virus should do. Receive file …"

"I don't understand a word you're saying," I say. He continues typing, ignoring me. He also continues muttering technical computer words under his breath.

"So, what exactly are you doing? This virus isn't going to

break his computer or anything, is it?"

"It could possibly make it explode," Peyton says as he types. "Like a small nuclear blast. But that isn't very likely."

"Wait, really?" I ask after a few seconds.

"No, of course not," he responds as if it is obvious.

"Good."

"And ... it's ... done." Peyton smiles and flexes his fingers.

"Really? You already hacked his computer?"

Peyton looks at me as if I'm an idiot. "No, of course not. We need to find a way to upload the virus to his computer."

"If you think I'm going to sneak into his house and plug some thumb drive into his MacBook, you're kidding yourself," I warn him.

"No, of course not," he assures me. "This isn't some *Mission Impossible* movie."

"Good." I breathe a sigh of relief. Peyton looks back at the computer and begins to type again.

"If you don't mind me asking," he begins, "why are you trying to hack your grandfather's financial portfolio? That's a little bit creepy—and illegal."

"I know that my grandfather has been involved with some bad people in the past. And I want to know if he's up to anything shady now," I respond.

He ponders this, then asks, "What kind of shady business?"

"He was working with some organized crime group," I say. "I don't think he knows what he's dealing with. I just don't want him to get hurt. That's why I'm doing this."

"Wow!" says Peyton. "Your grandfather's a mafia boss? Emit, I'm breaking into a mafia computer. Am I going to get whacked? Am I going to wear concrete galoshes?"

"Don't be silly, Peyton," I say, trying to sound surer than I really am. "That's just in the movies and books."

"What are you going to do if it turns out he is doing business with these guys?" asks Peyton. "Get him arrested?"

"To be honest, I don't know," I say. "I'm just focusing on finding out if anything's going on."

"What's his email address?" Peyton asks out of the blue.

"Who? My grandfather?"

"Yes, of course," says Peyton. "Use your brain."

"Sorry," I say. "One minute." I pull out my phone and search through my email history for a message from Opa. I finally find one, and I show the address to Peyton.

He types it in. "OK, I'm going to attach this file with the virus to an email. If your grandfather opens it and clicks a link, the virus will be uploaded to his computer. If all goes well, we will have complete access to his computer and his stock portfolio." Peyton sits back, pleased with himself.

"Cool!"

"What's a believable email that Opa would actually open?" Peyton asks.

"Ummm … how about an email from his phone company?" I suggest.

"I guess that would work," he says. "Do you know what phone company he uses?"

"Verizon, I think. I remember him talking about that."

Peyton takes a few minutes to register and create a new email address that could plausibly be from Verizon. "I also need to create a fake email from Verizon, with the link to the virus," Peyton says. "That won't be that hard, because our family gets emails like that from Verizon all the time. They're always trying to get us to sign up for something. I'll just doctor one up in HTML and add the fake link with the virus."

"You can really do that?" I ask.

"I think so," he says.

For a few minutes, he does computer stuff that I don't understand. Then he smiles proudly. "Here goes."

"Done with it already?" I ask.

"Yup. Here's what it says: 'We would like to speak with you about a new service option, Verizon Speed. This service will offer a faster connection in more remote locations, at a cheaper price. Please click here to be placed on our preorder list. Thank you for your continued loyalty to Verizon.'"

"Nice," I say. "You're good at that. You would make a great criminal."

Peyton presses send. "Now we wait for your grandfather to open the email. He may not do it. There are a million reasons why he wouldn't do it, why he'd be suspicious. But you can't say we didn't try. And I'll accept my fee now, if you don't mind."

"What?" I ask. "I have to pay you?"

"No, I'm just kidding," he responds, smiling. "The look on your face!"

"Yeah, you got me," I admit.

"I was just playing around." He looks back at his computer, then exclaims, "Wait, he just opened it!"

"Really?" I peer over his shoulder at the computer.

"Let's see if he clicks the link," says Peyton. We both stare at the screen. Suddenly a notification appears, and the screen changes color to black.

"He clicked it!" says Peyton. "I can't believe he did it. I have to admit, I didn't think he was going to do it."

"Can you hack it?" I sit forward, staring at the screen.

"I think so. Hang on a minute." Peyton pulls up another black command prompt screen and types quickly.

Suddenly his face falls. "I'm sorry, Emit," he says. "I can't do it. I thought this was too easy, and I was right. For an old guy, he's smart about security. He has two-factor encryption, and we don't have the encryption key. The key is a number that appears once you're into your account. But we don't have it. Dang it. So close." We look at each other and smile glumly.

"Peyton, hang on for a second!" I stand up, run out of his room, and go across the street to my house. "Hi, Mom," I say as I run by her up to my room. "Bye, Mom," I say as, thirty seconds later, I run back by her and out the front door, holding a folded sheet of paper.

Back in Peyton's room, I ask, "Might this help?" I hand him Opa's financial statement that I stuffed in my pocket when I was in Opa's secret room.

Peyton examines it. "Bingo," says Peyton. "I can figure out

the encryption key from those codes right there at the bottom."

After about forty-five seconds of typing, a new window pops up showing a bunch of graphs and numbers. "This is it," says Peyton. "This is his stock portfolio. Unbelievable."

"Super," I say. "Peyton, you're awesome."

I gaze at the screen in confusion. "Peyton, do you understand any of this?"

"To be honest, only a little," Peyton says. "This over here"—he points to the far left column—"shows the timing of different stock transactions, or stocks or options bought and sold. To the right of that is the amount that was purchased or sold."

"What's the far right column with all the letters though?" I ask. "Could that be company names? The companies that the stock belongs to?"

"I think so. Most of them just say 'AAPL,'" states Peyton. "What is that? Apple?"

I shrug my shoulders. "Probably." Peyton looks it up on Google. "Yup, Apple," he says.

"This is weird," he continues. "Almost all of the transactions happen on January first, April first, July first, and October first. And they all happen at 4 p.m. exactly. It's not approximately 4 p.m. It's 4 p.m. to the second. They're all Apple options. Sometimes he buys call options. Sometimes he buys puts."

"What are puts and calls?" I ask.

"That's weird that you're asking about that, Emit. I've recently been having fun messing around a bit in the market myself with an online trading account. Twenty-five bucks here, and twenty-five bucks there. So I've been trying to learn about this. I'm about even so far. It's like legal online gambling."

"So what are puts and calls?" I repeat.

"They're types of stock options. They give you an option to buy or sell a stock at a later date, until the expiration date. Buying a put allows you to sell a stock at a certain price in the future. You buy them when you think that the price of a company's stock will go down. Let's say you buy a put to sell a stock at forty dollars; then the stock price declines to twenty-five dollars. You can buy the stock for twenty-five dollars and then go sell it under the put for forty dollars. You make a quick fifteen dollars."

I nod. "OK, and a call?"

"A call is the opposite. A call lets you buy the stock at a certain price at a later date. You buy calls when you think the stock price will go up. So let's suppose you buy a call that lets you buy a certain stock for, say, eighty dollars, and then the value of the stock increases to one hundred dollars. You can buy the stock under the call for eighty dollars, then turn around and sell it for one hundred dollars. You make a quick twenty dollars multiplied by however many call options you bought."

"This is legal, right?" I ask, still slightly confused by all this financial stuff.

"Oh, yes, of course. One reason that people use options is that it allows you to make as big a bet as possible that a stock will go up or go down. If you have a certain amount of money to bet on a stock, you can make a lot more money using options if the stock goes up, compared to if you just bought shares in the stock. But using options is a lot riskier than just buying stock. If the stock price doesn't do what you expect, you lose a lot more money with options than just buying the stock."

"How long has he been doing this?" I ask.

"It looks like years," says Peyton. "Why is he doing this like this?"

"I don't know," I say. "We need to figure out why the transactions are once every three months at the exact same time. And we need to figure out why he's buying puts sometimes, but calls other times."

"Yes," Peyton says. "Let's look up the dates and AAPL on Google and see if they're connected somehow."

He pulls up a new window and does a search for Apple financial documents. "Here!" he announces. "It says that Apple Inc. releases its quarterly financial reports on January, April, July, and October first."

"I'm guessing they release the reports at 4 p.m.?"

He digs a little further. "Yep," he confirms. "So if your grandfather is buying right at 4 p.m., he must be one of those crazy financial guys."

"Huh?" I ask.

"There are these guys on Wall Street who access the reports as soon as they're released, and then buy stocks, or puts and calls, an instant after the reports come out. If the financial reports have good news, they expect the stock price will go up. So they buy calls. If the reports are bad, then they buy puts.

They make money if they can transact before anyone else does, before the market price reacts to the news."

"OK. How much has my grandfather made by doing this?" I ask.

"Well." Peyton scrolls down the screen. "Over the years that he's been doing it, it looks like he's made over forty million dollars, just on the Apple stock options."

"Forty million!" I shake my head. "That's a lot of money. No wonder he can afford a Mercedes."

"Yeah," Peyton agrees. "I still don't understand how he reacts so quickly to the quarterly financial reports. If he's buying the options at 4 p.m. on the dot, he's probably one of the first people to respond."

And it hits me. Opa slows time the moment the financial reports are released. He reads through the entire report, prepares his option order (puts if the report contains bad news, and calls if it contains good news), returns time to normal, and immediately places the order. He is the first one to respond.

"Uh, I guess my grandfather has really fast reflexes," I offer, not wanting to explain the real reason he's so quick to buy the options.

"Sure," Peyton responds skeptically. "Wait, is your grandfather a good coder?"

"You mean computer coder?" I ask.

"Yeah. Maybe he's created a computer program that can quickly analyze the reports and place the trade immediately. But hold on. He does it in less than a second. I don't think even a computer program could analyze the reports and make the trades that fast."

"I don't know." I shrug. "I don't think he's that good of a coder. But then again, I didn't know he'd made forty million dollars trading stock options."

"Well, maybe he knows how …" Peyton pauses. "Wait, Emit, look at that trade," he points to the most recent transaction at the top of the list. "Geez! The last trade isn't for Apple stock. It's for the S&P 500."

"What's the SNB 500?" I ask.

"The S *and* P 500," he enunciates, "is an index of five hundred stocks whose performance is supposed to represent the overall stock market. People like my parents like to buy it because you don't have to bet on how any one stock will do. You just have to expect the overall stock market to improve, and over time, the stock market always goes up."

"Then why is it so unusual that he bought it?" I ask. "It sounds like a smart thing to do."

"Because he didn't buy it," Peyton explains. "He bought puts, betting against it. Forty-eight million dollars of puts. He must be betting everything he has, his whole fortune."

"So he thinks our economy is going to crash?" I ask. "Why would someone do that?"

"Who knows." Peyton shrugs. "People don't usually bet against the US economy. I mean, I heard that Osama bin Laden bet against an industry before the 9/11 attacks. He knew that the planes crashing into the World Trade Center would wreak havoc on the airline industry. People wouldn't want to fly anymore. So he bought lots of puts on airline stocks. He was right. When the planes hit the World Trade Center, airline stocks went down a lot, and he made millions of dollars."

"But Opa's betting against the whole economy, not just an industry," I say.

"He must feel really sure that something really bad is going to happen soon," Peyton continues. "The puts have an expiration date. If the market doesn't crash before then, then he loses every penny that he spent on the puts."

"Peyton, what bad thing could happen so soon?" I ask.

Without having even heard my last question, Peyton looks at me with wide-open eyes. "He's done it through a VPN alias emanating from Argentina! He's used a VPN!"

"What's that?" I ask.

"It's a way to buy securities anonymously so that they can't be traced to you. I've heard that organized crime people use a VPN alias for money laundering, to hide drug money."

"Why would Opa be using a VPN alias?" I ask.

"I don't know," says Peyton. "For some reason, he doesn't want people to know about all of the puts he's buying."

"Peyton, why did Opa buy all of these puts?" I ask again. "What huge horrible thing does he think is going to happen so soon? Do you think my grandfather knows of some imminent terrorist attack?"

Peyton shrugs his shoulders. "I hope not," he says.

A hundred possibilities of terrorist plots involving Opa

flash through my mind. None of them seems realistic though.

"Can you think of anything?" Peyton asks. "Something like this could be horrible. If we figure it out, maybe we could tell people and save a lot of lives."

"Think, think," I command myself frantically. I search my thoughts for anything I might have seen or heard at Opa's house. Nothing comes to mind.

"Nope," I say. "I've got nothing."

I pause. Then a thought occurs to me. "Peyton, I think you said that puts have expiration dates. The puts he chose, when do they expire?"

"Let me check," says Peyton. He clicks some keys. "Thursday, February sixth."

"You mean, February sixth next week? That's soon, Peyton. Very soon. What's happening in the next week and a half?"

I suddenly remember my conversation with Mr. Zachs. "Peyton, isn't President Brown's State of the Union speech next Tuesday? That's two days before the options expire."

CHAPTER 25

"Thanks," I say to my mom as I jump out of the car the next morning at Opa's house.

"How long do you think you'll be?" she asks.

I shrug my shoulders. "I don't know. I'm just going to talk to Opa for a while. I'll get him to drive me home, or I'll take an Uber."

"OK. Love you. Gotta run. A yoga class waits for no one." She drives down the block and turns the corner, back to the YMCA.

I walk up to Opa's front door and knock twice. "Hello? Opa, it's me." I wait. "Are you there?" I knock twice more. "Anyone home?" No answer. That's puzzling. Unless they tell us they're travelling, Opa and Oma have always been here when I drop by, so I didn't even think to call ahead. Nor did my mom even think to wait before she drove off to yoga.

"He's not home," says a voice to my right.

Startled, I turn toward the voice. "Oh, hello," I say. "I'm sorry. Who are you?"

"Oh, sorry," says a middle-aged man in a green coat and khaki pants as he comes up the driveway next to Opa's house. "I'm Henry's neighbor. I'm Harold Jones. Are you his grandson, Emit?"

"Yep. That's me."

"I remember him talking about you several times." Mr. Jones pauses. "Anyway, your granddad asked me to keep an eye on the house. They'll be gone for a few days."

"Oh, really?" This was unusual for Opa and Oma not to tell us about a trip. Usually they let us know if they're going to be away, so that we can check on their house. They usually ask us, not a neighbor. "Mr. Jones, did they say where they were going?"

"Let's see," he says. "I think your grandmother said they were going to Washington, DC. She said that they were going to look around museums and art galleries. They hadn't been there for a while."

"Did my grandfather say anything about what he wanted to do in DC?" I ask. "Or did my grandmother do all the talking?"

"I don't remember your grandfather saying much."

"Really? Are you sure? He didn't say anything?" I ask, perhaps a little too eagerly.

"No. The only thing we talked about was the upcoming State of the Union Address. We talked about that yesterday when I saw him, and also this morning, just when they were leaving."

"Mr. Jones, could I ask what Opa said about it?"

Mr. Jones smiles. "I don't think your Opa is a big fan of President Brown. He was saying that he doesn't think much of the new bill that Brown wants to get passed."

"I'm sorry, what new bill?" I ask.

"You know, the one that they're talking about on TV all the time," says Mr. Jones. "The one that cracks down on hate speech. It would crack down on white-supremacists saying racist stuff. President Brown thinks that they can get a bill through Congress now, after the Jewish school shooting.

"Anyway, your grandfather doesn't like the bill, to put it mildly. Hasn't he talked with you about it?"

"No," I respond. "I don't remember him saying anything."

"Really? He was talking my ear off about it." Mr. Jones uses his left hand to touch his left ear. "I guess it didn't quite come off. It's still there," he says with a smile.

"Anyway," he continues. "He says it would be a dreadful attack on freedom of speech. He says it reminds him of what happened in Germany, when he was growing up there. What the Nazis did."

"Wait. What?" I ask. "He told you that fighting against racism is the same as what the Nazi's did? I don't get it."

"Yeah. He's pretty alarmed about it. He says the bill is just like the Nazis. They started controlling what people could say and burning books. People didn't fight back. And then you got the Holocaust. He's distressed about it. He thinks the bill is the start of the slippery slope to fascism. He thinks people need to do something."

A cold shiver runs down my back. "Oh, right," I say. "Thanks, Mr. Jones."

"Good luck finding your Opa. Please give him my best if you see him. Tell him I'll bring his mail in and keep it at my house."

"Thanks again, Mr. Jones." As Mr. Jones walks toward his house, I turn toward Opa's front door and pull out my phone to call my mom for a ride. I change my mind and turn back toward Mr. Jones. "Mr. Jones, the State of the Union Address is in Washington, in the capital, isn't it?"

"Yeah. It's held in the Capitol Building, in front of the US Congress and a lot of other important people. The Supreme Court judges are there too, I think. It starts in—" he looks down at his watch "—about six hours. You can watch it on TV. Or you can watch it on the web." He turns and walks inside his house.

I turn back toward Opa's house. Opa must be up to something. Otherwise, he would have let us know he was leaving town. He always does that. Is Opa going there to interrupt the speech? He could really disrupt the speech if he used his slowing ability. Hmm. What would I do if I wanted to disrupt a major speech? I start to smile as I think of how fun that would be. Maybe unplug President Brown's microphones? Unplug his teleprompter? That would stop everything. Maybe slow time and then reprogram the teleprompter. Maybe I could make President Brown say embarrassing stuff. Probably not. Brown is smart enough to stop talking if he sees that the text on his teleprompter has been changed. Also, I wouldn't know how to hack the computer for the teleprompter, and I wouldn't have Peyton with me.

I force myself to stop thinking these thoughts. I'm good now. I don't do bad stuff anymore. That's kind of a shame. It was pretty fun to be bad.

That must be why there's so much evil in the world. If you've got power, it's so much more fun to be bad than good. With great power comes great fun from being bad. It's no wonder that the villains in superhero movies have way more fun than the heroes. The Joker has a great time creating his evil schemes, cackling and laughing all through it. Batman's the opposite; he acts like a depressed person who's off his meds. Not a lot of smiles from Batman.

Emit, stop letting your mind wander. Focus. What's Opa going to do at the State of the Union speech? He must be going to do something. That's why he was in such a rush to finish training me. And does this have anything to do with him betting that the economy is about to crash?

It becomes clear what I need to do. I need to get to Washington and figure out what Opa's up to. But there's no way my parents will take me, and I don't have the money for a plane or train ticket. There's only one person I can ask. I pull out my phone.

"Hello, Emit," says Mr. Zachs.

"Hi, Uncle Dimitri. Ummm … this is a lot to ask, but would you be willing to drive me to Washington, DC?"

He laughs. "Washington, really?"

"I know it's far …"

"No, it's just that it's such an amazing coincidence. I actually have some things I need to do there anyway. I was going to go there later today and stay overnight. I'll be happy to take you," Mr. Zachs agrees.

"Really? Wow! That would be awesome. The sooner the better for me."

"What's up, Emit? Why do you need to go?"

"Can I not talk about it now? It's just really important. Can I tell you later?"

"OK, Mr. Man of Mystery," Mr. Zachs says. "I'll pick you up as soon as I can get to you. Where are you? Your house?"

"No. I'm at my grandparents' house, at Opa's house."

"Ah, yes. I'll be there soon." Mr. Zachs hangs up the phone. As I wait, it occurs to me that this is all strange. It's strange that Mr. Zachs knows were Opa's house is. He's never been here, as far as I know. And it doesn't seem likely that my parents gave him the address. How could he know?

Now that I think about it, it's also odd that Mr. Zachs could take me to Washington on a moment's notice. It's usually hard to get a grownup to drive me to a place across town, much less to another city.

Yikes. I forgot something: what am I going to tell my mom? A couple seconds later, I pull out my phone and text her to ask if it's OK if I spend the day with Opa, and maybe sleep over. I'm not technically lying. I very much hope to spend the day with Opa—if I can catch up to him and find him.

Mr. Zachs's car pulls up outside about half an hour later. Through the car's passenger window, I see that he's wearing a wool jacket that I haven't seen before. "Hey, Emit," he says through the open car window, calling to me where I am sitting on Opa's front steps.

"Hi, Uncle Dimitri!" I jog down to the car. I jump in, and Mr. Zachs slowly pulls away from the curb.

"Uh, Uncle Dimitri, I hate to ask this, because you've been so nice to agree to drive me, but can we drive fast? I'm kind of in a rush."

"Where do you need to go?" he responds.

"To the Capitol Building in Washington. I've got to get there before President Brown's State of the Union Address."

"Oh, then we do have to hurry. OK, I'll drive fast," he promises. "Why are you going there?" he asks, puzzled. "Emit, you can't just walk in there. The public isn't invited. I think it's only for people in Congress and the Supreme Court. That's great that you're interested though. Why don't we just stay in town here and go to a restaurant and watch it on TV?"

"I don't need to go in the actual State of the Union speech," I respond. "I just need to talk to my grandfather. He's going there, I think. It's just really important that I talk to him before he gets there."

"Ah. I see." Mr. Zachs nods stiffly, then clears his voice as his face loses its smile. He pauses. "You know … Emit. I've been waiting to tell you something for a while." He pauses again. "I know quite a bit more about your grandfather than you think."

"You do?" I ask. "What do you mean?"

"Well, I know that your grandfather has special abilities," he says, watching me closely. When Mr. Zachs sees that I'm not confused, he continues. "I'm guessing that you have the same abilities."

"How do you know about that?" I ask quickly. "I've never told you anything."

"Well, I've been suspicious since the strange incident with your teacher's book disappearing," he begins. "And then, lately all of your questions about Kennedy and Hitler have pretty much confirmed it."

"Wait, do you know about how Opa's involved with all of that?"

"I do, or at least I think I know most of it. Emit, I've known about your grandfather since he was a boy, not much older than you. As I'm sure you know, your grandfather was a Nazi soldier when he was young, and I was a young soldier in the Russian army."

"Yes," I recall. "When you told me that the dying sniper talked about a 'slow person,' I was stunned. Uncle Dimitri, I call myself a slower. I call myself that because I can slow time. I don't know if you already know, but Opa and I both have this slowing ability. He calls himself a slower too."

"I expected as much," says Mr. Zachs.

"When you told me what that soldier said to you, I couldn't help thinking that it sounded a lot like a slower," I say. "Then my Opa told me they used the same term in Germany."

"Emit, that's very perceptive," says Mr. Zachs. "When I was telling you about the sniper, I was guessing that you might figure it out. Let me tell you about what happened after my encounter with the sniper. I told my superiors about what the dying sniper had said."

"What did they say?" I ask.

"They didn't say anything, at least at first," he continues. "They just wrote down my account of what happened and then sent me back to my unit at the front. But then, in 1942, about a year after that, something did happen. In late 1942, I was ordered to leave the front and report to Moscow. I was taken to a big official-looking building that had nothing on the outside indicating what it was. It turned out that it was the headquarters of the NKVD. This is the Soviet secret police."

"That must have been terrifying," I say. "Didn't the NKVD kill about a bazillion Russians during the Stalin purges?"

"Yes. I was scared. I didn't want anyone standing behind me. I thought I might get a bullet in the head. But it turned out I didn't need to be scared. I was stunned by what they told me. I was not the only person who had encountered mysterious references to something to do with slowing time. They had started getting strange reports about incidents that seemed impossible. For example, a British major general was giving a speech in a church to a thousand officers. As he was speaking at the lectern, he suddenly keeled over and died, with blood streaming from his head. They found a bullet in his head and gunpowder residue in his hair."

"So?" I ask. "What's the mystery of that? Couldn't he have just been killed by a sniper?"

"No," Mr. Zachs shakes his head. "Gunshot residue in the hair means he was shot from point-blank range. But there was absolutely no one near him. The closest person was twenty feet away.

"Another time," Mr. Zachs continues, "one of our Russian bombers was taking off to bomb Berlin. We didn't have very many bombers, but the NKVD had borrowed this one from the British. We had intelligence that Hitler was in his Berlin Führerbunker, so that was the target. The payload was special bunker-buster bombs. The pilot was the only person in the plane, and he communicated with the tower as he started accelerating down the runway. But then, instead of ascending into the air, the plane slowed down and rolled to a stop. When officers got to the jet and unlatched the glass canopy over the cockpit, the pilot was still the only one inside, but he had been stabbed and killed."

"That must have been crazy to hear. Like a *Twilight Zone* rerun," I say. "So what did they want from you? How old were you then? You were still a little kid, weren't you?"

"By then, I was eleven years old."

"Only eleven, and you were killing people on the battlefield, and talking to the secret police?"

"It was a different time," he says. "No time for growing up. I was ordered to join a new group that they had set up to try to figure out what was going on with this. It was called the Special Activities Division. It was completely top secret. They had a bunch of secret police in it—investigator types.

And also scientists and anyone who had anything to do with these weird incidents. The government was really worried about this new German weapon. They were terrified that the Germans had access to something powerful that would win the war. What if thousands of these incidents started happening everywhere on the battlefield? It would be like fifty years before, when armies that had machine guns could slaughter armies that didn't. We didn't know whether it was some kind of technology. Or maybe it was magic. That was a really dreadful thought for our leaders: that the Germans might have been able to figure out how to harness magic and the supernatural, and they were now using it to kill our leaders and soldiers."

"How terrifying!" I say. "But the Germans were losing the war by then, weren't they?"

"Yes," he says. "By 1942, we had started pushing them back. Our group was told that we would win the war, unless the Germans developed some new technology. We thought that the mysterious killings that we were investigating might be evidence of Germans having a new technology. Our scientists knew that the Germans and the Americans were working on an atomic bomb, which required lots of applied work with Einstein's nuclear theories. Our scientists also knew that Einstein's theory of relativity showed that, under certain circumstances, time could slow. So we were really scared that as part of their nuclear program, the German scientists had discovered how to slow time."

"You really understood this, even when you were eleven years old?" I ask.

"Like I said before, we didn't have the luxury of being allowed to grow up then. The existence of our country was in the balance. The Germans were slaughtering our war prisoners. Little kids had to be soldiers and shoot guns. We also had to help out as best we could against this German secret weapon. We had no choice. It was do what we could to help out, or our country would be destroyed along with all of us.

"But, Emit, finally we got a lead from a high-ranking German commander whom we had flipped into an informant. He told us that there was a Nazi soldier that could literally slow time. Of course, we didn't believe him at first. But we eventually accepted it. We talked to the scientists in our group, and that was the only way that the strange events could be explained. During the war, we could never figure out who the slower was. We figured that it must be a senior officer. We never suspected that it could be a boy."

"So what did the Russians do?" I ask.

"We got to work combatting the slower," he says.

"But how?" I ask.

"It was tricky. Since we didn't know who he was, we designed several traps to kill him, even if he was slowing time. We would stage events where important Russian officers would be and plant many agents in the building. We hoped to kill the mysterious slower as he attempted to kill the officer."

"What happened?" I ask.

"Nothing. We never caught him. The slower killed several of the Russian officers, but the slower always escaped the traps."

"Of course he did," I nod. "When he's slowing time, he's faster than any trap you could make."

"Yes, I know that now," he agrees. "Well, before long, the war ended. The Russian army was reorganized, and our Special Activities Division was eliminated. I was assigned to Military Resource Collection. This meant that I struck deals with local people in other countries so they would provide food, water, and shelter for our soldiers who were stationed in the other countries. It was a tedious job. I didn't feel like I was helping much of anything.

"So after a few months, I'd finally had enough," Mr. Zachs continues. "I made up some story to get a meeting with my commander; he was four steps up the chain of command. When I got there, I asked for a new job. He yelled at me for going around the chain of command. He then asked me what I did during the war. We were supposed to keep everything the Special Activities Division did a secret, but I told him the truth. I explained that I had been on a team searching for a young Nazi soldier who could slow time."

"Did he believe you?" I ask with a smile.

"No. He laughed and sent me back to my work site. But four days later, the commander summoned me back to his office. He had done some digging and realized that what I told him was the truth. He offered me a new position. I alone would be tasked with hunting down the slower."

"And you took it?"

"Yes. It was a good job, and it paid a lot of money. I had to get a normal job as a cover, but I also received a lot of additional money from the Russian government, paid through an escrow account in Switzerland."

"What's an escrow account, Uncle Dimitri?"

"I was worried that my support from the Russian government wouldn't continue. So I had them put a large amount of money into a trust account in a Zurich bank. The bank pays me a substantial amount every month. The Russian government has no control over it."

"I've always wondered how you could afford your big house and awesome cars," I say. "But what did you find out, Uncle Dimitri? What happened?"

"After years of investigating, I figured out who the slower was. It was your Opa."

"I know that too, Uncle Dimitri. I haven't known it for very long. But I know it now."

"Your grandfather moved to America. So I moved here too. The KGB arranged my immigration papers. I have carefully lived near your grandfather ever since. And that's what I've been doing for the last sixty plus years. I've kept doing it, even after all of the changes in Russia. I could probably stop if I wanted. But I don't want to. Stopping the slower is my life's work. I'm not going to stop. My job is my obsession."

"But, Uncle Dimitri, I thought you loved us. You didn't. You were just spying on us. Using us."

"I do love you, Emit. I do love your family. This has been a wonderful side benefit of my job: I got to know you and your family."

The smile vanishes from Mr. Zachs's face. "I hate to be the one to tell you this, but your grandfather has done many bad things. He's murdered a lot of people, some important people. He has protected bad people. He has committed many other crimes too."

"I know that, Uncle Dimitri. I know that."

Mr. Zachs's face turns cold. I have never before seen him with such cold eyes.

"Emit, I need to ask you something. Something very serious. And you need to answer me truthfully."

"Sure," I say, confused. "Just ask."

"Has your grandfather tried to recruit you to try to help him?"

"Yes, he has," I respond. "He said that we would make a terrific team. We could change the world."

"What did you tell him?" Uncle Dimitri continues. "How did you respond?"

"I wanted to help him. He's my Opa, and I love him. It's true he has done so many horrible things. But he said that he had no choice. He said he would be killed if he didn't do them—him and his family. And he said he's changed as a person."

Uncle Dimitri clenches his jaw. "What did you tell him, Emit?"

"I told him no. I couldn't help him."

"Really? You told him no? Are you telling me the truth?"

Suddenly I look down at Uncle Dimitri's chest. As he steers with his right hand, his left hand is in the left pocket of his coat. My eyes focus on a pointed object that Uncle Dimitri's left hand is holding in his coat pocket. I observe the end of the object pressing against his coat. It occurs to me that the end of the concealed object is pointing at me.

"Uncle Dimitri, why are you driving with only your right hand?" I ask slowly. "What are you holding in your left hand in your coat?"

Sweat glistens on Uncle Dimitri's face even though the car is cold. "Emit, are you telling me the truth?"

"Yes, Uncle Dimitri. Yes! What's in your hand?"

He won't answer me. Tears glisten in his eyes, merging with the sweat. I stare at the object in his coat. It begins to shake.

"What is in your hand?" I repeat.

"You didn't promise to help him?" he says. "It must have been hard to refuse your Opa."

"I said no to him!" I say, my voice rising with fear. "I said no! You've got to trust me! I said no!"

The tension in Uncle Dimitri suddenly leaves. The object in his pocket relaxes against his coat. His face soothes. Uncle Dimitri pulls to the side of the road and stops. He pulls from his left pocket a shiny black handgun. He switches on the safety and returns it to his pocket.

"You were going to kill me? You were going to shoot me with that? I'm Emit. Your friend." My breath gets heavy as I realize what just happened.

"If you were going to help your grandfather, I was going to kill you. The stakes were too high to follow my feelings. If you had decided to help your grandfather, there would have been great danger for the whole world. Opa by himself was able to do many horrible things. It is hard to imagine the deep damage that could be done by two slowers working together. I had to stop you. Even …" He pauses and looks away from me. "Even if it meant killing you. The only way that I can think of to stop a slower is to kill. A slower who is alive can always slow and escape."

"But I told you I wasn't going to help him," I say. "I told you, Uncle Dimitri. You still almost shot me."

"You said you weren't going to. But I didn't know whether to trust you. I have watched you recently. I know you've done lots of bad things. Cruelty. Dishonesty. I've watched you lie. I've heard you lie to me. You were becoming like your grandfather. I worried. I worried, Emit, that you had become like him, that you would follow him. I worried that you were lying to me when you denied it." The cold tension returns to his face. He clutches the handgun again in his left hand and switches off the safety. "Are you lying to me now? Are you lying, Emit!"

"No, Uncle Dimitri! No! You've got to trust me." I clutch his right hand in both of mine. "I'm sorry, Uncle Dimitri. I found out about Opa's powers only recently. I found out what he's done; the killing, the stealing, the lying. That made me see that I was doing the same thing. I have to admit that it was fun for me. The power made me happy, like some drug; like a horrible, addictive drug. I loved the power over people, the excitement— even if I hurt people. But I snapped out of it, Uncle Dimitri. I beat the addiction. I beat the drug." I start to cry. "The bad way was the easy way. But it wasn't right. I'm not going to do that. I'm not, Uncle Dimitri. You've got to trust me. If I wanted to, I could have slowed and escaped. I don't want to. That's why I'm still here."

Uncle Dimitri places the gun in the console between us. He brings me close to him, and gives me a hug. A big Russian bear hug. The best hug ever. I hug him back. The hug continues in silence for what seems like a wonderful eternity. In reality, it's probably only a few seconds. I think how I've known Uncle Dimitri my whole life, and my parents have known him even longer. That whole time, he'd been watching us. Or not watching *us*, necessarily, but watching my grandfather.

"Uncle Dimitri, two things. First, let's start driving again."

"Right," says Mr. Zachs as he starts the car and pulls into traffic.

"Second," I continue, "why haven't you killed Opa?"

"The simple answer is, I didn't want to. I was fascinated with his abilities. After the war, I decided I wouldn't kill him unless it was absolutely necessary to prevent him from killing someone else. And that situation never arose."

"Yes, it did," I insist. "He killed Kennedy."

"True. But you must know that I'm Russian. I love Russia. It's my homeland. So I was no fan of Kennedy. It was the height of the Cold War. Kennedy was fighting a war against Communism, which meant a war against the Soviet Union. If you remember, he was responsible for planting missiles in Italy and Turkey that were pointed at Mother Russia. In response, we began installing missiles in Cuba, just ninety miles south of Florida and within striking distance of the US. But then that led to the Cuban Missile Crisis. Kennedy decided to send the US Navy to enact a blockade around Cuba, preventing any more Soviet ships from reaching the island. There was a showdown among the ships at sea, and many people thought we were on the verge of World War Three. But nothing ever happened, and Kennedy and Khrushchev, the Soviet leader, reached a deal where we agreed to dismantle our missiles in Cuba. The US agreed to not invade Cuba—which they had done before in the Bay of Pigs invasion—and Kennedy secretly agreed to remove the missiles in Turkey. So even though the deal ended the standoff, the Soviets hated Kennedy. To be honest, the KGB wanted Kennedy dead too."

"I see," I nod, understanding, even though I'm a little disappointed in Mr. Zachs.

"And the other things he's done since then haven't resulted in anyone's death," Mr. Zachs explains. "I know he's hiding some paintings the Nazi's looted during the war: Raphael's *Portrait of a Young Man* and Degas's *Five Dancing Women*. And I know he recently stole the Gutenberg Bible from the museum in Moscow. And yes, those things infuriate me, but they aren't murder."

"Yes, I know," I say.

"Emit, why do *you* think Opa's going to the Capitol?" Mr. Zachs asks.

"Well," I begin, "I think he's angry about Brown's push to make criminals out of the neo-Nazis. He thinks it's persecution, not prosecution. I guess he's still really loyal to the Nazi cause." I think for a minute. "I don't know exactly what he's planning to do, but I do know that he bought a bunch of put options on the S&P 500, and the options expire a couple days after the State of the Union speech. He's betting that the economy will crash soon."

"Really?" asks Mr. Zachs.

"Yeah. So I would guess he's planning something big. Something that would wreck the stock market."

"Something like killing the president?" Mr. Zachs asks quietly.

"Yes," I say quietly. "I hope not." I pause. "But I think so."

We both sit in silence for a few minutes.

"So the question is, Emit, will we have to kill your grandfather today?" Mr. Zachs looks at me to judge my response.

I turn away, gaze blankly out of the window, and try to figure out an answer to the most difficult question I have ever been asked. I turn back.

"Maybe. I've thought about it a bit, and I think you may be right about what you said before. The only sure way to stop a slower is to kill him. Otherwise, they can always use their power to get away."

"Maybe we can think of a way to stop him without killing him," Mr. Zachs continues. "We'll do that if we can. But we have to be prepared to kill. Could you do that, Emit?"

"I think so. I've thought about it hard. I think so."

"Emit, thank you," Mr. Zachs says. "I know this is deeply sad for you, and stressful. To fight your own grandfather. Maybe kill him. A fourteen-year-old should not have to do this. I wish you didn't have to. But there's no other way. Only you have the skills."

"That's OK, Uncle Dimitri. I know I might have to do it. You had no choice but to fight in the war when you were ten. I have to step up when I'm fourteen." I pause and clasp my hands together. "As far as I can see, the only way to beat a slower is with a slower. For example, only I can sense when Opa slows time. When I feel that tingling in my neck, I've learned to slow time too so that I can join him in slowed time. It's called simul-slowing." I smile nervously. "Opa taught me. I'm thinking he might regret that."

"You know, Emit," Mr. Zachs looks at me again. "Sometimes bad people have to die so good people can live."

"I know," I agree softly. "There's no other way."

"But we will only take that step if we have to," says Mr. Zachs. "Agreed?"

"OK, that sounds right. I agree."

Soon we're in downtown Washington. The traffic is terrible. What's worse, the Capitol is surrounded by tons of security and blockades. "How are we even going to get in the Capitol?" I ask.

"You can slow time, can't you?" Mr. Zachs reminds me.

"Yes, *I* can. But how are you going to get in?"

"Here's the plan," says Mr. Zachs.

CHAPTER 26

"Ready?" I ask nervously. We have left the car in a handicapped parking space about two hundred yards from the entrance to the Capitol. With all of the security blockades, that is as close as we could get. We have walked inside a bus stop kiosk. The sides of the kiosk shield us from view of the Capitol's entrance.

"Yeah, I'm ready," Mr. Zachs says. "Please hurry. It's only five minutes until the start of the speech."

I grunt with effort as I lift Uncle Dimitri over my shoulders in a fireman's carry, with my back and shoulders supporting his weight. I support his head with a hand to make sure my movement in slow time doesn't break his neck in normal time.

"Here goes nothing," I say. I slow time. Carrying Uncle Dimitri, I climb the long Capitol steps. Mr. Zachs is heavy. This is hard. I find the official entrance, and I carefully slip past the frozen security guards outside the doors, and into the building.

We then pass the security check, moving to the outside of the metal detectors to ensure that they won't be triggered. Because we entered on the upper floor, we are already near the

House Chamber, where President Brown's speech will occur. I find a deserted corner of the building, as near as possible to the centermost of the back entrances to the main floor of the chamber. I try to picture what the scene must be in there now; I have a pretty good image from watching last year's State of the Union Address on TV with my mom. President Brown will be standing on the podium at the far side of the chamber. The speaker of the house and vice president will be sitting right behind him. The senators, congressmen, and Supreme Court justices will be arrayed on the main floor in a semicircle in front of him in many curved rows, all the way from his left to his right. The Republicans will be on the right, and Democrats on the left. There are five aisles that run from the back of the main floor, converging on the podium. A balcony runs around the room's entire circumference.

I will try to position us at the back of the center aisle of the main floor. That's my best guess of where Opa would be if he were to try to attack the president.

I find a deserted section of the hallway, fifty feet or so from the various entrances to the chamber; almost everybody has left the hallways to enter the chamber. I put Mr. Zachs down and return time to normal.

"Owww!" says Mr. Zachs, cradling his neck. "Didn't I say to support my head?"

"I did," I insist.

"Well, not well enough," mutters Mr. Zachs.

"We better hurry," I remind him. "Someone might come

down this hallway and see us."

"Don't worry," he responds. "A lot of people are invited to this. How could they know we aren't?"

"Everybody's inside the chamber already. We stick out like a sore thumb out here in the hall by ourselves. It doesn't help that I'm the only teenager here, and I'm wearing jeans and a T-shirt." I glance at my green T-shirt and wonder why I had to wear the shirt that mom gave me from the library fundraiser. It reads "Dinosaurs didn't read. Look what happened to them."

We hear applause. "Uncle Dimitri, I think President Brown just came in. The speech is about to start. We've got to go in. Now."

"Emit, if anything happens, you can just slow time, pick me up, and we can escape." Mr. Zachs puts his hand on my arm. "We'll be fine. Don't worry." He stands up and glances around. "We go this way." He points and starts to walk briskly down the corridor that winds around toward the chamber's central rear entrance.

"Let's go in this entrance up ahead. It's in the center on the main floor," he continues. "We can't use the balcony; there's no quick stairs from the balcony to the main floor."

"I wonder where Opa is now," I whisper as we walk.

"If he's really here, he's probably doing the same thing we are," responds Mr. Zachs.

"It would be easier for him, though, because he's alone," I say. "No offense."

Mr. Zachs smiles. "None taken. But you're probably right;

it would be much easier for you if you were by yourself. You could just slow time and walk in there until you find him."

"Speaking of, what are we going to do when we get into the actual chamber where the speech is happening? It's big in there, isn't it? Hundreds of people there. Opa could be anywhere."

"Yes, you're right," Mr. Zachs agrees. He thinks for a few minutes and adds, "We just need to do the best we can. We have no choice. You can slow time and have more time to look around."

Mr. Zachs pushes me against the wall and shushes me.

"What?" I mumble.

"Shh," he says again. "Look."

I peer around the next turn in the hallway. Two uniformed armed guards stand in front of a closed set of large double doors. A sign above the doors says "House Chamber."

"That's the entrance to the back of the chamber, right in the center. How do we get past them?" I ask. "They're standing too close together for me to get through with you on my back."

"We have to get by them to get into the chamber," Mr. Zachs says.

"We could just tell them the truth: that we think an assassination attempt on the president is imminent and we need to get in," I suggest.

"No, we can't do that," says Mr. Zachs. "The Secret Service agents have no chance against an assassin who can slow time. And anyway, you think these guards would possibly let in two random people who claim they could stop the assassin, but may actually be the assassins themselves? They'll just detain us. That will leave Opa free to kill the president."

I think for a second. "I know what to do," I say. "See you inside the chamber."

"Just a second, Emit," says Mr. Zachs. "Before we go in, could you get me a gun? I'd feel better armed. I was really dumb, and I left my gun in the car."

"Yes. Good idea," I say. "If things go right, the next thing you'll know is that we'll be inside. Wish us luck." I slow time.

With time slowed, I walk around the corner and up to the left guard. I squat, grab the guard around the waist in a bear hug, and wrestle him a couple feet to the left, clearing an opening in front of the left of the two doors. Whoa! He almost tips over. I carefully reposition him so that the officer is standing in a stable way. I carefully remove his handgun from its belt holster and stuff it in my pocket. I hope he doesn't immediately notice. Oh well. We'll try to be fast.

I walk back around the corner to the frozen Mr. Zachs. I lift him over my shoulder as before. Wow. He is just as heavy as before. I carry him to the space that I have created between the two guards in front of the left door. Grunting under Mr. Zachs's weight, I push open the door and slip inside.

The doors open into a two-part red velvet curtain. The two parts are drawn to cover the door. After I carefully close the door behind me, Mr. Zachs and I are in a narrow area between the doors and the curtains.

Then I return time to normal. To a startled Mr. Zachs, I

explain what I have done and where we are. I hand him the officer's gun, and he places it in his jacket pocket.

"Great work," says Mr. Zachs. "Will the guards be OK?"

"Yeah," I answer. "I just moved one out of the way. I hope he doesn't notice."

"Good," Mr. Zachs nods. "I'm glad that we haven't had to hurt anybody. At least if we get caught, we won't get a much longer prison sentence."

I gulp. "Prison sentence?"

"I'm afraid so. Think how it looks, what we're doing. We're breaking into the Capitol. We're evading security. We're wrestling law enforcement officers around. We're stealing their weapons. We're carrying weapons as we enter the room where everyone important in the government is sitting."

"Well, now that you put it that way ..." I say. "I don't really want to go to prison. But we've got to take the risk. No choice."

"Look," Mr. Zachs says, putting his hand on my shoulder, "we just have to keep going. I hope we won't get caught. But it's not because of me that I care if we get caught. It's because of what might happen to the country and the world."

I hear the muffled voice of President Brown through the curtains, beginning his speech. He starts by acknowledging each of the groups that have assembled.

We part the curtain slightly to see into the chamber. The room and the people in it are just as I envisioned, except the scale is much smaller than I expected. TV makes it look bigger than it really is. Nobody seems to have noticed our entrance.

Everyone's focus, including the TV cameras, is on President Brown, who is behind a lectern on the raised podium down the aisle directly in front of us, about fifty feet away. He is standing. Thank goodness he is still alive.

"Do you see your grandfather?" whispers Mr. Zachs.

I look around. "No."

"Maybe he hasn't arrived yet," he says.

"Maybe he's not coming at all," I say. "Maybe we were all wrong about him. Maybe he was just planning to visit the Holocaust Museum."

"I hope so," says Mr. Zachs. "But I don't think so."

"Let's watch the rest of the speech, but be ready."

President Brown finishes his opening acknowledgements. He now turns to his speech's substance. "My fellow Americans," begins Brown, "tonight I have come to address the State of the Union and our plans for the future. Now, you all know our country has suffered unimaginable loss with the recent school shootings."

Mr. Zachs nudges me with his elbow. "Watch the crowd carefully. I don't know if your grandfather is here. I don't know if he's going to attack. But if he is, I'll bet it will be during this part of the speech."

"What's even worse," President Brown continues, "this loss is the result of hate; hate born from the ignorant misunderstanding of others and the refusal to accept those that are different from us. This will not stand!"

The Democrats applaud with enthusiasm. The Republicans

generally applaud too, although with less enthusiasm.

"I'm going to use every power at my disposal to stop this hatred," President Brown continues. "My administration will be instituting new educational policies to foster acceptance and an appreciation of diversity in our schools. I am also supporting a bill and a constitutional amendment that will allow police to arrest and prosecute people that engage in certain forms of hate speech. Now, I know that the First Amendment protects most speech, hate speech included. However, it's time, as a nation, that we recognize that hate speech has consequences, devastating consequences. At best, it creates separation and suspicion. At worst, it leads to violence and death."

"Should I slow?" I whisper to Mr. Zachs.

"No. Just watch," he says.

I look around for Opa, but I see no sign of him.

"Maybe we can't see him because he's slowing," I whisper.

Mr. Zachs breathes out. He reaches into his pocket to reassure himself that the pistol is ready.

"We must act now, and here is what me must do," Brown continues, about ten minutes into his speech. He mentions something about the better angels of our nature. But I'm not listening carefully. Instead, I'm frantically scanning the crowd for any sign of an old man in a wheelchair.

Why hasn't Opa attacked by now? Were we completely wrong? Is Opa even here?

A tingle runs down my spine. That's the signal that I was dreading, but also hoping for. I instinctively slow immediately.

Opa, in his green wheelchair, is rolling down the aisle directly to the left of the central aisle where I am. He has moved past the frozen guards at the back of the aisle and is rolling toward President Brown fifty feet away.

CHAPTER 27

"Opa!" I scream. Standing at the back of the center aisle, I'm separated from Opa's left center aisle by a section of spectators that is about ten people wide.

He turns, sees me, then rolls faster down the aisle toward President Brown, who is still standing behind the lectern.

"Opa, stop!" I yell as I hurry to my left behind the last row of spectators. I then turn right, down the left center aisle after Opa. He has already stopped about fifteen feet in front of the president, within shooting distance. He pulls a handgun from under his seat, aims carefully, and pulls the trigger.

Anticlimactically, instead of a normal shot, the bullet slowly slides out of the gun and travels forward at a velocity of about a foot per second.

I run down the aisle past Opa and catch up with the bullet about five feet from the president. I nudge the bullet so that its trajectory is now toward a point safely above the president; it will hit the wall about five feet above the vice president, sitting behind the president. I dare only nudge it; if I tried to stop it, it would rip right through my hand. As it is, even nudging the bullet hurts intensely. It feels like catching a fast baseball throw with your bare hand. I'm reminded of playing soccer with Peyton behind his house, and changing the path of a soccer ball. But that seems like a different life.

I turn back toward Opa and walk toward him. "The velocity of a bullet is determined by the internal mechanism that ignites a small explosive charge," I say. "It doesn't matter that you squeezed the trigger at one thousand times the normal speed. We're on slow time, so the speed of the mechanism and the explosion doesn't change."

"Of course, I know all that," Opa says. "I think you might have deduced that this is not the first time that I have shot somebody while slowing. But it is the first time that I've had to do it with the distraction of another slower. But I have to tell you, Emit, that you're really no more than a minor annoyance. You won't be able to stop me. I'll just get to point-blank range, so you won't be able to swat it away. I'm sure you know about the handicap ramp that gives wheelchair access directly to the back of the president's head. Handicapped assassins are entitled to accessible facilities too."

"Wait," I say, trying to stall until I can figure out what to do. "Please be careful. Firearms can be dangerous. Lucky I was here, or you could have hurt someone." I stand directly between Opa and the president, about four feet from Opa, standing in the way of any possible shot.

"You'd be surprised how many people I've killed with this thing," he responds.

I look closer and realize that the gun he's holding is an antique German Luger. I'd read Lugers were the standard-issue pistol for German soldiers in World War II.

"That's your Nazi gun," I say. "I saw it on the shelf in your secret room. Your pride and joy?"

He nods. "That's right. This is the first and last handgun I'll ever own."

"How did you keep it in such good shape?" I ask casually, continuing my attempt to stall.

"Well, obviously, I've had to replace a few parts …" he says.

"Opa, you need a different hobby than collecting Nazi weapons, and taking target practice at the president," I say. "How about golf? You could use slowing to cheat, and you could get a hole in one every time. Just hit your drive, slow time, and go and pick up your ball and drop it in the hole."

"Emit, this has nothing to do with you. Don't get in my way," Opa demands.

"Opa, he's the president of the United States. He's the leader of our country."

Opa continues to aim at President Brown, with me blocking his shot.

"Opa, you lied to me," I hiss. "You said that you were forced to help Hitler. You said that you were forced to kill Kennedy. You said that you were going to do good now. So this is your idea of doing good? It's your idea of doing good to kill the president just to make money on the stock market? Goodness gracious, I'm so glad I decided not to follow you." I look at Opa's Luger, which is pointed directly at my head. "What are you going to do? Kill your own grandson so that you can make money on the stock market?"

"Emit. Get out of the way. You're really starting to annoy me."

Suddenly a question dominates my brain. "Opa, I have to ask you this. Are there other slowers? You made me think there were others. Or are we the only two?"

"Emit. Get out of the way. Brown's an unjust leader who is supporting a policy that will persecute free-thinking people like me, intellectual heirs to the Third Reich. I've got to admit that Himmler went overboard with the Jews. Hitler wanted the Jews just relocated. He didn't want them killed. Hitler's ideas were good. Our ideas are spreading because they are good and powerful ideas. The president and his Jewish sympathizers know that they can't win in the fair marketplace of ideas. Our ideas are too perfect. Our ideas are too powerful. Our ideas are too convincing. So Brown knows that he can't win a fair debate. So instead he wants to shut the debate down."

"Opa, you're wrong," I say. "You're so wrong."

"No, Emit. Brown is taking the first step to fascism. This is exactly how it started for Lenin and Stalin. Put everyone who disagrees with you in jail. I can't let it happen. Imagine how much better the world would be if someone had killed Lenin and Stalin in 1917. I am that hero here. Brown needs to be stopped before it's too late for our country. I'm the only one who can do it."

Suddenly Opa disappears. He's slowed further and changed position! He can get to the president unless I quickly slow time further myself and stop him. Using my training in variable slowing, I slow further myself. By the time I get to Opa's speed, he has wheeled around me, down the aisle, advancing within ten feet of the president, about five feet from the low wooden barrier around the edge of the podium. He points his Luger again and shoots.

"No!" I sprint past Opa, down the aisle, toward the progressing bullet. I scramble up and over the wooden barrier onto the podium in front of the president's lectern. I am able to deflect the shot up and away from president, just before it hits him in the face. I scramble back down and plant myself right in front of Opa, again blocking any shot at the president.

Opa scowls. "Not going to make this easy, are you? Apparently, I taught you too well. Emit, that was really a fine bit of slowing that you did just now, to find me in time when I slowed."

Suddenly I disappear. Opa had been looking straight at me in front of him. Now I'm not there. "I know what you're up to," Opa mutters. "You think you can slow time further and, before I react and slow time further too, get behind me and take my gun. It won't work. I'm too fast at finding you in time."

Opa quickly slows to my slowing speed, but I am not directly behind him. I am running down the center aisle, twenty feet away from Opa's left center aisle.

"What are you doing there?" Opa demands, confused.

"No, Opa. Stop!" I yell, not answering his question. "You must stop." I continue running down the center aisle. If I can only get in front of him before he fires again …

"You know I can't do that," he responds, rolling his wheelchair farther down the aisle to just in front of the podium, five feet from President Brown. "This man is going to push through a law that will punish us just for saying what we believe," he says, waving his gun at Brown. "We don't deserve that."

"Opa, your so-called brothers killed six million Jews for no reason other than their culture or religion," I respond, stalling. I reach the front of the center aisle and turn left toward Opa at the bottom of the next aisle over. "They *certainly* didn't deserve that," I continue.

"You don't understand …" Opa begins.

"I do understand!" I say as I desperately squeeze between Opa and the podium, blocking Opa's line to the president.

"Emit, you're being very disrespectful right now."

With sweat moistening my face, a product of both my anxiety and my recent sprint, I force a laugh. "I bet the president would say the same thing to you."

And then, out of the corner of my eye, I see movement to my left from behind Opa, from the rear center of the chamber, near where Mr. Zachs is standing. There they are. As Opa starts to justify the Holocaust, I see two bullets travelling toward us. Slowly, but they're coming. The closest one is about sixty feet away, a few feet in front of the other. During the time when I further slowed time and disappeared from Opa's view for a few moments, I had run back to Mr. Zachs and grabbed the gun from his jacket pocket. I had taken careful aim at where I guessed Opa might end up, and I had quickly fired two shots. I had then placed the gun back in Mr. Zachs's pocket. I had done this rather than take the gun with me toward Opa, because I knew that Opa would soon search for me in time and find me. If he saw me with a gun, he might quickly try to kill me or the president.

Suddenly Opa punches me hard in the stomach, and I crumple to the ground, gasping for air. I'd forgotten how strong he is. That punch was worthy of his many hours in his weight room.

When I regain my breath and my eyes clear, I see Opa staring down at me from his wheelchair. "I don't want to hurt you, Emit. Stop getting in my way," he commands. And then more thoughtfully, "I don't understand why you care so much, anyway. Why do you care about Brown? You don't even know him."

"Opa, he's innocent. He doesn't deserve to die." I struggle onto my feet and place myself once again directly between Opa and the president. From this position, I can once again see the bullets heading in our direction. The lead one is about thirty feet away now.

Opa lifts the gun and presses it firmly against my chest. "Emit, I'm going to give you to the count of three to get out of my way. Then I will shoot you if I have to."

"I don't believe you. You wouldn't shoot your own grandson," I insist.

"I'd rather not," he says. "I'd rather my grandson stop this foolishness and work with me instead of against me." He pauses. "Emit, did your parents tell you that I picked out your name?"

"No," I respond. The lead bullet is twenty feet away.

"Well, I did. And what does your name spell backward?"

"T-i-m … oh, *time*," I say.

"I named you that because I hoped you would share my abilities. I hoped you and I could work together."

"Opa, please stop this," I plead, suddenly feeling the power of our bond because of this power that we share. A feeling of great love for my grandfather surges through me. "Please don't do this," I say. "We can just leave right now and go back to normal."

"One," Opa begins his countdown. The lead bullet is ten feet away. I see that it will now miss Opa, traveling a foot or so behind his head.

"No, Opa, please. I don't want any of this to happen. Please leave with me."

"Two," he continues.

"Opa, you're hurting me." I slowly push his wheelchair back a foot from me. Opa continues to press the Luger's muzzle against my chest.

I look from the gun to his face. I'm searching for clues about whether he really has the will to kill me.

"Opa, please," I plead softly, one more time. But when I see the cold determination in his eyes, my resolve hardens. I don't have a choice.

"Three." Opa's finger slowly begins pulling the trigger. But all I can see is the bullet now only a few feet from his head.

"I love you, Opa," I say as I lean toward him, clasp his shoulders, and adjust his position perfectly into the path of the oncoming bullets.

He hesitates, looking into my eyes. He slowly begins to lower the gun. Is he changing his mind? About me? About the president? But it's too late. I'll never know. All I see is a slow-motion burst of blood as the bullet enters the back of his head.

CHAPTER 28

"No, no, no," I whisper. "No, no, no." I stare down at Opa's body. He has slumped back in his wheelchair with his head and face covered with blood. I'm so confused about how to feel about him, about my grandfather, about the only person who will ever be able truly to understand my abilities, about the person who had done such awful things and had such vile ideas. Maybe, in his final moments, he had changed his mind and was lowering his gun. Or maybe he was going to shoot me anyway.

Something is bothering me. Something about the current situation. Something about the shooting. Maybe it's just seeing my dead grandfather on the ground, and I killed him. But I think it's something else.

It's about the shot, the shot that killed my grandfather. The shot that I had fired with Mr. Zachs's gun. But what is it? Think fast! Think fast! I run what happened again through my head. Opa and I were talking, and the bullet killed him. It had all happened so fast. It took an instant for that bullet to kill my grandfather. It had taken just an instant for me to fire the bullet.

Wait, there were two bullets! I suddenly remember: there was a second bullet! A hand suddenly reaches around a couple inches in front of my neck and deflects the remaining bullet over my shoulder.

"Ow!" says a familiar voice. "That really hurt."

"Wait. Is that …? Is that …? No. Wait."

I turn to the voice. "Yes," says Ellen.

"But you're … But you're not a …" I struggle to find the right words. "Am I dead right now?" I glance around at all the frozen famous politicians and security guards, then down at Opa's body. It doesn't feel like I'm dead. But how could Ellen be moving around here and talking with me here? She's not a slower.

"I'm sure you have many questions," she says.

I look at Ellen. Then I look down at the wheelchair and Opa's body in it, slouched to the side. His lifeless eyes, still open, stare at me. A large exit wound on his left cheek is still oozing his blood, blood that I spilled.

I start to shake. I start to sob. Ellen reaches out and holds me in her arms. With two fingers on her right hand, she closes Opa's eyes. "Rest in peace, Opa," she says, as her face reddens and her tears flow.

"I love you, Opa," I say, amid sobs. "I'm so sorry, Opa. I'm so sorry."

Ellen turns me so that I can no longer see Opa.

Ellen holds me, and I hold her. We cry together uncontrollably. Two children, next to their grandfather's corpse, alone together in an adult nightmare.

After what seems like hours, but was probably not long at all, Ellen pulls her head up and looks around. I look up too and confront the frozen stare of President Brown just a few feet away.

"We better get out of here," she says. "And also, my hand hurts."

She holds up her left hand, which is very bloody, and it looks as if the webbing of her thumb was sliced in half.

"What happened?" I say, looking at her wound.

"Yeah, sorry," she responds, thinking I'm reprimanding her for the close call. "That was a little close, wasn't it? I got here just in time."

"No, not that," I say. "I'm so grateful that you came out of nowhere and rescued me. You saved my life. What happened to your hand?"

"Oh, that. Well, when I—" she searches for the right word "—deflected the bullet that was about to make a big hole in your neck, it really cut into my hand. I was able to redirect it, but if I had gotten here even a second later, we wouldn't be having this conversation right now." She shakes her bloody hand. "My technique for deflecting bullets is not very good."

"How did you get here? How are you—" I open my hands wide "—slow?"

"C'mon, Emit," she responds. "You honestly thought you and Opa were the only people in the world who had this power? You didn't think you were that special, did you?"

"I … I … Yes, I did. Can you explain what's going on, please?"

"Later. Right now, we need to leave. And this blood is not going to clean itself up. Come over here and help me."

"OK," I say. "But first let's try to fix up your hand as best we can." I find a water pitcher in front of one of the senators and rinse off the cut on her hand. Luckily, it's not as bad as it looks. It has stopped bleeding on its own, and we leave it open with no dressing. That will have to wait.

"Now, we've got to do what we've got to do," I say. "We have to try to clean this up as best we can. I know it's not going to be perfect. Investigators are going to go over this all with a fine-tooth comb. But let's do our best."

Ellen nods in agreement. "That's all we can do," she says.

Trying not to look at Opa's face, I help Ellen prop Opa up more securely in his wheelchair. Then I walk up the aisle and out the door and find a janitor's closet. I collect some towels from the closet, return to the chamber, and begin to clean up. We're lucky. There's surprisingly little blood on the rug. What blood there is was mainly soaked up by Opa's clothing. Contrary to what you see in the movies, not all head wounds cause a blood bath. Or maybe with time slowed, the blood has not had time to come out yet.

After we sop up as much blood as we can, we place several towels over his head to soak up blood that might otherwise fall on the ground. We then tuck the crimson towels into the wheelchair, next to Opa's body, and we start to roll him up the aisle. It's hard to believe, but the floor looks clean. It will be interesting to see whether anyone notices anything.

"We forgot something," I say. "There are four bullets that we should try to find. There are two that Opa shot at the president, and I deflected. Then there's the one that hit Opa. And there's the one that almost got me and hurt your hand." I look around carefully, and I soon locate four small bullet holes. The two from the shots from Opa are in the dark wood molding behind the lectern, above the seats for the vice president and speaker of the house. The two that I shot are in the wood molding at the front of the podium.

"Don't you think we should leave them be?" responds Ellen. "The holes are really small, and they're in parts of the wood molding that have lots of details. I bet nobody notices them for a long time."

"I think that's right," I say. "We could try to find a screwdriver and pry them out, but that would just draw more attention. Where's Opa's gun?" I say. I locate the Luger on the ground and stuff it in my pocket. I also pick up the two shell casings.

We then push the wheelchair up the aisle and carefully make our way out of the chamber through the aisle's rear door. We are especially careful because I have not been through this door before. I entered through the door one aisle over.

When we are in the hallway outside the chamber, we look at each other and think exactly the same thing at exactly the same time. "What are we going to do with Opa's body?"

"Yes, what are we going to do?" she repeats.

"We could bury him?" I suggest.

Ellen shakes her head. "No. People will be suspicious if they find an old man with a gunshot to the head buried in an unmarked grave. They'll identify him and start questioning everyone, including you."

I still don't respond. I'm still thinking, looking down at Opa.

I look up. "I have an idea," I say. "I know what to do. Follow me."

"What is it?" asks Ellen. "What do you want to do with him?"

"Please just follow me," I say. "I'll show you. I learned something from my political science class last year. The unit about Congress."

I grab the wheelchair and push it toward the center of the capitol. First, we move through a high-ceilinged hallway, lined with armed guards every twenty or so feet, all frozen. Then we enter a domed hall ringed with marble statues of political leaders from the past. We pass a life-size bronze of a man in a 1940s military uniform.

"With time slowed," Ellen says, "the statue of President Eisenhower looks just about as lifelike as the frozen real President Brown that we just left."

"This is the National Statuary Hall," I say. "I remember that from the class. Next is the Rotunda." We enter the large round area under the Capitol's dome. Because of the security for the president's speech, the Rotunda is empty except for guards standing in the center and around the perimeter. We push on out of the far side.

"Where are we going?" Ellen asks.

"Now it's time to go down," I respond. "Way down." I head for the top of the large marble staircase.

"Shouldn't we use the elevator?" Ellen asks. "The stairs will be a pain with the wheelchair."

"The elevator won't work in slowed time," I respond. We bump down the long staircase.

At the bottom of the stairs, we encounter a tall arched opening. At the top of the arch, painted gothic letters announce "Crypt." Peering through the opening, I see a large windowless circular room containing stout floor-to-ceiling columns every ten feet. Upward-facing lights on the columns cast overlapping shadows on the ceiling's vaulted curves. Stern statues of founding fathers scowl into the room from its perimeter. In the gloomy light, two frozen guards resemble the statues. A three-foot circle of glass is embedded in the floor at the room's center.

"The Rotunda is on top of us," I say. "This crypt is exactly the same size. The columns in this crypt support the Rotunda."

"Are dead people buried here? In the Crypt?" asks Ellen.

"I don't think so. They bring tour groups down here for a thrill. But no bodies. We're not stopping here," I continue. "We're going all the way down, if I can find the way."

We step back out of the Crypt, and I push the wheelchair down a dimly lit hallway to the right. After fifty feet, I spot a modest stone staircase, only five feet wide, with a cramped ceiling.

"Here it is," I say. I turn the wheelchair down the stairway and begin to bump down it, with Ellen behind me.

At the bottom, we look through an arched door into a circular chamber, twenty-five feet across with a stone ceiling fifteen feet above the stone floor. No lighting fixtures illuminate the room. They are either off, or there aren't any. The only illumination is the shaft of light that shines from the Crypt above through the three-foot circle of glass in the ceiling.

Through the arch, we see that the shaft of light frames the chamber's only structure. Directly in the center is a rectangular waist-high pedestal, crafted of black granite, intricately carved. On top of the pedestal is an unadorned rectangular sarcophagus also made of black granite slabs, two inches thick. The pedestal is wider and longer than the sarcophagus, extending a foot beyond it on each side. Above the arch, a sign reads in faded gothic letters "George Washington's Tomb."

"Really? Is George Washington really in that coffin?" asks Ellen as we push into the room.

"No," I say as I push the wheelchair through the arch. "The chamber was designed and built for him. You can see the coffin down here through the glass circle in the floor of the Crypt upstairs. George Washington agreed that he would be buried here, but then he changed his mind. He decided instead that he wanted be buried at his house at Mount Vernon, next to his wife. After he died, people in Washington tried for thirty years to get his family to move the body here, but they always refused. The coffin is empty. It's been that way for two hundred years."

"Are you thinking of doing what I think you're thinking?" asks Ellen.

"Yeah," I respond. "It will be a perfect resting place for Opa. He'll be in a place of honor. He'll be in a public place, but invisible. That's just like he was for a lot of his life when he was slowing."

"Why do you want to dignify him so much?" asks Ellen. "He was a horrible man. He deserves to be interred in a dumpster."

I pause, unable to formulate an answer. Then I turn to her. "He did awful things. But he's our Opa. I love him. I don't understand why I love him. But I do."

"But how are we going to get him in there?" says Ellen. "Won't he be discovered when he stinks up the place when he decomposes?"

"I don't think so," I say. "At least I hope not. I'm thinking a good granite coffin will create an airtight seal that won't let any smell out. That's how it must have worked for all of the dead kings that have been put in stone coffins in old churches for thousands of years. Let's see if we can get him in there."

I climb on the pedestal and stand next to the coffin. I push on the coffin's top. It refuses to move.

"Ellen, can you jump up here and help me? Jump up on the other side, opposite me." I reach across the coffin, grab the top's far edge, and brace my feet. "Now you push, and I'll pull. Ready? Now!"

We each apply all of our strength. Nothing happens. We stop for thirty seconds and look at each other.

"Again, now!" I say. This time, the top begins to slide. "Don't stop," I grunt. The top continues to move.

"That's enough," I say. "That opening's big enough. We pull it any farther, and it'll fall off on top of me."

"Now, let's squeeze him in there," says Ellen.

I jump down and take a deep breath. "I'll grab him under the arms," I say. I grab him from behind the wheelchair. I just can't bring myself to bear-hug my dead grandfather from the front. "Ellen, you get his feet."

We push and pull and grunt in a desperate wrestling match with Opa's corpse. Somehow we triumph. Once he's in the coffin, we lie him on his back and turn his head to the left, to obscure the wound on his left cheek. We take one final look. Somehow our struggle to get him in the coffin has contorted his mouth and face into the position of smile. I smile back.

"Goodbye, Opa," I say.

"Yes, goodbye," says Ellen.

With a groan, we slide the top back over, sealing the opening. Using some paper towels from a nearby restroom, we do our best to clean off the blood and grime that would evidence our struggle. Not perfectly clean, but it will have to do. The stone's black color helps hide the stains. We have to hope that the room's dim lighting and remote location will hide our secret.

We then wrap the paper towels in the remaining bloody cloth towels and place them on the wheelchair. After I feel the bump in my pocket, I retrieve Opa's Luger from my pocket and add it to the bundle.

As we leave the room, I look back. There is Opa's tomb, glowing from the shaft of light from the glass circle above. Each day, thousands of tourists in the Crypt will look down through the glass at Opa's marble sarcophagus. I wonder how a private man like Opa would feel about that.

We turn and drag the wheelchair back up the stairs. It is much lighter now. Just as we're reaching the Capitol's exit, I suddenly remember. "Mr. Zachs!"

"Huh?" grunts Ellen, but I am already gone. I race back to the rear of the House Chamber, where Mr. Zachs is standing frozen in the shadows.

"Ugh," I grunt as I hoist Mr. Zachs onto my shoulders. The gun in his jacket pocket clatters to the ground. I briefly put Mr. Zachs down again, pick up the gun, open the door, and replace the weapon in the holster of the officer from whom I borrowed it. I hope that he doesn't notice that two bullets are missing. He has not moved from the spot where I placed him, a little bit to the side of where he originally was. He must not have noticed anything. Now that I think about it, very little normal time has passed since I took the gun. For me, it's been forever. But for everyone else? A few minutes? Or maybe just a few seconds? I remember one final thing. With a careful search of the area, I retrieve the two spent cartridges from the rug. I pick up Mr. Zachs and carefully, and with great effort, make my way back to Ellen.

With Ellen watching in surprise, I put frozen Mr. Zachs on top of the bloody wheelchair and begin to push toward the exit. Near the exit, we pass a long mirror. I grimace as I see our reflection. Streaked with blood, Ellen and I are pushing a wheelchair that contains a stiff body. Except, unlike the chair's former occupant, this body is alive.

"Why is Uncle Dimitri here?" asks Ellen as we thread our way through security, leave the building, and head down the long exterior stairs.

"He drove me up here," I answer. "I learned lots of stunning things about him today."

"I also know Uncle Dimitri very well," she says. "He was one of the first people to help me with my powers."

"I'm stunned that you have powers," I say. "I thought it was just me and Opa."

"Well, Opa's the other person who helped with my powers. Although 'helped' is not really the right word for it. Instead, he taught me a couple of lessons. He was trying to harness my power so we could be very powerful together and do great things. Eventually, about a year ago, I started feeling weird about the whole situation. Somehow Uncle Dimitri figured out that I could slow, and he talked with me about it. He warned me about Opa and taught me a little bit more about my power. Or rather, *our* power."

"So you've known about being able to slow down time for a while?" I ask.

"Yep. A couple of years," she says. "I had trouble sleeping and concentrating. But then I figured out that it was because I was slowing down time without knowing it. That was certainly a shock to find that out. Because of the accidental slowing that I was doing, everything was slow and boring."

"Yeah," I say. "That's exactly what happened to me too."

"Then why didn't you tell me that you were like me?" I ask. "I'm totally embarrassed. Ellen, you must know about all those times that I used my power to prank you. Or when I used slowing to make you do things I wanted you to do. All those times, you could see me?"

"That's right."

"Even when I planted that fake note from Coco about Jake cheating on you? Could you see me the entire time?" I ask, feeling stupid. I notice that the conversation is distracting me from my task of pushing the wheelchair containing Mr. Zachs safely: after reaching the bottom of the steps, I push the wheelchair over a curb into the street at full speed, causing Mr. Zachs's head to bang against the wheelchair's handle.

"Be careful, Emit," says Ellen.

"Sorry, Uncle Dimitri," I mutter.

"I remember, while you were writing the note, I accidentally blinked normally. You came up really close to my face and stared at me for a long time. I'm surprised I didn't burst out laughing."

"So that explains why you didn't get mad at Jake when you saw the note," I say. "I expected that you would get furious at him."

"That wasn't a nice thing to do," says Ellen.

"I'm sorry. I feel so dumb now. I'm really sorry I did that. I don't really know why I did. I guess I was jealous that you were spending so much time with him. I got carried away with how fun it was to use the slowing power."

"That's OK, Emit. I was mad at you for a while. You were really acting like a jerk. It was hard to be around you." Her face suddenly brightens. "But you made up for it now. You were a jerk to my boyfriend, but you saved the life of the leader of the free world. You did good."

"Thanks, Ellen. I'm sorry about what I did. I don't know why I did that." I pause to think. Then I change the subject. "But why didn't you tell me you are a slower?" I ask. "Why didn't you just tell me?"

She glances over at me. "I was afraid."

"Why? What is scary about telling me that you are like me?"

"It's not you that I was afraid of," she says. "I was afraid of Opa."

"Why were you scared? Did he hurt you?"

"No. He didn't do anything to me," she clarifies. "But he did threaten me. When I first discovered what I could do, I wanted to tell the world and be a famous superhero. Opa did not like that idea. He explained that if I went public with my powers, many people might be able to link me to some of his crimes. I don't know if you have figured it out, Emit, but Opa has done a lot of bad things. Really very bad."

"Yeah, I think I found out at least some of what he did," I say.

"Apparently, a lot of people, including several intelligence agencies, are looking for Opa," Ellen continues. "Anyway, he said that if I told anybody about our powers, he would kill me. And I believed him, so I kept his secret, and mine. But everything changed when I found out that you were like me."

"How did you find out?" I ask.

"I knew you could slow before you did," she answers. "At school, when you were bored in Ms. Beans's class, you would accidentally slow without knowing it. I would watch you do it. You would get bored, and then time would slow accidentally. I saw you steal Ms. Beans's book during one of those episodes. I think that was the day when you figured out you could slow time."

"I must have looked crazy weird when I accidentally slowed," I say. "How embarrassing."

"Not embarrassing at all. I learned in school too, a little younger than you. The class was so boring that it created the perfect conditions for learning to slow."

"I saw you slow time a bunch of other times," she continues. "I could see it when I was over at your house, and you slowed. And of course, I saw it when you were trying to prank me."

"That's creepy to think you were watching me. I thought I was the one who was secretly able to watch people. That's one of the great things of slowing: you can look at people without them knowing. But you were secretly observing me. The secret watcher was secretly being watched."

"I wanted to tell you that I was like you," she says.

"I should have figured it out by myself," I say. "The clues were all there. How you and I were the only two people who were so bored in Ms. Beans's class. How you look older than your age. And then how you blinked when time was slowed. I'm an idiot for not figuring it out."

"I told Opa that I was going to tell you," she continues. "But he was worried about being found out. He told me that if I said anything, he would silence us. I took that to mean that he would kill us."

"I hope when I get to be a grandfather, I'm a little more loving to my grandkids," I say.

"Once, when we both were at your house, I was sitting with you and your mom and Opa. I slowed time, and I told him that I didn't believe him when he said that tough-guy stuff. I told him that he would never hurt his family. I told him that I was going to tell you that day."

"You were talking to him with me and mom right there?" I ask. "How come I didn't slow too and hear you?"

"You hadn't learned to slow yet," she answers. "You hadn't learned yet to feel the tingle when someone was slowing, and then slow too."

"What happened when you said that you were going to tell me?" I ask.

"While time was slowed, Opa pointed a gun at your head from about five feet away and fired. He waited until the bullet was an inch from your face; then he deflected it away. He said that if I tried to tell you again, he wouldn't stop the bullet next time. I didn't test him."

"So that's why there was a hole in the kitchen wall," I say.

"My mom thought it was from a bee."

"No," Ellen says. "A Luger. Sorry about the hole, but it was almost a lot worse. The hole was almost in your head."

"Well, thank you," I say.

"For what?"

"For not letting him kill me," I say.

While we're talking, we've failed to notice that we've walked past the Supreme Court building, and we're now a half mile into a residential neighborhood.

"I think we're far enough away now," I say. "Let's take Mr. Zachs out of the wheelchair and get rid of it. We can get rid of the bloody towels and Opa's gun too. How about that dumpster there? The one next to the gas station across the street?"

"Good idea," responds Ellen.

We put Mr. Zachs on the grass beside the sidewalk, not too near to a frozen woman who's pushing a frozen baby in a stroller and waiting with a plastic bag for her frozen dog to defecate. I cross the street and dispose of the wheelchair and the towels. Finally, I toss the Luger into the dumpster. I can't help thinking of all of the carnage that that gun has caused. The world will be a better place now that it's being retired.

"Should we stop slowing now?" I ask Ellen as I return.

"Yes," says Ellen. "I'm starting to get a bad headache. You too?"

"Yeah," I answer. "I hadn't noticed it in all the excitement, but I'm getting a really bad slowing headache."

"Before we stop slowing, let's try to clean up a bit first," says

Ellen. "You've got blood on you from moving Opa. You can't really see it on your jeans, but you really can see it on your shirt."

"Your shirt is all bloody too," I say.

We think for a moment.

"I know," I say. "I'll put Mr. Zachs's jacket on over my shirt."

"How about I just borrow dog lady's coat," she says, pointing at the coat that's draped over the handle of her stroller.

"Fine," I say. "I don't want to steal anymore, but it's an emergency."

After we put on the coats, we carry Mr. Zachs to a hidden area that I noticed next to the gas station. We place him between us, with each of us holding one of his arms. We look at each other, nod, and resume normal time.

"Where are we?" asks Mr. Zachs, looking around.

"About half a mile from the Capitol," I estimate.

"Ellen, why are you here?"

Suddenly Mr. Zachs reaches down and feels the back of his pants. He raises his hands, and his eyes widen as he discovers that the dampness is blood.

"Don't worry, Uncle Dimitri," I say. "It's not your blood. It's from Opa. He's dead. I shot him. The president is safe. I can fill you in as we walk back to your car. It's still parked in the handicapped spot next to the Capitol, where we left it."

We fill him in during the slow twenty-minute walk to the car. We tell him about what happened in the House Chamber and how Opa died. When we tell him about Opa's final resting place, Mr. Zachs smiles. "I'm glad George Washington's Tomb is finally getting some good use, even if the place of honor in the Capitol is now occupied by a Nazi assassin. Opa devoted a lot of his life to hating the US government. I can't help smiling to think of him spending eternity at the center of it, with millions of tourists admiring his coffin."

Mr. Zachs looks at me. "Why are you sad, Emit? You had to do it."

I shake my head. "I don't know. I think at the last minute, Opa may have been changing his mind. I don't think he was going to kill me. He may have even changed his mind about the president."

Mr. Zachs places his hand on my shoulder. "I'm sorry, Emit. But we don't know. We can't know. You did what you thought was right. You did the only thing you could."

"I know," I say softly.

Mr. Zachs turns toward Ellen. "I'm glad you made it. I was a bit worried about that," he says.

Confused, I look at Mr. Zachs. "You knew she was coming here?" I say.

"Yes. She and I arranged it."

"W-what?" I stutter.

"When you called me to ask me to take you here, I didn't know whether you were working with Opa," Mr. Zachs says. "I hoped you weren't, but I didn't know. So I immediately called Ellen. I asked her to come to DC too. She would be there as a backup to protect me. And she could protect the president. The only way to protect yourself from a slower, or slowers, is with another slower."

"Before Mr. Zachs picked you up, he drove to my house and got me," Ellen adds. "He dropped me off at the train station, and then he got you. The train wasn't as fast to get to DC as the car. I just barely made it from Union Station in time. That was close."

As we get in the car, I look at the clock. It shows that since Mr. Zachs and I left the car, only thirty-four minutes have passed. President Brown must still be in the middle of his speech. I guess we did a good enough job of cleaning up. I don't hear any sirens. Nobody has noticed anything out of place. Amazing.

"Well, I'm glad you both finally know that there's another slower in the world," says Mr. Zachs.

As we get in the car and drive off, I wonder if there are any others.

EPILOGUE

"Emit, wake up," says Mr. Ratworth.

"Oh, um … sorry," I say, apologizing and rubbing my eyes.

"This is the second time this week. See me after class," he orders. "Now, where was I?"

"The terrorist attack," a girl in the front row reminds him.

"Ah, yes," Mr. Ratworth continues. "As tenth graders, you are mature enough to analyze current events, no matter how gruesome they may be. Like the one that happened this morning. Now, what do we know about this awful attack so far?" he asks the girl.

"Well, it happened at the main building at the Centers for Disease Control in Atlanta," she answers. "Only one criminal was spotted, but the police think there must have been several more, because bombs went off at the same time in many places around the building."

"Yes," Mr. Ratworth says. "Any survivors?" he asks a boy.

"None found so far," the boy replies. "The building went down just like the World Trade Center on 9/11."

"OK, what's important about the Centers for Disease Control, or the CDC?" he asks the boy again.

"That's where we keep all of the weird diseases from around the world, isn't it?" the boy asks. "Like Ebola and smallpox and stuff."

"Yes, that's right. The CDC has always been a possible terrorist target because of the possibility of creating biological weapons from the diseases that are stored there. The CIA has–"

Suddenly the intercom interrupts Mr. Ratworth.

"Mr. Ratworth? Mr. Ratworth?" asks the voice of Ms. Burner from the front office.

"Yes, this is he," Mr. Ratworth replies.

"Please send Emit Friend to the front office."

"Sure." Mr. Ratworth points at me and then at the door. "He's on his way."

I nod to him and head out the door. I slouch down the hall, looking at the floor, trying to figure out which bad thing that I've done is sending me to the principal's office. I don't think it's sleeping in Mr. Ratworth's class; he's dealing with me on his own after school. And I haven't done very many bad things recently.

It's nice to be back in these halls after the summer, even though I've already gotten in trouble twice in the first week for sleeping in class.

Since Opa died seven months ago, I've been depressed. I often think about whether Opa was changing his mind about killing the president when he died. I could have stopped that bullet, to give him time. But I didn't.

It's also been hard not being able to tell anybody else what really happened to Opa. It was especially tough not being able to talk about it with Peyton, who had unknowingly helped me so much in my efforts around slowing. To everyone except Ellen and me and Mr. Zachs, it appears that Opa simply disappeared. On the day before the State of the Union speech, Oma and he had driven up to Washington, DC, for a week to see some museums. The morning after they arrived, Opa told Oma that he had just found out that he needed to attend some meetings that morning, but that he would be back for lunch.

He never returned. After a day, Oma called us. My dad went up to be with her and to try to find him. But they couldn't find him. The police couldn't find him. Oma said that this wasn't the first time that Opa had traveled away for a week or two for meetings. But this time, he never returned. For a while, people thought that since he was so old, he might have just become confused, but that he would return, or someone would find him. But no.

In June, Oma and my parents finally had a memorial service for him. Nobody much showed up except my family and Ellen's family, and of course, Mr. Zachs and Peyton and his family. My dad and Uncle Ethan talked about how he was a great husband, father, and grandfather. They asked me to speak, but I declined; I said I was too emotional to do it. In dad's speech at the service, he said that he expected Opa to make a grand entrance and tell everyone that his disappearance was part of a big prank.

It makes me sad to think that I took away someone that they loved so much.

Much to my surprise, nobody other than Mr. Zachs, Ellen, and me knows about the assassination attempt in the House Chamber. It's stunning that nobody noticed the bullet holes. And nobody noticed our lame attempt to clean up the blood. It's so strange that nobody but us knows how close we came to losing the leader of the free world.

Being back in school has helped me start to get my mind in order. Life is simple in school. I can just be a regular tenth grader with no worries about assassinations or Nazi time manipulators or Russian spies. It reminds me of the way it was before I ever realized I had these abilities, when all I had to worry about was grades, bullies, and girls.

It's like before hanging out with Peyton. It's nice, too, that things are back to normal with Ellen. Well, not really back to normal, but better than before, because we know about each other's slowing skill and can support each other about it.

"Emit!" I look up and see Ms. Burner, the front office assistant, poking her head around the door and motioning for me to come in. "The principal will see you now."

"OK." I walk quickly past her and into Mr. Zachs's office.

Mr. Zachs, typing intently on his computer, looks up at me. "Emit, please close the door and sit down."

"OK," I say. "What's up, Uncle Dimitri? Oh, hey, Ellen," I say as she walks in.

"Have you seen this?" asks Mr. Zachs. He motions to the

muted TV on the wall. On the screen is a breaking news report with the words "Terrorists Destroy CDC Building" scrolling across the bottom.

"Yes," I answer. "Mr. Ratworth was just talking about it in class."

Mr. Zachs looks grave. "I think we have another one."

—

ABOUT THE AUTHOR

An author of both fiction and non-fiction, Ted recently won a national award from the SIFMA Foundation for his financial writing. He lives in Atlanta, Georgia with his family. *Slower* is Ted's debut novel.

To find out more about Ted, please visit Ted-Shepherd.com.

Made in the USA
Columbia, SC
01 September 2021

44685578R00193